The Oaths of Land and Sea

EVELYN A. BERNARD

EVELYN A. BERNARD

OATHS OF LAND AND SEA

First edition. February 25, 2025.
Copyright © 2025 by Evelyn A. Bernard
ISBN: 979-8-230-47466-1

EVELYN A. BERNARD

To T.M. for believing in me, to M.V. for his help with this book,
and to my dad, thanks to whom not all my book dads have to be villains.

EVELYN A. BERNARD

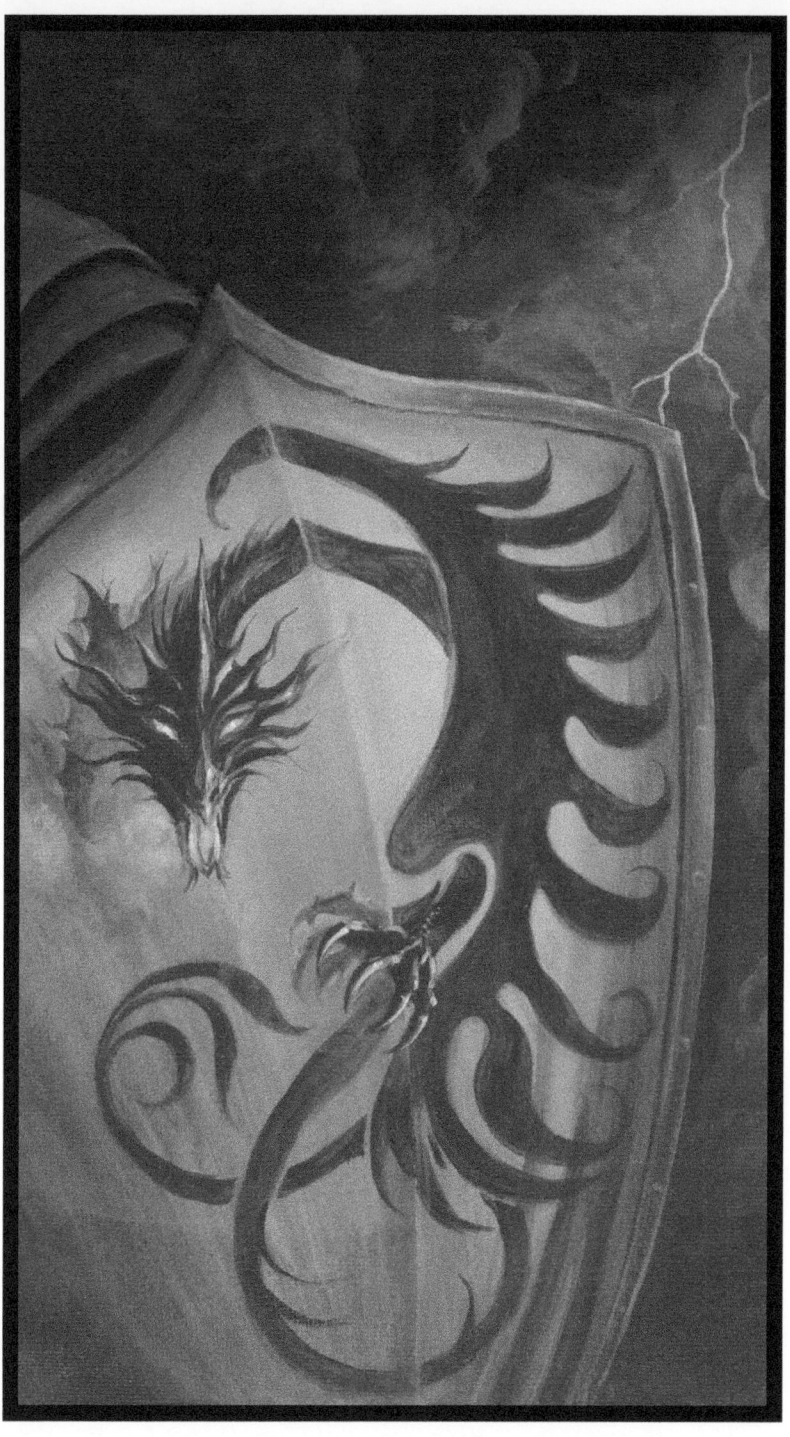

EVELYN A. BERNARD

Chapter 1

Life was good. Cassandrea liked it the way it was. Not simple, but cosy. She owned a nice home in Borve, the capital of Ordeara, the southern kingdom ruled by a dragon king and his two sisters. A kingdom of mild weather and pleasant people, where humans and magical creatures coexisted peacefully. So there was nothing to complain about.

Cassandrea's life was wonderful. She even had a kind husband who was anything but boring. No kids yet, but that could change soon. She wouldn't mind it changing. Of course, with the war raging on the northern borders, things could get complicated, but it had been going on for centuries, with only minor gaps in between. By now, Cassandrea doubted many people cared—aside from the soldiers fighting on the frontlines, and the spies working behind them. Naturally, she cared about the second because her husband was one of them. However, she didn't mind his occasional absence. It gave her time to go about her own business.

So life was good. Until the night she woke with a rope around her neck.

*

Panic. It was sudden and overwhelming, and stole the breath from her lungs. Cassandrea tried to wrench her fingers under the rope, but it was wound too tight and coated with something caustic that stung and boiled her skin like it was set on fire. Choking and frantic, she let her instincts kick in and shoved her hands behind her head. Long, sharp talons extended from her fingertips, and she slashed viciously at her assailant. Once the talons found purchase, she heard a scream that shot cold iron through her veins. Then turned it into pure, distilled rage. Because that voice... She tore into skin, muscle—anything she could find. Neck, face, arm—it didn't matter; she was shredding like a wild animal, her legs kicking and thrashing, the bed wailing underneath as she tried to find some footing. Her world was ebbing and turning dark from the edges, but Cassandrea refused to give up. And with an agonised cry, she heaved herself off the bed and to the ground, taking the man with her.

This was the end. A small part of her knew that. Surprising. Undeserved. Painful. One of those words stuck, shining like a

beacon in the darkness that was slowly taking over her mind. It was undeserved. Unfair. And she wouldn't die like that. She would fight it. With everything she had. In truth, she knew why it was happening, but this wasn't the way it should have ended. She genuinely loved her husband and didn't want to hurt him. But now, it seemed Ryker left her with no other choice.

It was hard to remember her training after all these years, and far harder for the hum in her ears and the darkness settling in. Her lungs were burning, and her hands were raw and blistering from the caustic rope, and she could feel her own skin peeling off. But Cassandrea remembered. She had to. She clawed at Ryker's face and turned her head to the side. Her elbow landed in the man's ribs and it gave her an inch to move the rope up, even if the rope burnt her ear in the process. The pain was enough to force a scream from her lips, but that was a good thing. It meant she was almost free. And she was still alive.

Ryker let out a stifled groan as the elbow jabbed him hard enough to make him recoil and his hands faltered from their grip. Cassandrea struck, simultaneously yanking from the coarse, coated rope and slamming her head backwards. Something cracked, and she hoped it was her husband's nose. The man grunted and reeled, enough that she managed to push her fingers, then wrist, in between the rope and her neck. Then, as the caustic coating scorched her cheek as it passed, it slipped from over her head, leaving her heaving and free. Cassandrea gulped in air like water and scrambled to her feet, nearly as fast as the man behind her. Her lilac nightgown was drenched in sweat and blood, but she didn't care to check whether it was hers. Not now. Not when she had to face him. Not when she had to meet those eyes—eyes she knew all too well.

Her husband had always been a very handsome man, by any standard. He had chestnut hair, the kind of wavy that always looked a little messy, facial features that were pleasant to look at, with a sharp, angular jawline, and a pair of sky-blue eyes that had always been playful. But not anymore. Right now those eyes were burning with nothing but hatred and disgust, his perfectly straight nose crunched to the side, and his lips curled into a snarl that only meant one thing: she was the enemy. Seeing him drop to a similar stance to hers, Cassandrea knew only one of them would walk out of this house alive.

She couldn't blame him. Had it been her, she probably would've done the same. But she couldn't help the pain that was stabbing her heart so hard it made her wince. She had been preparing for this. Mentally. For years. And part of her wasn't sure if she could actually finish it. Him. If she could finish him.

"Don't do this," she pleaded.

But Ryker immediately lunged at her, aiming to finish the job. He tried to catch her arm in the coil, but she was faster—she had always been faster. With a swift and merciless manner, she weaved to the left and aimed her heel into his knee pit and made him buckle down to his knees. Ryker scrambled to intercept her knee strike with his arm, but she dropped her elbow straight to his temple instead.

With a dull thud, her husband went down.

Cassandrea took a step back. She knew she should finish it. A blade was lying next to her husband's head, where he had dropped it. A tool to an end. A clean slate. Cassandrea looked at it. Leaned down to pick it up. Yet she couldn't bring herself to do it. Instead, she just stared at him. With his eyes closed, all the rage had disappeared from his features, together with the unbearable hatred for her that she knew she would never forget. He was handsome. Peaceful. Calm. And in the end? He was innocent. She was the infiltrator. The traitor.

Grasping her chest, Cassandrea tried to calm her breathing, but she couldn't. The darkness of this new world was overwhelming. Pressing. Drowning her in the new reality. Ryker was her husband. And he decided to execute her. Just like that. Without hesitation.

And Cassandrea knew she should repay the favour. To protect herself. Her king. Yes, she should repay the favour.

But instead, she got up and stumbled towards the mirror. She looked awful. Her golden hair was dishevelled and messy, and the rope had left it uneven where clumps of it had snapped off. Her bright green eyes were wide with shock and filled with tears. The once beautiful, sensual mouth was twisted in agony and disbelief. Her chapped lips lead to a horrendous disfigurement of her cheek and her neck. Her face was burnt badly. That rope had been coated with a thick layer of Hurom's blood, a viciously corrosive herbal tincture that was used in torturer's tools. A tincture she had used many, many times before herself. And now, her entire neck was wreathed by a scar she knew would never fade. A burn that would forever mar her otherwise flawless appearance. And while it was the least of her worries, she couldn't help but hate what she had become. For what good was a siren without her beauty?

The man stirred. There was no time to waste. Cassandrea threw on a tunic and a pair of riding pants, pulled on long, comfortable boots, and a dark cape to conceal her mangled face. She took only one look behind her as she strapped her twin swords, *Dusk* and *Dawn*, to her back and gave her home one last glance before she vanished into the shadows of the night.

*

Eight days later, Cassandrea started to feel better. She was almost at the northern border, taking forgotten, winding paths through the deep forest of Eberanth and along the coastline of the East Sea to avoid the frontlines. With no contact to her superiors, she had no idea where the brunt of the fighting had shifted to, but she knew that Eberanth, with its magical beasts and the rocky cliffs along its eastern edge, were nobody's favourite path to walk. She didn't mind, though, as she was one of those beasts. And she wouldn't be surprised if she learnt that her grandmother, or some other ancestor on her mother's side, used to sit on those very cliffs, luring fae and men to their doom.

While wading the rolling hills, thigh-high grass kissing the leather of her pants, Cassandrea took in the scenery. She had been here once before, long ago, and not a whole lot had changed in those decades. The landscape was untouched, wild. As it deserved to be. The area was ruthless and teeming with beasts of fable, creatures many human mothers warned their children about in tales of disobedient boys and girls going missing, snatched by the wildlings of the East.

Yet Cassandrea wasn't afraid. She was safe—at least safe enough to rest while taking proper precautions. She couldn't risk manifesting her wings and taking to the skies: the frontlines might be closer than she realised, and a single stray arrow could bring her crashing down. Worse still, there could be poachers. Sirens were rare enough on the mainland as it was—mystical beings known for their seclusion and fierce guardianship of their waters. But a paleblood like her? She was an anomaly, a prize even among her kind. Her voice, a weapon capable of charming and mesmerising, made her a weapon many would kill for. And her body, crafted by nature to allure and enchant, was a trophy for those bold enough to hunt her kind. She knew all too well how her beauty and song could be exploited. After all, hadn't she used them herself? They had ensnared her human husband, delivering not only his affections but also the secrets she so desperately needed.

And she had done it all in the service of her king. His kingdom, her homeland.

Ryker Weller had been picked because he was an Ordearan spy. A target of high value. And for years, Cassandrea had lived a comfortable life, sending occasional letters to her 'uncles and aunts' living far away, detailing her mundane life with her mundane husband. However, each message contained important intelligence, details and messages she had uncovered. Counterintelligence, they called it.

Still, she had loved Ryker dearly, and her heart was breaking at the thought of never seeing him again. Never touching him again. Never hearing his voice. His beautiful laughter, which used to light up his eyes and shone whenever he took her into his arms. The scent of him, the silky strands of his hair in her fingers—all of that was gone. And the only thing laughing at her now were the waves hitting the sharp rocks some thirty yards below her. Laughing and calling to her. Beckoning her. *You should have killed him.* They sang. *You should have killed him. Treacherous, lying men. You could end them all.* Cassandrea snarled at the call and wandered away from those roaring cliffs. Back into the forest, where their voices couldn't reach her.

Her mind was so busy ignoring those tempting words that she noticed the stench too late. Blood. A lot of it. And not the animal kind. There was a red patch in the middle of the path, slowly leaking into the dirt. And a bit further away, as if somebody had dragged the body after it was already ripped open and bled dry, was lying a human corpse. Decapitated. With the head nowhere to be seen.

Cassandrea's eyes darted around the forest floor, then immediately to the bushes and the tree trunks. She dropped to a low prowl, prepared to bolt off. Her instincts screamed at her to fly away, yet some primal fear told her not to, else it might be the last thing she would do. She leaned closer to the blood and touched it to determine how long ago this poor soul had met his fate. The liquid was fresh enough, still to be pooling and warm enough to say this was recent. Cassandrea sniffed and then recoiled as a sudden cold gust of wind blew the stench straight into her face, together with the smell of pines and resin.

It wasn't good. Whoever killed that human could catch her scent if she were standing upwind. Her ears caught a faint rustle, and Cassandrea immediately drew her twin blades from their sheaths while her eyes were scanning the area.

Yet, nothing came out of the bushes, and the rustling slowly died out. A curious animal, perhaps. Or a killer circling its prey. Her.

Cassandrea had only two options. She could either trail the blood to wherever the head had gone or she could very slowly and very carefully back off towards the cliffs and hope that whatever killed the human man came out of Eberanth and disappeared again under its thick canopy.

Given that she had already had one hunter on her trail, Cassandrea decided to backtrack towards the sea and roaring waves. They were the safer option. Especially for her if she suddenly needed to fly.

The scent of blood accompanied the siren all the way to the cliffs, and she wondered how it was possible that she had missed it in the first place. Not that it mattered. It would have ruined her plans all the same. She cursed. The sun was already setting and she had to forget about her original plan of finding a place to settle for the night. Instead, she would have to keep walking long after the dark fell to be on the safe side. After witnessing the decapitated corpse, she doubted stopping before daybreak was an option. Whatever killed that human was big. Strong enough to rip his head off. A troll, she suspected, but a troll wouldn't have left the body. But she spied nothing moving on that grassy plain, and there was no sound beyond the roaring sea.

Cassandrea let out a slow, careful breath and straightened up. The crashing waves called to her again. She wandered across the grassy plains, doing her best to ignore that call, but the wind brought scents that washed away the blood from her mind, only to have the smell of brine fill it with memories of times she would never get to live again. Ryker loved the sea. He had always enjoyed fishing and sailing, and he had proposed to her during one of the cruises they'd taken on a big ship that sailed between the continents. During a sunset similar to the one that was currently painting the world with peachy orange tones on its slow way behind the horizon.

Cassandrea took a deep breath and felt the burns on her neck and cheek sting violently. It'd been eight days, and the wounds still felt raw and fresh. Sheathing her swords, she took another step towards the cliffs. Come nightfall, she would have a far worse chance of finding herself a place to rest, but she was also less likely to be spotted from the sky. So, she might risk flying.

*

The sun gave way to the moon, and Cassandrea's progress

slowed down. The coastline was ragged, and there were huge holes in between the rocky plates, some leading all the way down to the sea. Another thing to worry about were the overhanging cliffs that could easily crumble if stomped on with enough force. So, the siren proceeded slowly and carefully on light feet and tried to ignore the persistent inner voice that kept urging her to get far from the human corpse as fast as possible.

Luckily, that healthy paranoia was all she needed to notice the new danger in time. The stench of blood became the first warning. Not as abhorrent and strong a scent as in the forest, but it was still there. Together with something else. Resin and autumn leaves. Something that should have been a while off still, as summer was at its peak. Yet, there it was, sailing to her on the cold northern wind.

And then she saw the beast.

It was little more than a towering shape against the starry sky at the very edge of the cliff. And it was huge. Even though it was sitting down, she could see it was far bigger than a human or fae.

Cassandrea froze for a moment, and she felt the air escaping her lungs. The terror was overwhelming, making her body fight each command she gave it. The stench of blood was pungent, almost enough to make her taste iron in her mouth, even if it mixed with the smell of autumn, a scent that made no sense to her. Why was it there? Why was that beast there? Was it feasting on its prey? She hoped it was. If it was still preoccupied with its feast, she might still have a chance to slip by.

However, Cassandrea wasn't going to bet her life on hope and wishful thinking. Instead, she forced her body to move, and stalked closer to the edge, away from sight, and sought to retrace her steps. Silent as a cat in the night, she held her breath. Bringing out her wings was out of question; the rustling of feathers would only draw the beast's attention.

Another careful step backwards and a seagull screamed nearby, almost giving her a heart attack. It seemed she had gotten too close to its nest. And that the gods weren't on her side.

At the seagull's shriek, the monster's head snapped in Cassandrea's direction, and even from a distance, she could see its two white eyes shining in the darkness.

The siren froze on the spot, trying to look as small as possible but deep down she knew it was pointless. The thing may not have smelled her, but it knew she was there. It tilted its head to the side, and only now she noticed it was holding something in its hands. Paws. Hands. Something round. Something that now dropped down the cliffs and fell into the upcoming tide with a quiet splash. And then the predator stood up. Definitely a beast by the size of it, but it had two legs and two arms, and from what she could see, clothes.

Cassandrea reached for her dagger, only to find it pointless, too. That thing was gargantuan. It could just rip her head off. No. A dagger wasn't going to work.

The beast was standing at the edge with too little distance between them. Not enough of a head start to run. But still Cassandrea's instincts screamed at her to do so. To run and never look back at this cursed land again.

She wasn't sure if the beast noticed what she was. The hood was covering most of her face, but she hadn't masked her scent, for she was still in the human lands. She had no need to do so. And now... what she needed was to run.

Taking another step backward, Cassandrea lifted her hands in the air to show she didn't want any trouble. Still, what good would that do? She could only guess what horrors would wait for her if that hulking mountain of a man got his hands on her. For a man he was. Despite his size, the scent she sniffed in the winds coming from the sea wasn't one of fur or scales. But it wasn't human either.

Cassandrea stopped. And waited. To see what the male would do.

He did... nothing. He kept watching her for what may have been ten seconds and seemed like an hour. Then he just turned away and looked back at the sea.

"I mean you no harm," the wind carried that strange autumnal scent towards Cassandrea together with a deep voice. One that was way more pleasant than what she had expected. "You may pass if you wish."

If she weren't so focused on the size of that beastly male, she would have sworn there was something sad in his tone.

A moment passed, and still nothing happened. Cassandrea dared to take a long breath. Then another. The male had turned his back on her. Either he was foolish, or he knew better. Knew that he wasn't in any danger and that he could still easily overpower her if he wanted to, even if she lunged at his back.

That thought made her uneasy.

But she had to keep going. She had to go home.

So she forced her legs to move slowly, one step at a time, to the other side of the cliff, but the cliffside curved steeply towards the edge, bringing her far too close to the male for her liking.

Cassandrea found herself wondering what kind of person he even was to have such authority in his aura, beside his size. Still, his voice was friendly, and it was the only interaction Cassandrea had with another being for over a week. So she kept her distance, practically trying to meld into the cliffside, but she spoke up, hoping not to challenge the male further but to warn him instead.

"Be careful. There is something dangerous out there."

Her voice rang soft, far softer than it should have. The siren used her magic to veil her words and charm the beast, if only to make him understand that she was no threat to him, either. He might not have been outright hostile, but the blood—that smell was still pungent on him. And Cassandrea had no intention to become an addition to that.

The male's only response was a quiet laughter.

"I am aware."

He still hadn't turned towards her, but as the path led her closer, she could see that despite his towering height and broad shoulders, he wasn't a beast after all. Or perhaps the shadows were playing tricks on her. Maybe... The wind caressed his black hair and the scent of autumn grew stronger. As did the scent of blood. And indeed, the sleeves of his pale blue tunic were dark and reeking of it. The blood of his victim. Cassandrea shuddered. But not because of the blood. She had finally recognised the last ingredient in his scent. He was fae. Dark fae, judging by the tone of his skin that was in stark contrast to the pale tunic. His skin was brown and tanned, making his features blend in with the night and impossible to remember.

"Where are you going?" he asked and angled his head enough that she could make out the line of his pointed ears.

Cassandrea found herself staring at the male intently, aware and ready for any sudden movements. That he was fae, wasn't making the situation any better. Definitely not for her. She looked like a human without her wings. And she hadn't heard any sympathy for sirens either from his ilk, so displaying her features might just agitate him into skewering her anyway...

"As far as I can, from here."

She admitted, her voice thick with the siren's veil. She wasn't planning to seduce or charm him fully. Only to make him not want to crush her as she was trying to pass around him. A few more steps in the silence and... She took the time to look at those pointed ears, then the dark, beautifully angled features of the male's face. It was a thing of lethal beauty. Brutal, yet mesmerising. She took another step. She was almost through.

"Not because of me, I hope," the deep voice rang with amusement, but the sadness in it lingered.

"Why are you here?" Cassandrea asked in return, not really understanding why.

She didn't care to know. But perhaps if the male kept talking, he would stay docile. Even though he must have caught her scent by then. Even though he most likely knew or would know what she was as soon as she stepped upwind. It was too late to hide her nature now. And she was too tired to do so anyway. Unavoidable. It was unavoidable. And maybe if he killed her, she wouldn't have to deal with the loss that was making her chest ache and her heart feel hollow. Maybe dying right there and then was for the best... Cassandrea took another step.

"I had a debt that needed to be paid." The male's voice was a little more than a whisper, barely audible over the raging tide.

His head turned after the siren, one of those white eyes keeping a tab on her wherever she moved. Perhaps he, too, wasn't sure whether she was going to attack. Yet her approach seemed to be working, as he hadn't ripped her to pieces, so it was worth feeding him another line.

She was right in the middle of pondering what it should be when he stole that wind from her sails.

"Why are *you* here, siren?" he inquired. "There haven't been any sailors in these waters for months. Though... I must applaud you. For having the audacity to test your spells on me."

His gaze was piercing. Firm. Amused. The gaze of a predator toying with his prey.

Cassandrea took another step. She was fully upwind now, which meant that she had an open path ahead, should she need to escape. It also meant that the reek of blood disappeared. Together with the warm scent of autumn surrounding the fae warrior. And just as the next gust blew past her and she looked towards where she was heading, the wind tore her hood off, revealing her mangled face and the sheer pain in her eyes. The shame.

"No, not because of you," she whispered. She knew the wind would carry those words and echo them for him like a choir. They had no veil in them, not this time. It was just her and her grief. She had no idea what she could answer to his latter question, or if she even should. If it even mattered now that he knew she had tried to charm him.

To hell with it, she thought. If she was going to die because of her wings, at least she would die with a wind in them.

"I'm just passing by," she said as the wings rustled out of her back like feathery sprouts, which then fanned open wide. She had always been proud of these creamy, white feathers that shone with bronze and golden brown patterns, leading to the darkened tips glimmering in the moonlight. So she lifted her chin up and met the male's gaze.

"I'm going home," she said.

The last few steps took her past him. Then, to the ledge she had been trying to reach. Finally, there was an opening in the cliffside where the downdraft wouldn't throw her right onto the rocks and crush her. She could ride that wind alongside the cliffs for a long time before she would need to go back to walking. This was her chance. She took one last look at that male and jumped.

She expected him to attack. Braced for the magic pulling her back and the paws shredding her wings. But none of that happened. Her wings caught an updraft, and she laid into it and soared high above the sea. High enough to risk a glance back.

The fae male was still standing in the same spot, his face turned up towards her. His eyes were shining, and she could almost swear there was something akin to admiration in his expression as the wind brought her his last words.

"Beautiful."

*

That last word haunted Cassandrea for weeks, echoing in her mind as she made her way back to the capital city of Alanthys. By the time she had soared into the night, the male's face had already blurred in her memory, but the weight of his voice remained, an imprint she couldn't shake. Her disfigurement—her lost beauty—was still burning as fiercely as it had the night she received it. And somehow, the weight of that final word, carried to her on the wind, made it ache even more.

Only when she approached the polished metal gates of Alanthys, that had always stood open to welcome a steady stream of visitors, Cassandrea finally managed to bury that pain deep within her heart, alongside the life she once knew. To be able to return home.

However, her home had changed. The gates weren't raised this time, nor were there visitors flowing freely through the main gate. Instead, fires burnt across the fields outside the city. Fires, tents, and soldiers filled the space, their banners flapping in the wind with the unmistakable sigil of her dragon king, Valderan. The capital was no longer a beacon of prosperity; it was a fortress. With an army poised to defend it at any cost.

ChapteR 2

There were five people waiting in front of King Valderan's throne room, even though none of them had been allowed in since the morning, so the mood was dire. One of the people there was a red-haired fae general standing motionlessly by the wall. The other four sometimes glanced at him with fear. Not because he was so terrifying, but because they knew that if even he hadn't been allowed in, the situation was beyond bad. The general didn't look at them. He wasn't interested in advisors, the aristocracy, or politicians. The only people he talked to were the two soldiers guarding the throne room. But their conversations were hushed and short and they didn't change anything. So the five people kept waiting. Until the very evening when the door on the other side of the corridor opened and let in a young woman with blond hair and a horribly scarred neck. All seven heads in the room turned in her direction and the four courtiers gasped for air. Because the young woman had somebody else with her. A prisoner. A beautiful noblewoman with long brown hair, now stuck together with blood clots. A lady, all four of them knew for once, she had been one of them. Not anymore. And as if the lady's presence alone could stain them, they recoiled, shuffling towards the walls, leaving a free space in the middle of the corridor for the two women to pass through.

Both of the ladies held their heads high, but each with a completely different expression. The blonde was walking with a proud and confident gait, smirking with the knowledge of a job well done. The brunette was walking to her death, challenging the people around her to witness it. But they didn't. None of the four. Only the general had given her a small nod of his head. The last acknowledgement. He was the only one who dared. And the lady awarded it with a smile.

"Out of all the people here, Torquil," she said. "I pity *you* the most."

"Save that pity for yourself," the blonde shoved the lady forward, "you are going to need it."

The two guards stepped out of their way to let the blonde one and her prey into the throne room, and as they opened the door, a strong gust of wind blew into the corridor carrying a mighty roar. A dragon's roar.

*

Cassandrea thought she knew her king, but after she had returned to Alanthys, even she found him terrifying. Unlike his counterparts, the three dragon siblings ruling Ordeara, Valderan rarely took on his human form. On most occasions, he preferred his dragon body, and the throne room was designed accordingly. It was a giant, mostly open area on top of his castle, with only a small, narrow portion protected from the elements. Everyone found it extremely painful to talk to the king there because of the merciless whipping of the winds and the northern weather alone. And when one survived that, then there was the dragon himself.

Valderan was a massive black beast the size of several ships, with a maw large enough to devour ten of his courtiers at once, and a voice that could shatter windows and eardrums. A mighty, ancient creature that left anyone beholding it in awe. His gargantuan black body was covered with thick, sharp spines. Some of them were worn out by age and shorter than others, but they were all as sharp as ever, ready to pierce through anything the king wished to crush. The dragon king's tail was as deadly as his head; the spined scales led to a bladed tip, like a scaled halberd, capable of cleaving through anything. Then there was the head itself. Marred by centuries of battles and wisdom, the wide head of the dragon was as beautiful as it was brutal. Its black as night scales shimmered with ancient magic and were decorated with runes, the origin of which was known only to the king himself. The wide brow of the beast was crowned with sharp, jagged spines, and two thick, tiered horns swept backwards from above the king's eyes. Eyes of smouldering gold.

But the king had never hurt Cassandrea. Not even these days when everybody was shaking in their boots, just thinking about talking to him. No. Valderan gave her clear orders; that was all. And she had carried them out as fast as she could. As always. He was her king. Her saviour. And she was his best spy.

"Cassandrea."

The growl coming out of his massive maw reverberated through her body. She let it. She loved the feeling of the dragon's power surging through her. It was that very strength that was protecting her. Protecting their entire kingdom. Until last week...

"My king," Cassandrea kneeled before the dragon, dipping her head and casting her eyes down. "I hunted down lady Aronea, as you wished."

She didn't rise. It would have been impolite. Not until a low growl let her know that she could. Then she looked up and saw the enormous golden eyes with cat-like pupils staring at her from so close that she twitched. He was within reach. Cassandrea could easily stretch out her hand and touch the tip of his nose. Not that she would ever dare to do that.

The lady next to her didn't bow. She was staring at the dragon, frozen by fear but still proud. Still defiant.

"Your rule is over," Aronea started, "king Terren-"

"Kill her," the deep voice bellowed.

"He will-" Aronea tried to finish her sentence, but Cassandrea acted without hesitation. *Dusk* whined as it was drawn from its sheath and plunged into Lady Aronea's heart. One fluid motion was all it took.

Cassandrea was well aware that it was all a test for her, but it made no difference. If the king needed to verify she was loyal, then it was his right. The lady was a traitor. She deserved to die. They all deserved to die.

What did startle her, however, was when the dragon opened his maw and devoured Aronea's body before it collapsed. Cassandrea barely had the time to pull out her blade and arm away as blood sprayed on the floor. For a moment, there was no other sound but the dragon's teeth grinding against the bones of his dinner. One horrifying crunch after another. No other words. No orders. So the siren took a step back to avoid getting her clothes dirty and she waited.

A few minutes later, her king moved again, and his golden eye came close to her head. The sheer size of the gargantuan head would've sent people running away. But Cassandrea looked straight at him. She wasn't afraid.

"You didn't ask why."

"She was a traitor, my king. Why should I ask for another reason?"

The golden eye blinked, and the place went silent, with only the wind howling through the empty throne room. Valderan had changed since she saw him before going to Ordeara. Cassandrea could tell. Maybe she was the only one who could. Who could see how deep that pain of betrayal ran. Who had felt it.

"You have to kill them all, Cassandrea," the dragon demanded quietly, "all of them. All who support Terren. All of those who betrayed us."

"I will," she said firmly.

"All of those who *would* betray us," the king continued.

"I will," she said.

And she would. She would kill them all. Especially Terren. The prodigal protégé who had dared to defy her king. To betray him. Betray a man who had been like a father to him. Who was ready to offer him an entire kingdom one day. But no, the young dragon couldn't wait. He had to have it all. Yes, he would pay for it, the siren promised both herself and her king. Terren would pay for it all. Dearly.

"I know you will," Valderan growled. "That I can trust *you*."

His hot breath hit Cassandrea's face. It stank of blood and death, but the siren didn't flinch. It was a blessing to be standing in front of the dragon and be seen. And she let her king pick up just how much those words meant to her. How important it was to her to be worth that trust. Her heart ached from joy and relief as she lifted her chin up to face the one true ruler of the land.

"I won't disappoint you."

"I have always believed in you, Cassandrea," the king's deep, rumbling voice sent chills down her spine, making the hair stand up on the back of her neck.

"I am most grateful for that," she managed to utter in response, despite the tremble her voice carried. "And it is an honour to serve you, my king," she continued, lowering her head to a humbled bow.

There was a gentle breeze, the same stench of death and blood, then silence. The steady thrum of the dragon's breathing was gone. And Cassandrea found her chin lifted up by the king's fingers. Her eyes widened as she beheld the greatest honour the king had ever bestowed upon her. His human form.

"Come now, child," the king's voice was still deep. Still eternally wise, and it rumbled like a storm on the horizon.

King Valderan was the most handsome man she had ever seen. A tall, broad-shouldered man with silky, ebony hair, wavy and elegant, and emphasising the regal, sculpted features of his perfect face. His eyes, bright and vibrant like molten gold, were hidden behind a veil of dark lashes and framed by dark brows that were not frowning at the sight of her. No, the king's sensual lips were curled to a smile.

Cassandrea knew at that moment that she would die happy, knowing that her king had smiled at her. She would dredge through a mountain of corpses, knowing that he had granted her that gift.

"You were very young when you were first brought into this court," the king's velvety voice continued.

Cassandrea nodded. She couldn't keep her eyes off the visage of her king. He was perfect.

"And I've watched you grow into the woman you are now, Cassandrea. You are not the blunt crushing weight of my army, or even the blade of the sword that cuts through our enemies, no." His hand moved to cup her cheek and Cassandrea felt her chest expanding.

"You are my shadow, child, my shadow that I send across the land to cut short the cries of the dissidents, traitors, and rebels," Valderan continued, those golden eyes still smiling at her.

"As you will it," she said, and dared to smile back.

The king's smile faded as his hand moved to her shoulder, gripping it firmly. It was not a fatherly encouragement or gentle gesture of a lover, but a grip made of iron with enough weight on it to gently bend Cassandrea's knees. It was a grip that demanded obedience. One that would not allow for a shred of doubt. The siren held her head high as she gazed at her king.

"I have shown you how to break them through pain," Valderan said and turned, guiding her towards the side of the throne room.

The wide, open terrace provided views of the sky, the vast, beautiful Alanthys with its countless twinkling lights, and the deadly fall down to the rocky root of the palace, which no doubt countless courtiers had faced after insulting the king. The wind was howling at them, and Cassandrea was relieved that she knew the air currents better than most. Trusted them. She wasn't afraid of them, not even this close to the edge, not even when it tugged and tore on her leathers and tried to snag her hair. The king's cape billowed like a mighty sail, and she could only stand there in awe of him.

"But it is time, Cassandrea, for me to teach you how to break them with fear."

Cassandrea took a deep breath. This was it. He cared. He cared enough to teach her.

"Fear," the handsome dragon said, "is the key to their souls."

Chapter 3

Three years later, Alanthys still hadn't been sacked, but, other than that, there was little reason for joy. Every single day since Terren's betrayal had been a brutal tug between the two dragon rulers, both grasping for control. Like two stags stuck together by their antlers, their battle for territory was so fierce, it ripped apart the very lands their war was trying to secure. Numerous cities were razed, countless lives lost. King Valderan had drafted every single capable soul to fight, regardless of their occupation or age. If they could fight, they would. And yet, his forces were no closer to winning the war than when it started.

Standing at the broken shores of Ithyren, a once beautiful coastal city and a jewel of the Western Weald that had been sundered to ash only a month ago, Cassandrea took in the surroundings. The port was filled with a mass of troops: soldiers, menders, mounted units, and their fae-seeker fiends—all tired and weary. The crowd, a sea of pale, creamy white armour, capes, and tabards decorated with gold details and trims, slowly ebbed towards the arriving ships that lowered their platforms to take the troops in. Several icon bearers were holding tall banners and standards with the gold and black royal seal of king Valderan's black dragon, roaring proudly in the gentle sway of the ocean breeze.

Cassandrea blended in perfectly. She was one of them—a rugged, worn-out soldier with scars on her face to remind her of the toils of the war. Clad in an identical cream tunic and with a hood that veiled her thick, golden hair, braided back for convenience. Yet, she was not one of them. Not in the way that she would fight on the front lines or face the enemy head-on. No, she was a saboteur, a spy, a guerilla unit that only answered to the king himself and to his most trusted generals. Valderan knew what she was and had used her gifts many times to gain an edge on a crucial battle or to tear out information from prisoners of war. He knew, and still relied on her to deal with some of the most delicate matters there were. In return, she wore that trust proudly and strived to further prove him right for relying on her. Even when others didn't.

Today, she was here in Ithyren, waiting for a boat to arrive to take the battalion she had been assigned to on board and deliver them to the battlefield.

Cassandrea hadn't received her orders yet. She never did, not before it became necessary, but her presence alone meant that the battle ahead was about to be particularly important.

The crowd moved, and Cassandrea boarded the ship, following her battalion. She wasn't sure where they were going. Didn't know why. Trying to keep track of the entire war was a task that was way above her capabilities. Not abilities, no. But nobody ever bothered to provide her with information that wasn't part of her mission, or show her the maps of the current situation. And most definitely, nobody ever asked her opinion on anything. The generals and commanders suffered her presence only because the king demanded they did. She was hiding her scent during the endless hours she was spending with the crew and the fae soldiers, pretending to be another human in their midst, completely unremarkable. But the general knew. Knew and hated it. Him and his closest circle treated her like some infected tool that was to be touched only by a five-foot-long pole. Cassandrea was well aware that if it were up to them, she would have been walking around with a gag, silencing her beautiful voice and the gift they feared.

They didn't want her mingling with the troops, either. Fearing what she could do and the disarray she could cause. Not that she wanted to do any of that. She had dedicated her life to her king and his kingdom, drowning the pain into work, and suffocating the screams of revenge in the blood-curdling thirst to act and do something meaningful. She had been ruthless. Cruel. Efficient. For Valderan. She had clawed her way to the person she was now. Someone important. Invaluable. And she desperately tried to hide the pain from feeling unwanted. Because everywhere she went, those who knew the truth were turning away from her, shielding their ears or eyes in the fear of her alluring call. So she served in silence, carefully tucking away her feelings and thoughts, never complaining, never questioning. Always ready.

Cassandrea walked atop the ship's bow, peering towards the glimmering horizon. The sun was about to reach its zenith, the distant waves were glittering like diamonds, and the gentle southern breeze promised soft, tender winds for their sails. It was relatively warm, even though it was still an early spring. Especially here in the north-western parts of the continent, winter was still holding the land in a firm grasp, and snow was coating the majority of the landscape. But the sea was clear and open. And today, the wind coming over the endless waves came with a gentle promise of a spring.

Cassandrea turned to look at the docks. Eight dreadnought galleons were docked in the ruined port, capable of transporting several hundred soldiers each. Approximately sixty yards long and sixteen wide, each ship was equipped with large sails and oars in case of a sudden lack of winds.

Ebongale, the ship housing Cassandrea, was being stocked and preparing to set sail. The fair-haired siren leaned on the railing and let the wind caress her cheek as the ship moved, and its hull resounded with playful waves drumming and splashing against the timber. She loved the feeling, loved the scent. Seaweed and salt, and a warm southern breeze—that was how home smelled to her. One day, perhaps, she would buy a small house somewhere on the western shore. Away from the men and fae both. Away from everybody who feared her. Alone. Or with somebody like Ryker...

A light cough interrupted her daydream.

"Miss?"

The siren turned around and laid her eyes on a young human man, an aide, who was keeping a respectful distance, most likely warned about her charm by his superiors.

"Yes?" she asked. Her eyes studied the man in silence. She could see the fear dancing in his eyes. Fear mixing with desire. Lust. Disgust. He tried to hide it, but it shone through his eyes, clear as day, every time he looked at her. A rush of warmth grew in Cassandrea's gut. And anger. For three years she had suffered being treated like this by the males who knew what she was. As if they thought she was some volatile mixture that could go off at any given time.

"What is it?"

Cassandrea imbued her voice with an extra layer of the siren's veil just in spite. She knew she shouldn't have, but she didn't really care. The aide's fear was making her blood boil. In moments like this, she didn't know why she bothered hiding her nature. She loved her dragon king, loved him fiercely for giving her a chance despite the usual prejudices, but dealing with people was torture on a good day. And this wasn't a good day. And she had far too little wine in her system to be nice.

The young man's gaze melted under her spell, and his voice became friendly and warm. Longing.

"The general wishes to talk to you, should you be inclined to accept his request."

Cassandrea let a small smile spread on her lips as she watched the man's posture shift, and his gestures become far less rigid. She inclined her head and nodded.

"Why, of course. We shouldn't let him wait," she said with a smile, even though the words were laced with irony. She had kept him waiting. Several times. Just to spite him. But today, she wasn't in the mood for playing games or entertaining his fits, even if it was somewhat satisfying to know that these men held no power over her; on the contrary. The king's decree guaranteed that she remained untouched. With one last glance at the glittering sea, she nodded. The galleon swayed gently as the waves crashed against the hull. The crew was finally done restocking, and, with her sails lowered, Ebongale was slowly leaving the harbour.

"I will talk to him," Cassandrea said to the aide, and as she passed the young man, she let her fingers brush past his cheek. It was only a second—all that she needed. The aide smiled, and, had she done anything more, he would have been rolling at her feet like a lost puppy, begging for attention. Like this, he was content with looking at her with heart-aching tenderness and desire.

The general's cabin was at the back of the ship, close to the captain's quarters. Cassandrea strode towards the double doors and gave the guarding soldiers a glance. Both of them bristled.

Clearly, they knew, too. She didn't acknowledge their existence as she knocked on the door, and, almost instantly, the door was opened for her. As if they were worried, she could speak up. She stepped into the cabin, the young aide in tow.

"Sit down," General Torquil uttered as a form of greeting, trying to silence her before she even got the chance to open her mouth.

Torquil was a seasoned fae warrior, almost six hundred years old, which made him Valderan's oldest general. Not necessarily the most popular one, though, as Torquil's personality was highly abrasive, and Cassandrea wasn't the only one who found the male insufferable. However, he was still handsome and not looking a day past thirty. The only markers of his true age were numerous white scars trailing his tanned face and his muscular arms. Bare arms, needless to say, as the man rarely wore anything more than a sleeveless jacket. Unless the battle was around the corner. Which it clearly was now, because he was in full armour, his long red hair tied into a knot and crowned with a leather headband.

"And I would appreciate it if you could release my aide from your toils," the general snarled, showing his sharp teeth in the process, "right about now."

Cassandrea gave him a snarl of her own and sat down on a free chair, giving a lazy nod to the man standing next to the general. A very thin human man. Old and wiry, his skin the colour and texture of a sun-dried octopus. Ualan, the captain of Ebongale.

"And I would appreciate it if you treated me with a bit more respect, general," Cassandrea replied, "but it seems none of us is getting what we want."

The general frowned, but he didn't try to push his luck. The siren had been chosen to be on this ship, whether he liked it or not. But Cassandrea wasn't really in the mood to drag this one out, so she shifted her stare towards the male and gave him a pointed stare.

"General Torquil, what is it that you want from me?"

Cassandrea saw no reason to stay in the company of those who detested her any longer than necessary, so the question came out a little sharper than she had originally intended. The reaction came immediately.

"For you to release my man from your spell, witch. And to shut your foul mouth," Torquil growled, "for long enough to hear what the king's orders for you are."

Cassandrea sighed but decided it was better not to argue at this very point. The young aide behind her took a sharp breath and turned red as a tomato. She didn't even have to look at him to know it happened.

"Much obliged," Torquil growled and pointed at some spot on his map, "now listen. We are about to land south of Renglow in two days. There we will drop you off, and you are to meet a contact on the shore. Somebody called Kerr. The two of you will prepare our landing in Renglow, which will happen in three days from when we drop you off. So get into the city, start a fire, disable their cannons, bite their mayor's dick off or whatever it is you do."

Cassandrea dug her nails into the fabric of her trousers not to bite Torquin's head off instead, but she managed to keep her voice levelled when she replied.

"Whatever it is I do, general, usually takes more than three days."

"This is all I can give you. We can't risk a storm catching us before the battle. Not to mention, it will be hard to avoid their spies as it is. Oh, and Cassandrea? There is no room on the ship, so you will be staying in the cabin with me while you are on board. Unless you'd prefer to share with the human soldiers." His eyes moved to the poor aide, who still had the colour of a radish. "And give them something to do."

Cassandrea took a small breath to calm her anger. She angled her head to look at the general and offered the male a sweet smile that didn't reach her eyes.

"There's no space for me on this ship? Then pray tell, general, why was I brought aboard it?" her words dripped of venom, and she had to stifle the urge to claw the man's face a new set of scars. "For your sake, I hope you aren't planning to try to get busy."

Her eyes narrowed at those words, and she shot the general a glance that mirrored the same exact distaste that was displayed in the male's grey-blue eyes. The captain recoiled at those words, and even though Cassandrea still didn't see him, she knew the young aide was glowing red like a piping hot stovetop.

"Anything else, general?" Cassandrea shifted her glare towards the captain, who more or less looked like he wanted to become a part of the furniture and found the wood patterns on the floor planks suddenly immensely interesting. The siren crossed her legs and laced her fingers over her lap. Slowly, a spiteful smile started spreading on her lips. She didn't want to feel so smug about it, and she certainly didn't want to admit it to herself, but seeing these males squirming was immensely satisfying. She looked back at Torquil.

The general didn't reply for a while, but he was the only one who hadn't averted his gaze.

"Trust me, temptress; if I had a say in this, you wouldn't be sailing with us. Or you'd be locked up with the cargo."

"Temptress..." Cassandrea's voice was dangerously soft. "It sounds a lot like you're uncomfortable around me because you're afraid of losing control."

She didn't bother to hide the smugness in her voice.

"Don't flatter yourself, sea-witch. I will have you gagged if you don't keep your foul tongue in check!"

Cassandrea chuckled. She had won. The general was not going to be able to sleep a single wink in the following two nights. That much was certain.

"Your choice, general. You can always find a nice empty cabin for me," she suggested innocently.

"Or I can decide to use your services," the man growled, partially losing his control already, "so shut. Your. Mouth."

Too far. Cassandrea had gone too far. It was time to withdraw before he actually decided to act on his threat. It was one thing to toy with the defenceless human men and a different thing entirely to provoke a six hundred-year-old fae general in the middle of his army. Especially with the results of her teasing already showing under the fabric of his leather trousers. She quickly stood up and gave the males a courteous bow.

"Later, gentlemen."

Air. She needed air.

Luckily enough, none of them said anything. And nobody tried to stop her as she hurried out of the cabin. Two days, she reminded herself as soon as she reached the upper deck and the warm southern air filled her lungs. Just two days. And then she would be free again. Free on the shore. Free to do her job. Well, not entirely free with this Kerr working with her. But maybe Kerr was a she. Maybe it was somebody who wouldn't hate her. Or at least somebody who wouldn't see her as nothing but a whore or a dirty rag to be discarded. Or a tool to be used, then forgotten...

Cassandrea took a deep breath and allowed it to soothe her. She could taste the breeze on her tongue. Filled with the scent of new grass and promises of flowers in bloom. Soon. Soon the spring would come, and maybe they could finally end the war. At least this war. It was a ridiculous one, she thought. There was a huge threat looming on the southern borders, and instead, they were fighting each other, shattering Entirie and giving their southern neighbour all the advantages. She didn't even know how the whole thing started. There was a rumour that the young dragon Terren killed Lord Ragnall, the king's fae ally and advisor, but she knew it was nonsense. Lord Ragnall was fighting deep in Ordeara with his army at that time, and Terren started his uprising all the way in the north, marching down to Alanthys. There was no rumour of the young dragon flying to Ordeara, nor of any betrayal in Ragnall's own ranks. Ragnall died on the battlefield from what she could tell, which was really bad timing, resulting in his army sitting tight and waiting for a new leader while Terren's people were seizing city after city and gaining new support for their campaign. Eventually, it was Valderan's own army that was sent north to stop their advance instead of protecting the capital, and it led to a lot of sleepless nights and uproar among the wealthy citizens of Alanthys, who felt suddenly somewhat vulnerable. Cassandrea herself went with that first wave to see the size of Terren's army and gain as much information as she could. And she had worked diligently for three years to help her homeland, her beloved king, her kingdom. And to her horror, she had witnessed Terren's numbers growing with each city they ploughed through, like some living plague that left nothing but doubt and treason in its wake.

Her thoughts were brought to a halt as the ship teetered against a wave. Cassandrea braced her hands against the wooden railing. They were sweaty. She had three days to change the tide in Renglow, and she could only hope that this Kerr would be able to keep up with her.

A strangely familiar scent rose from the waters as the ship crashed against a particularly rough wave, making the humongous hull bump against it. The brine and smell of seaweed mixed with something she couldn't quite place. Something she knew she should recognise. And she finally did, as she glanced down at the waves. Merfolk. Gleefully swimming alongside dolphins and white-finned sharks, racing with them, playing with them. Cassandrea grimaced as she leaned over the wooden beam and peered into the waters. Beautiful things. Beautiful, terrible things. For as much as the sirens and the harpies were considered cruel and savage, merfolk had gained only a slightly better reputation among the other magical creatures. Not among humans though. Humans loved them. Perhaps it was that vibrant, beautiful fishtail that glimmered with prismatic scales, or their ethereal faces, or those alluring, black almond eyes that made them somewhat more tolerable. Or perhaps... It was because merfolk could not leave the waters, whereas sirens and harpies could fly. Yet Cassandrea knew that the better reputation was wholly undeserved. Merfolk were exactly as vicious and predatory when it came to hunting sailors. Oftentimes, they even dared to steal a siren's prey. So, Cassandrea didn't wave. Didn't consider this a lucky encounter. She was watching their rainbow tails with careful distaste while imagining one of them dragging General Torquil to the bottom of the sea. Maybe she should offer him a nice song after all. Maybe...

Cassandrea blinked those thoughts away. As obnoxious as Torquil was, he was still Valderan's general and skilled at his job. Something rattled, and Cassandrea raised her head just in time to see a red-haired fae female pulling back a soldier who was about to jump overboard.

"Moron," the fae girl hissed and slammed the man against the main mast, "if you want to hug that fish, better make sure you grow gills first."

Cassandrea peered over the railing again, and there was indeed a young mermaid with beautiful breasts all on display, her pretty face distorted by anger while she was hurling insults in the old tongue at the fae redhead. However, the girl didn't just take it. She shouted back, and within a second, she had a bow in her hand and an arrow on the rest, drawing the bow and aiming... The mermaid didn't like that. She swiftly parted with a rude gesture towards the archer and disappeared beneath the waves, the other merfolk in tow. The redhead laughed and returned the arrow to her quiver with a smooth and well-practiced move.

"It would have been a waste of a good arrow," she said.

At first, Cassandrea thought the words belonged to the soldier or to nobody in particular, but then the fae girl turned and smiled, and the siren realised they were meant for her.

"Colossal waste," she replied, not really knowing what to say, "humans, right?"

Apparently not the right answer. The fae girl blinked and shook her head.

"It is not their fault, is it? Not really. They don't have defences like we do," she replied as soon as she helped the soldier up and sent him below deck.

"So, you are watching over them?"

"Kind of," the redhead laughed, took a step towards Cassandrea and to the siren's surprise, she held out her hand, "I am Mairi."

Cassandrea hesitated. She knew the name well, although she had never seen this female in person before. Mairi. Torquil's very own cousin. Only a few decades younger than the general and more than a capable warrior herself.

And as if Mairi knew what thoughts were going through Cassandrea's head, she moved her hand up and down, reinviting the handshake with a quiet laugh.

"Come on. I am not a second Torq. I promise." Her voice was bright and light, like a crisp spring morning. A breath of fresh air.

Cassandrea hesitantly took that hand and shook it once. Twice. She couldn't help but smile, as she realised the female hadn't indeed been snarling at her, hissing insults or wishing her to be tied up to the front of the ship. Mairi was painfully beautiful, with a freckled face, wind-kissed cheeks, and that flaming red hair that shone in the sunlight like a halo around her head. She, too, had the same grey-blue eyes Torquil did, but hers shone with a different light. Unburdened. Friendly.

"Cassandrea," the siren's reply was soft, and while she didn't want it to be, wary. Very few knew about her disposition. She wasn't sure if Mairi did. The female *was* a cousin of Torquil's, but surely she wasn't prancing around the command table just because of her relation to him.

"Just Cassandrea?" Mairi asked. Her voice was willowy, and her smile was charming. Challenging. Cassandrea felt her heart freeze over. Mairi knew. She had to.

"Cassandrea Thalarin," she said.

The girl was still holding her hand, and as the last name was spoken aloud, she beamed a smile and finally sealed the handshake with one more firm nod. The last name was a lie, of course. Sirens did not have last names. Cassandrea had taken her father's mother's maiden name only to blend in. Normally, sirens carried no family names, and to take her father's name was to curse the entire flock. Or so was sung in the sirens' chants and canticles that were passed down through aeons of history onto the next generations. Even for half-bloods like Cassandrea there were rules. Sacred rules that were never to be broken.

"So how long have you been running the 'human protection services', Mairi?" the siren asked, and she couldn't help but feel conflicted about it. Something about Mairi's smile was so disarming. She felt a little poke of guilt in her heart for enchanting that aide.

Mairi let out a laugh.

"Someone's got to watch out for them. They're good people, but utterly helpless sometimes."

There was no mockery in that voice. Or in the words. Strange words, coming from a fae of such a high status. Cassandrea let out a small hum and glanced over the railing. The merfolk and their pets were gone.

"Since the war started," Mairi shrugged, finally answering the question.

Cassandrea took her time to study the redhead. Especially the blue eyes that suddenly turned grey in the evening sun, as if something weighed heavily on the girl's soul. It was the same shadow that constantly lingered in her cousin's eyes. War? The long lifespan? Cassandrea didn't know, but before she could figure it out, the female shook that thought off and beamed her another smile.

"We need every able body and soul to keep up the fight, right?"

Mairi grinned at Cassandrea, and although there was neither malice nor judgement in her eyes, the siren felt another poke at her conscience. She hadn't really thought about that. Selfish as she was, she had only thought about her own comfort, or the lack thereof. The poor aide did nothing wrong, except for knowing about her origins and being human.

"Right," she growled and kept hypnotising the sea, unable to look at the gorgeous and kind fae.

However, her attitude did nothing to ruin Mairi's mood. The female just beckoned towards the sea and smiled.

"It's good you are on the lookout as well. Call me if they come back?"

"Sure."

Cassandrea wanted to add something. Wanted to tell Mairi that she was the last person who should be put on guard duty. But before she could figure out the right words, Mairi was gone. So Cassandrea stayed. Long into the night, she remained on the deck, watching the waves coming and going until her eyes hurt from it and she started seeing fishtails in every shadow. It still felt like the right thing to do. To help. Just a little bit. Plus, it was a nice clear night, and the stars were bright and laughing down at her. She loved watching them. Loved the way the moonlight kissed the waves and turned them into sparkling silk.

Only when the guards changed again, the siren realised just how tired she was and how heavy her eyelids had turned. She sighed. It was the time to face the general. Or preferably, sneak into his cabin and fall asleep without him noticing. Cassandrea kept her footsteps light, even when she cut through the deck and passed the marines on their night watch. She didn't smile, but nodded at those who acknowledged her. At the door, she nodded at the guards again. They were alert, fresh, and just arrived at the shift. Their eyes scanned her, and she hated what she saw in them. Amusement. They thought they knew what was going on. She didn't bother to answer them, even though every cell in her body told her to scream at them that they knew nothing. But she didn't scream. Didn't say anything to them. She just quietly opened the door and slipped in.

There was only one flickering light in the cabin, a small stump of a candle seated in a candlestick. The wax had already pooled around the rim and base, indicating that it had been burning for a long while, undisturbed. Cassandrea gave the cabin a look around. It was quiet like a tomb, the silence only broken by the crashing waves and the snarling of wood and occasional groan of a rope from the sails. The cabin wasn't large, but certainly larger than some of the others on the same corridor. It was furnished modestly and decorated with a very frugal taste. The desk that sat at the back end of the wall was filled with maps and piles of books and stacks of parchment, quills and sextants, and pins scattered all around them. The inkwell was sunken into its nest, and although it had been corked, there were several ink stains around it.

None of that mattered to Cassandrea, though, because the best part of it all was that the general was nowhere to be found.

Worried she might stumble over a trunk or a chest or the fluffy, thick carpet on the floor, Cassandrea took a hold of the candlestick and let the flickering, warm light give her a little bit more visibility when she approached the hammock that was suspended between a support beam and a wall hook. There was a bed as well, unmade and with a thin blanket scrunched up in a corner, but that sleeping arrangement clearly wasn't meant for her. So, she opted for the hammock and was just in the process of removing her leathers when the door creaked open and the general strolled in.

Cassandrea froze.

Wherever the man came from, he was barefoot and wearing only trousers and a white shirt. She cursed. She hadn't noticed his armour or jacket lying around, so he must have tucked it into one of the chests. How long ago? And what was he doing outside at this hour? A night walk below decks? A mistress among his soldiers? Had he gone to relieve himself? Cassandrea blushed against her will. She didn't want to think about that part of him. At all. And seeing his feet made her uncomfortable. Seeing skin she wasn't meant to see. It felt oddly intimate.

"Have you decided to grace me with your presence after all,

sea-witch?"

Cassandrea couldn't stop the shiver that ran down her spine. Even his voice was abrasive. And there was something... ancient in him. She wasn't born yesterday herself, soon to round her first century, but compared to him, she was a toddler. In fact, there weren't many creatures walking their world that would be older than this warrior. Save for the dragon king himself, of course, and a couple of nightmares nobody ever wished to meet. And she had dared using her voice on him! Him! Stupid. Stupid siren.

Cassandrea swallowed heavily. She didn't want to show the general just how nervous she was. Or how seeing him like this impacted her far more than she had wanted to. However, she wasn't sure what else to do. She didn't want to turn her back to the male, for she was wary of what he might do, but she didn't want to start undressing in front of him, either. So she halted her hands and lifted her chin up.

"I thought you wanted to lock me up with the rest of the cargo," she said, although the intended edge in her voice was so mild it became negligible. She didn't look at him. The shame was burning her guts, and she really didn't want the old warrior to see that.

"You saw fit to try to humiliate me in front of the captain and my aide?" Torquil's voice was dangerously silky for the words used.

Cassandrea swallowed and bit back the snarkiest of her replies. She closed her eyes and craned her head upwards, as if she were saying some silent prayer in her mind. Then she turned to look at the male, who was now standing only an arm's length away from her. Her response got stuck in her throat, and she tilted her head in a warning. Her cheeks were burning, and the siren had no idea where to look; she didn't want the male to think she was trying anything, but she also didn't want him to think she was afraid of him. Which... she was. And she was more than certain the warrior could sense it in her. So she steeled her heart and held the general's stare.

"What do you want?" she demanded as she weaved a little backwards, but instantly the hammock snarled as it bowed and conformed against her back, leaving her stranded between the general and its knotted net.

The candle in her hand was the only thing she had to protect herself. Her twin blades were resting against the knee-high cabinet next to the wall, and her dagger was too far down now that her belt was partly undone. The belt. She could use the belt. She thought of a thousand things she could say to defend her earlier actions, but scurrying behind the King felt almost juvenile, like a child huddling behind her mother's hem. Besides, she had tried that already, and it didn't work.

"I want you to learn your place," the general snarled, "like all the soldiers in my battalion."

He took another step, his face almost touching hers, and Cassandrea dropped her hand and grabbed the belt buckle, readying to pull it out. But thus far, the male hadn't attacked. He was just staring at her with such intensity that she felt her bones melting. Maybe she could throw the candle in his face and melt him instead.

"So instead of prancing around and ensnaring my men, you'll be locked here and thinking hard on your assignment and how to deliver the city to me. And if you can't do that, if you can't keep that veil of yours in check, if you don't shut up upon receiving the order to, I will bend you over this bed and show you what it leads to when you get exactly what you've been asking for. Do you understand that?"

Cassandrea could barely hear anything from the thumping of her heart and the blood that was thrumming in her ears. Her breathing shallow, she swallowed her pride and humiliation. She was lucky, she reminded herself. Lucky beyond reason that the general didn't take the last step. Still marvelling at that fact, Cassandrea forced herself to meet Torquil's gaze. The male was a fair bit taller than her, which made her crane her chin upwards awkwardly to be able to look him in the eye. Probably exactly what he had intended. She felt small. Insignificant. Even if the general wasn't exceptionally large in the grand scale of fae, he had several inches on her, which wasn't really that much of a feat. Sirens were known to be smaller than an average fae, dwarfed only by humans by an inch or two.

"Perfectly."

Her breathing still shallow, Cassandrea managed to keep her voice from wobbling uncontrollably, but she couldn't stop her hand from trembling. She was at the mercy of an ancient fae. A male far more powerful than what she had ever dared to imagine. Her cockiness could've cost her dearly. Luckily, the general hadn't acted.

He did move though. But not towards her. No. Before she batted an eye, the man was gone. Gone to his own bed, the crumpled, thin blanket covering everything but his bare feet and a halo of red hair.

Cassandrea let out a quiet, relieved sigh, put her candle on the small cabinet her blades were resting against, and blew it out. She couldn't bear the thought of Torquil seeing her undress, even if it meant she had to fumble about in the darkness. So only when the candle hissed and the cabin was swallowed by a pitch-black void, she finally moved her trembling fingers to her belt and took off her leathers.

Chapter 4

The morning of the third day was exceptionally gloomy. Heavy fog was rolling over an unusually calm sea, and there was absolutely no wind at all. This close to the enemy city, the fleet was stripped of the option to maintain a safe distance from each other through the use of their fog horns, so when Cassandrea walked out on the deck, there was a line of fae soldiers both on starboard and portside, straining their eyes into the mist to give a timely warning.

The siren thought that the weather was both good and bad. Sure, they couldn't see each other, but the enemy also couldn't see them when they were about to land. Provided they could find the shore. Either way, she couldn't wait to leave the ship. And she would leave it today, even if she had to swim.

The previous day wasn't quite as bad as the day before, regarding the general's attitude, but she hated that she was literally locked in his cabin while all the wind and the sea were out there waiting for her. At least he didn't threaten her again, and he also hadn't tried anything. And Cassandrea made damn sure that she hadn't given him any reason to. Abrasive or not, the siren had to admit the old fae male had honour. Honour to keep his word to the king, honour to not harm her... even if she had provoked him into it. And some small part of her, somewhere deep within her, respected that tremendously. And was grateful for it.

Less so, was she grateful for the weather. The thick fog was making everything damp, sparing neither their clothes nor the wooden surfaces, leaving the deck and stairs treacherously slick. But none of that bothered Cassandrea. It was the offputting calmness of the sea, the almost nonexistent little lapping against the ship's hull, and the complete lack of seabirds. They should've been close enough to hear the seagulls screaming. But there was nothing but silence.

Perched over the railing overseeing the bow, Cassandrea took in the scents from the direction where the shore should be. Yet she could sense nothing. Just the salty brine. Where was the wind? She heard quiet murmurs in the back as the captain ordered the oars to be pushed out. They'd have to continue by rowing if the winds didn't carry them any further. Then she finally heard something. A bell, somewhere in the distance, punctured the silence with a metallic ring. Then another. And another. It wasn't a warning. More of a call. It could have been a temple bell, calling for worship. Or a school bell, herding the children in. An odd sound, either way, echoing through the mists and coming from all sides at once. Cassandrea hated this feeling of unease. It made her skin crawl, and she couldn't place it. So she turned around and headed for the general.

She found him leaning over a map on the upper deck with the captain at his side. Ualan was peering into a spyglass aimed towards the shore, where the bell was still ringing, but she doubted he could really see anything, spyglass or not. Torquil shifted his weight at another bell chime, equally uneasy about the eerie silence.

"General," Cassandrea addressed him quietly.

"Mmh?" he didn't even look up from the map as he replied, too busy measuring the distance with a sextant and a compass, both of which he was frowning at.

"I can go now. Alone, " Cassandrea whispered. She looked behind her, as if to make sure nobody else would hear her.

"I can jump off and fly-"

"Absolutely not." Torquil still hadn't looked at her.

"Why not?" She protested. "It makes the most sense. If you cannot find the shore and land safely, if we don't know how far the city is..."

"She's making sense," Ualan said suddenly and lowered his spyglass. "We are not getting anywhere in this, and we cannot wait for the fog to lift. We have to be far away from the shore when that happens, or else we will be spotted. And heading out on the open sea right now will also protect us from crashing into each other, which is at the top of my worries."

Torquil finally deemed them worthy of a look. And a growl.

"We don't know how far from the shore we are."

"Exactly," Ualan countered.

"And she doesn't know where to meet the contact."

"I will find him," Cassandrea said with way more confidence than she felt.

"Mhm."

"I *will* find him, general."

This time she actually managed to make her voice sound firm.

"And I will prepare the city for you."

"Fine," Torquil growled again, but he let go of the measuring tools and pointed into the fog on the portside. "That's where you are going. We shouldn't be more than a mile or two from the shore, but I can't give you my word on that. We were supposed to meet your contact in a small bay, or a cove, more likely. Not wide enough for a ship, but adequate for a boat. That's where Kerr will be waiting for you. If you can find it. However, I cannot even tell you if we are currently south or north of it."

"I'll find him," Cassandrea said again.

It was easier to repeat the same sentence over and over, then think of something new and smart to say. She had a feeling the general saw right through her fake confidence anyway.

"Right," he snarled, "just go."

It felt both freeing and humiliating to nod at that. So, to spite the male, Cassandrea didn't bother stepping to the railing to take off. Instead, she flashed her wings right into his face, lifting half of his map with the sudden gust of wind and knocking his sextant off the table. The tool rattled on the ground, and Ualan granted her a colourful curse. At that same moment, she realised she had made yet another juvenile mistake of trying to aggravate the general. However, the curses grew distant as she was already soaring high above the deck, going up, and up, and up, until there was nothing but mist and her. The bell chimed its last tone and left her with a faint echo still dying away around her. And then, a few seconds later, there was nothing. Nothing but a milky silence.

*

The fog was both a blessing and a curse. And after twenty minutes in it, Cassandrea was leaning heavily on the curse side. There was no wind helping her to carry her weight, so she had to work extra hard to stay in the air. To add to that, once she soared high above the waters, she soon couldn't tell where was up and where was down. Not to mention the high humidity, and cold, and that she had utterly failed at trying to reach the upper end of the mist. So, she opted to go down instead. To find the waves and follow their direction. Towards the shore, she hoped, as there was still some time before the high tide.

Ten more minutes, and Cassandrea started seriously doubting her own theory. She couldn't see anything through the mists.

Nothing to mark her surroundings with, and everywhere she looked, she saw only that cursed white void. An unpleasant, eerie feeling was starting to make its nest somewhere in the back of her head, whispering to her that this mist wasn't natural. Someone had created it to trap them. And they had sailed straight into the centre of it. Her eyes hurt by how hard she was staring into the void, and her ears twitched at the faintest of sounds, but still, she heard nothing but the wind rustling her feathers. Nothing. Then, finally, she noticed it. It was soft and gentle, but it was definitely there. Waves, lapping against something stationary. Sharpening her every sense, Cassandrea attempted to locate the source of that sound and veered to the right. But once again, she saw nothing. Not until the very last moment when she flew straight into the boat's oar and tumbled over it, plummeting into the waters with an unceremonious splash.

"Ugh," a deep male voice chuckled, "that could have gone better."

That was all Cassandrea heard before the sea swallowed her and closed its cold grip around her body. For a moment, there was nothing but that icy blue darkness, and the siren didn't know which way to swim, but then she noticed a flash of light. An odd one. Blurred, blue and dreamy. She lunged towards it because, for some strange, otherworldly reason, she felt that was the way to go. And a second later, she felt strong fingers closing around her wrist and pulling her into the boat.

"Aagh! It's cold!" the siren yelped, jumping back to her feet almost immediately, shaking the sea water off her wings, and crying with discomfort at the wet clothes sticking to her body. She didn't care who her saviour was; she didn't care one bit what he looked like or who he was, if he was human, fae, or a beast. No, all she cared about was that everything was freezing and wet, and she hated her clothes and hated her skin.

"Sit down," the male laughed, "you are going to rock the boat. I have some spare clothes in my bag on the shore if you want to change. It's a few minutes at worst."

"Ok! Ok, ok."

Cassandrea fought the insistent voice screaming at her to shed her clothes and forced herself down on the seat. Then she finally looked at the man. And if her jaw hadn't already been chattering with cold, it would have dropped to the floor. For the male, currently working the oars to get her back to the shore, was absolutely stunning. Almost too stunning. He was roughed up by the weather, just like she was, but had lost none of the charm. If anything, it had made him look even more handsome. His rich mane of brown hair was dishevelled, wet, and decorated with a light sea foam the tide was carrying around. A few loose strands were stuck to his forehead and falling into his eyes. Eyes that were... red. Not bloodshot, no. His irises were bright red, redder than the setting Sun. He looked young, but Cassandrea could tell he was no boy. No. This was a man who had peered into hell, and it had shouted back at him. Or maybe he was born in it and spat out, for she knew exactly what he was. The eyes were a dead give-away. And suddenly, she wasn't quite so sure that him saving her was a save at all.

"You're a-"

The male tilted his head to the side and gave her a light, careless laughter.

"And you are a siren," he countered softly, "is that fear really justified?"

"No. I mean... maybe?"

The fear was definitely justified, Cassandrea thought. Even with that smooth, deep, perfect voice that was inviting her to lie down and forget about everything... No! Especially because of that.

"What was that light?" she demanded.

"What light?"

For a second, he looked genuinely confused. How? Was she going crazy? Was she still flying through the mist and just imagining all of this? Wasn't he... a kelpie?

"There was a blue light just a minute ago," she uttered, her words slurry and jagged, and her teeth clattered so fiercely she could barely hear anything over it. The wings started retracting, and she shuddered as the remaining droplets ran down her spine.

"You hit your head pretty hard there. You sure about that?"

He didn't look like he had a clue what she was talking about, and Cassandrea was too exhausted to press him about it. She hugged herself and fell silent for a long while, focusing on trying not to whine too much. She had messed up enough already. Her yapping and yelping must've been heard all the way to the shore, if her rotten luck would have it.

Sulking and cursing her catastrophic blunder, she tried to keep her eyes away from the stranger. But soon, her curiosity got the better of her, as she gave the male a third glance. He was dangerously handsome to look at. She could feel it in her heart— the primal urge to hear him speak, to feel the touch of his fingers trailing up... With a sharp pinch to her own arm, she kicked those thoughts out of her head, recoiling from them. She had never felt anything quite like this, and she wasn't entirely sure how to handle her thoughts or the strange desire to get closer to the male. Realising this may have been exactly how males usually felt around her, she studied the bright red eyes for a moment longer.

"I always thought kelpies were women. Or animals."

It wasn't meant to be an insult or a pointed question. There was genuine curiosity in it, even if she tried to hide it, especially once she realised this must have been her contact—Kerr. She was about to spend the next three days with him. And she hadn't even noticed how her own voice had gained a subtle veil to it. One born out of fear.

The male's red eyes shifted to her as he kept rowing, although now he was listening to something. Perhaps that veil in her voice.

"I'm supposed to work with you, not kill you," he finally replied, with a slightly amused tone.

Cassandrea swiftly looked away. Was he immune to her charm? It would make sense. He had his own veil, after all. But would she be immune to his? And what if-

A gentle hiss of sand was their first indication before they reached the shoreline. The male jumped out of the boat and pulled it ashore, and Cassandrea followed in suit. Her feet sank into the soft, wet sand, and she blinked as she looked down. The sand was pitch black.

"Something wrong, love?"

The siren swiftly snapped out of her surprise and gave the kelpie a snarl. A snarl that somehow turned into a sigh as soon as her eyes actually landed on his form. He was perfect. A tight-fitting dark blue jacket, high leather boots, black trousers, and a white shirt made of some pricey material that was stroking his body beneath the jacket's opening and accentuating his slender, yet muscular figure. And all of that was crowned with a rascal's smile that seemed to be all but glued to his lips despite the crappy weather.

"You are Kerr, aren't you?" she managed to ask.

"Well, yes. Do you think anybody else would be waiting for you among all this lovely-smelling kelp?"

Confident. He was insufferably confident. She wanted to punch him for that, but all she managed was to stare.

"Alright," Kerr continued as if he hadn't noticed, "hold on a second; it should be here somewhere."

He disappeared between the rocks on the beach, and that gave Cassandrea the reprieve she so desperately needed. The most embarrassing part was that she didn't feel any mesmerising spell being used on her. No. As far as she could tell, the male was just... painfully handsome. And that was somehow making it even worse.

"There," Kerr emerged again with a leather bag and started pulling dry clothes out of it, "try not to get used to them. It is a bit too early for shirt sharing between us."

He laughed and offered her a set of trousers and a shirt. A white shirt. Made from the same soft material as the one he was currently wearing. An impossibly soft material, just asking to be caressed. Gods, was there anything about this male that didn't feel that way? Cassandrea dug her fingers into the white fabric and ripped it out of his hands.

"Don't worry, I will return your precious shirt. If you are lucky, I will choke you with it. Now turn around," she ordered.

"Careful, love," the arrogant bastard chuckled, "you're tempting me."

But he did turn around as she had requested. In fact, he did so with such casual grace that it made her gulp.

Staring at his straight back and broad shoulders, she finally stripped off her cold, wet clothes and tossed them over a nearby rock. They landed with a wet slap that made Kerr laugh.

"No surprise you were so eager to undress. You're-"

"Just... don't talk." Cassandrea demanded through chattering teeth and immediately felt bad about it. Although she wasn't quite sure whether she felt guilty for reprimanding the kelpie or for not obliging Torquil when he requested the same from her.

Another laugh let her know Kerr wasn't about to oblige her either.

"As much as I enjoy imagining your naked body, you've passed on the polite way to introduce yourself, love."

"You know my name already, I am sure."

"Then what's the harm in telling me?"

Cassandrea sighed and cursed when she reviewed just how baggy his trousers were around her form. No matter what magic she performed with her belt, keeping them from sliding down to her ankles was the best result she got. It got only slightly better with the shirt. The fabric was extraordinary, and she could spend hours just hugging herself to feel it against her body, but it was too big, and the male open-neck made for a pretty big cleavage. A laced window, more like it. She tied it up as best as she could, but that left her looking like a white and brown sack. If any seduction was supposed to happen for the success of her mission, she was going to need a lot more graceful dress.

"You can look now," she allowed Kerr, "and my name is Cassandrea."

The male turned, and Cassandrea gritted her teeth. He must have noticed how ridiculous that outfit was. Yet whatever he thought, he didn't say it or show it in his face, offering the siren nothing but a warm smile.

"Cassandrea," he repeated, and her name sounded soft and lovely on his tongue. "Much as I'd love to spend some quality time with you on this beach, we have to move. Renglow is ten miles north of here."

"Ten miles?!"

That thought hurt. Almost as much as knowing how her feet were going to look after ten miles in wet boots.

"As close as we could get without your ship being spotted. The coastline swerves here, and the line of sight is clear all the way to Renglow. Well, when there is no fog."

"Lucky us," Cassandrea said pointedly and grabbed her clothes, wringing the water out of them into the black sand.

Kerr was watching her, biding his time while leaning against a tall, sharp rock at the edge of the beach.

"Well," she asked him, "can't you turn into a horse and carry me there?"

A soft laughter caressed her ears.

"So eager to ride me, love?"

Cassandrea's heart stopped for a beat, and she looked at the male like she just ate something particularly sour. The audacity of the handsome kelpie was infuriating.

"Stop that," she said firmly, but even though she tried to make those words sound annoyed, her lips curled into a smile against her will.

"And you haven't answered," she reminded him as she finally bundled up those wet clothes into a ball and held them in her arm.

The sand was sucking her feet in with a soft rustle each time she took a step. Biting down a thousand curses and cries about her discomfort, she took a deep breath to calm herself down. Kerr gestured towards the small patch of bushes at the edge of the black beach, and she followed suit as the male started to move. Cassandrea felt humiliated. She had no idea how she had managed to both miss the boat and come utterly unprepared with only one set of clothing on her back. Not that the spare clothes would've helped; they would've been soaked as well. But there was one thing she could do to maintain some semblance of grace and dignity: she wouldn't complain. She was a saboteur, sent by the king himself. And she would not let him down.

"Well, what can I say? We go by many forms," the rich, deep tone of Kerr's voice punched through her thoughts, peeling her back to reality. "I thought sirens had snake tails and gills."

He gave her a sidelong glance, and that delectable smile grew wider as he glanced at her feet. Cassandrea tilted her head and scoffed. And smiled.

"Some do," she admitted, her voice still shuddering from the cold as she continued. "But the sirens of the depths never leave the waters."

Cassandrea could see her breath misting up, and she sensed Kerr watching her closely. There was something in those bright red eyes that she thought she recognised, but every time she could almost name that thought, it escaped her again. But that damned, cursed mischief in his eyes was infuriatingly irresistible. And somewhere deep within, a similar playful spark ignited in her. Fine, she thought. Two could play this game.

"Besides, I prefer having legs; they're far more practical. And while a tail could come in handy sometimes, I think legs can do just as many tricks, if not more."

She offered Kerr a playful smile as she strode by his side and noticed with a surprise that now, while she was focusing on him and the talking, she almost stopped feeling the soggy socks and wet boots. One thing was becoming crystal clear to the siren: she enjoyed talking in general. And she enjoyed that nobody was trying to muzzle her for once.

The sand turned to a small muddy slope, then to a flatland, and soon they left the fog behind them. As if it, itself, was a creature of the sea and unwilling to part with the shore. The snow had started to melt, dark patches of soil dotting what Cassandrea assumed to be fields for wheat or rye. She saw pale stalks of some tall plants crushed against the mud, waiting for the spring to clear the snow out and bring new life in. The further away from the beach they walked, the warmer it got. However, Cassandrea was still freezing. Her wet hair caused her head ache and her skin prickle. She was all too aware of how dreadful of a sight she must've been for the perfect kelpie. And for some reason, that annoyed her far more than it should have.

Soon they looped around a grassy hill, and a gentle, warm southern breeze greeted them, bringing a whiff of the new season with it—the scent of freshly tilled soil, melting snow, and the subtle songs of birds migrating back. Cassandrea smiled softly at the wind, wordlessly thanking it. She had missed the southern spring. This far north, the arrival of spring was as sudden as its end. It came late and stayed only for a breath before summer swept over it. Cassandrea always eagerly awaited the first, brisk spring winds to stretch her wings after the long winter and soar above the awakening land.

"Do you have a plan?" her eyes found Kerr's when she asked that question.

"Should I?" the male teased. "I've been told you were the brains of the operation."

"I-"

"Don't fuzz, love. Let's get you warm first."

And he must have heard some of the discomfort in her voice, because, with a nonchalant grace, he took off his jacket and offered it to her.

Cassandrea wasn't sure whether to hate him or love him for it. For a brief moment, she considered not accepting, but then her teeth chattered again and the sense of self-preservation prevailed. She took the jacket, still warm from his body and smelling of sea and kelp, and wrapped it tight around her torso.

"Thanks," she muttered. And feeling much better already, she added, "What's the situation like in the city?"

"Eh," Kerr took a deep breath and stuffed his hands into his trousers' pockets, "all sort of problematic. Terren's forces arrived six weeks ago, and the locals greeted them with glee. Ever since then, they've been preparing. Renglow is currently Terren's most southern fort, and for us it is the most accessible. From the sea. They know we are going to attack. Which is bad, I won't lie. The only positive thing for us is that Terren doesn't have a fleet. And that he is not currently in the city himself. His forces in Renglow are led by general T'aar. You've probably heard of him."

Cassandrea nodded. She had indeed heard of the giant general with horns, who was rumoured to have some fomori blood in him. And who was as terrifying as he was strong. And utterly savage.

"How many men?" she asked.

"Two thousand soldiers. Both humans and fae. Plus the locals. And the city has strong walls. And cannons to defend itself."

"You are making it sound almost impossible to breach."

"Oh, I haven't even told you the best part."

"Which is?"

Kerr laughed.

"We have to get inside first."

Cassandrea looked at Kerr, questions in her eyes.

"Of course... If they're expecting an attack, they're not going to keep their front door open." Cassandrea muttered, her tone indicating disappointment.

"Front door, back door, and all the small side entrances too. They're all sealed shut. Tight as a goblin's purse."

Cassandrea let out a curse, sour enough to curdle milk. Nodding, she used her free hand to massage her arm to warm it up.

"Good news is, we have more troops," she tried to sound optimistic. "Almost double the amount in the dreadnoughts, all prepared for an assault. Bad news is that with a few good cannon shots, they can disable the ships and leave them unable to dock, or worse, sink them before they reach the bay." She bit her cheek as she thought about it. "So we can't let them get those shots in. We need to level the playing field as much as possible if we are to confront their forces. The cannons must be disabled."

Cassandrea's eyes moved back to Kerr. The kelpie male studied her as she spoke, and she gave him a small smile. How she had missed having someone look at her with something other than disgust. Even if it was directly work-related. Some part of her desperately longed for more of that.

"I'll take you to an overlook where you can get a view of the city first. I think you need to see the situation before we start drafting a plan," Kerr said.

"Sounds good to me," Cassandrea replied.

There was a long silence between the two, which Cassandrea filled with her thoughts. She felt rather tense. And she could recognise that tension as fear. But not the kind one feels when encountering a wild beast in the forest. No. This fear was different. It was the primal drum in the heart of the forest, warning a trespasser not to take another step. Terren's forces were already in Renglow. Cassandrea had already known that the green dragon had made a move and conquered the city, but Kerr's words didn't sit right with her. The citizens of Renglow had welcomed the troops with open arms? Embracing them as if... as if Terren was some sort of saviour. That thought frightened the siren beyond anything else. How could the green dragon inspire that kind of adoration in people? How could whole cities turn into traitors in such a short time? What horrible, dreadful weapon did Terren wield that he had made good Entirie citizens fall to their knees?

"Up ahead, there's a marshland that's still thawing. You'll need to follow me closely if you don't want to drown," Kerr's voice interrupted her thoughts and turned them towards more pressing matters.

"Drown? Marshes aren't usually that deep."

The male smiled at the silliness of that question and shook his head.

"That's firstly not true, and secondly, this specific bog is known to house a few particularly feisty kappas. But keep your wits about you, and you'll be fine," Kerr's eyes twinkled as he spoke, and Cassandrea found herself smiling at the tone of his voice.

Kerr was a kelpie. She hadn't forgotten about that. But somehow, when he smiled, the fact stopped feeling so terrifying. So she just nodded and continued her enquiries.

"What else can you tell me about the situation? Do we have any other notable shifts? Where are the supply lines coming from?"

"Renglow served as a breadbasket for Alanthys, so Terren and his troops have more than enough supplies in the city itself. The granaries are running low after the long winter, but they could easily hold for another few weeks."

Kerr wasn't looking at her when he replied. His eyes were on the marshland ahead. The wind intensified, blowing straight across the boggy plain with no windbreakers in its way, and it wrapped Kerr's shirt tighter around him, causing its broad sleeves to billow around his arms. If the male was cold, he didn't show it. He pulled his hands out of his pockets and slowly bowed towards the marshland.

Nothing. Except for a small movement a few yards ahead. But that could have been a frog. Cassandrea shifted her weight from one foot to another.

"Should I bow as well?"

"If you want to."

She didn't want to, but she did it anyway. It felt appropriate.

Kerr smiled and offered her his hand.

"You will feel safer this way."

"With a kelpie dragging me into the marshes?" Cassandrea chuckled. "Forgive me if I disagree."

"With a kelpie," Kerr half-closing his eyes, laughter ringing in his voice, "protecting you while you're treading through these marshes."

Cassandrea hesitated. Something was urging her to give him her hand. Urging her to trust him. And the wind clearly liked him. *Her* wind liked him. Oh, what the hell...

"Don't get any ideas," she warned him while his warm hand closed around hers, "the king would have your neck for getting me killed."

"Ah," Kerr laughed, "and here I thought you loved water."

"I do love water," Cassandrea protested, while trying to avoid stepping into any of the deeper bogs that would fill her already wet boots to the rim. It was a hard task requiring her to balance each step atop a grassy mound or a heather-crowned mound. Neither of which was very stable. "Just not in my boots."

Kerr suddenly tugged her closer, preventing her from stepping on a tiny carnivorous plant. Cassandrea snorted as she was forced to step into the water instead.

"I doubt that would have killed me."

"No. But you might have killed it. And they are precious."

"That's-"

Cassandrea was about to snarl something mocking at the male, but when she looked into his eyes, she changed her mind. He wasn't joking. Or making fun of her. For some reason, he actually cared about that tiny bog plant.

"Never mind."

Another step, and she was back to her balancing exercise. It was terribly demanding, and she detested that Kerr looked like he had no trouble with it at all. Granted, he wasn't trying to keep his boots dry, but she could swear that even with the lack of effort, his boots simply weren't sinking quite as deep into the bog as hers were.

"Have you ever seen a kappa?" Kerr asked suddenly. His voice was quiet now, and Cassandrea presumed he didn't want to disturb the marshland's inhabitants.

"Not properly. I know of them," Cassandrea said and leapt off a mossy rock to a teetering lump of hornwort. She had to grip Kerr's hand tightly to hold her balance and found, to her surprise, that the strength with which he held her and supported her felt indeed quite safe. Far safer than what she had expected.

"Hold on," Kerr murmured.

Cassandrea stopped and looked around. Something was terribly off about this place. She felt the need to draw her swords but seeing that Kerr remained calm, she, too, stilled her mind. The marsh was indeed thawing, and it seemed like most of the wildlife had not yet migrated back for the summer—if this marsh was even inhabited by anything else but monsters. The bleak landscape of muted browns and greys was peppered with mounds of snow, and thick sheets of ice covered some of the larger bodies of water. The sun was hiding behind clouds, making the whole bog look washed out and pallid, like a dead man's skin. There was an eerie silence, only broken by an occasional frog's croak and the wailing wind that made the few still standing, dead, skeletal trees groan and tilt closer towards their doom with every gust.

Suddenly, Cassandrea felt Kerr's grip tightening ever-so-slightly, and she held her breath. Something moved in the bog nearby.

There was a clicking sound, resembling that of a frog's croak, but it was more rhythmic, and it came with a tone. And when Cassandrea saw the source of these clicks and ribbits, the hairs on her neck stood up straight. About a hundred feet away, the surface of a large pond broke, and a tuft of black hair popped from the murky waters—a mane belonging to a creature of nightmares.

The thing's unnaturally long limbs were covered with mossy, green, slimy scales and ended in four-fingered, webbed hands. Its legs were slightly shorter, but its feet both had terribly long, sharp claws instead of nails. The creature's messy, dark hair was matted and resembled a mass of tangled kelp that draped the face like torn curtains, clinging to its skin. Partly concealed was a hollow in its crown that contained stagnant water—the very life force of this being.

The kappa moved in a strange, languid manner, as if it were drifting under water, using its hands and feet to move forward. Each step made a disgusting squelch, until the creature stopped and lifted its head. Or rather, her head, Cassandrea realised, for she was a female. The creature's face was expressionless and unnaturally still. Terrifying, with wide, empty eyes—milky white and unfocused.

The kappa lifted her head and sniffed the air. And, as the wind carried the scent of the two travellers towards her, her face split into a dark maw, filled with razor-sharp, jagged teeth that were meant for tearing flesh from bone.

"Easy," Kerr said. His voice was calm. Too calm to be real.

Cassandrea wasn't sure who he was faking it for—for her or for the swamp monster.

The horrendous clicking and croaking echoed over the marsh again, and the kappa turned towards the two, angling her head like a wild beast. Then she spoke. And the voice she spoke with was quiet and raspy, and echoed through the bog like small droplets in a damp cave.

"Who goes there?" she croaked.

Cassandrea's blood froze over. The sound ground her mind and painted promises of a cold, painful death. The fact that Kerr stood tall and that he was still holding her hand was the only thing that kept Cassandrea from drawing her blades or bursting out her wings to fly away. But the male next to her showed no desire to flee. Or fight.

"Those who call from darkened shores," Kerr replied to the

kappa, and his voice made Cassandrea shudder. It had changed. No longer the careless laughter. No longer the lover's whisper. It was still deep and full, but there was something else in it now. Something cold. Beckoning. Deadly. Hearing it was like staring into the dark waters of a loch on a starless night. Tempting. Hollow. Terrifying.

"Those who sing of sunken dreams," Kerr continued, his words effortlessly dampening all the other sounds of the marshes. "Those who beckon beyond the foam."

Silence fell after the male's third sentence, as if it were some kind of spell stopping the time and life itself. But the next second, the kappa laughed and leaped towards them, landing only a yard away. Water jetted out beneath her feet, showered Cassandrea's trousers, and made her curse internally for having the second pair soaked, too. The creature clicked its tongue and reached towards Kerr with its mossy, green paw. The move alone would make Cassandrea scream if it were aimed at her, but the kelpie didn't stir. Not even when the webbed hand reached his cheek. It was a strange touch. Gentle, like a caress, but leaving slime and goo in its wake.

"I know you," the kappa croaked, "Lord of the Moonlit Mire. You are far from home. Far from the Wraithbound Marshes."

"So are you," Kerr replied softly.

"Oh yes, but don't we both know why?"

The kappa turned her ugly head towards Cassandrea, and she sniffed.

"You, I don't know, but you smell of those you should feast

upon. Half-blood."

Cassandrea forced herself to face that nightmarish pair of eyes.

"I am Cassandrea," she said, and although she willed her voice calm, her hand felt suddenly clammy and cold in Kerr's warm grip.

The kappa's nostrils flared as it took in the siren's scent. The unseeing, white eyes somehow still finding hers.

"The unforgiving northern wind is with you," the creature croaked, its lips letting out a strange hiss. The smell from its mouth was an abhorrent mix of fish, algae, and decay.

"I was born in the northern winds," Cassandrea confirmed.

The kappa hissed again; this time, the gesture was aggravated.

"Cold, cold wind! Bringer of winter and frost... and death."

Cassandrea raised a brow.

"Why aren't you further south, then?" Cassandrea looked at the kappa, but just as much as she craved an answer from her, she wanted one from Kerr, too.

The kappa leaned closer to her, and Cassandrea did everything she could to steel her will and not bend backwards and yield. The scaly hand moved closer to her face, but not close enough to touch. Until she found her hair, and ran one of those long claws alongside the strands, and lifted them up.

"To gain something is to give something. Humans shake hands, do they not?" the kappa smiled lifelessly, her hand moving forward.

Cassandrea felt Kerr squeezing her hand, as if warning her.

And she understood.

"They do, but humans do not shake hands without knowing the name," she replied to the monster.

The kappa shifted. Her webbed hand twitched a little, a small sign of frustration, before it fell down again.

"I can taste the change in the waters, delicious Lord. Why do you travel with one of diluted blood?" the kappa asked from Kerr, turning from Cassandrea, as if she were nothing but a fallen leaf on the ground.

"I like her," Kerr replied, lightness creeping back into his voice.

"A human girl? Again? Have you not-"

"Oh, she's hardly a human, isn't she?" Kerr interrupted the creature.

On purpose, Cassandrea felt. He interrupted her on purpose. He didn't want that sentence to be finished.

The kappa stared at the kelpie for a good minute, the milky eyes seeing something that wasn't for human eyes.

"Tell your king we are waiting," she said finally. "As long as the rains swell these waters, and the mist rolls thick, we will watch from beneath. But when the night grows darkest, and the reeds shiver with unseen hands, let him know no one who treads this land will see dawn's light—again."

Kerr hesitated as if it took him a moment to decide whether those words were a promise or a threat.

"Thank you...?"

The kappa croaked with laughter, and raised her paw to caress

Kerr's cheek once more.

"How handsome you are, Lord of Moonlit Mire. We shall meet again."

And with a giant leap, she was gone, the rusty waters closing above her head.

Kerr shuddered and let go of Cassandrea's hand, in order to kneel down and wash the slime off his cheek.

"What did that mean?" Cassandrea demanded, still staring at the spot where the creature had disappeared.

"Let me know when you figure it out," Kerr laughed, his voice playful and teasing once more.

But Cassandrea didn't buy that. Not this time.

"I think you know exactly what it meant," she said pointedly.

Kerr wiped his face on his sleeve, and got to his feet.

"Your guess is as good as mine. I am only hoping it was an oath of allegiance. But it might as well be a death threat."

Cassandrea snorted.

"Does everybody and everything you meet swoon over you?"

"That's a loaded question, coming from a siren."

"Yet you still haven't answered it."

"Are you falling in love with me?"

"No!"

"Then no. Not everybody."

Cassandrea stared at him. Stared and stared until Kerr gave up and laughed.

"Come on. It was funny."

But Cassandrea didn't laugh. She pointed her finger at the

kelpie's chest.

"Where are the Wraithbound Marshes?"

"So many questions."

"Where are-"

"Ok!" Kerr shook his head, an amused smile still on his lips. "But then you are answering one of mine. Wraithbound Marshes are southeast of here. The local humans have a different name for them, though. They call them The Swamps of Borban. Now me."

Cassandrea didn't get a chance to reply, as the male started walking again, expecting her to do the same.

"Why do you do this job, instead of, I don't know, living the life of a free siren on some small island in the middle of a sea?"

Cassandrea followed Kerr and hurried to his side. His question wasn't something she wanted to answer. To anyone. Ever. She tried to hide the tinge of pain behind her eyes, but most likely Kerr had caught it. So she looked away to the far end of the bog, trying to buy herself some time before she had to answer. But the swamp was silent, and she found no satisfying lie to tell him, so she opted for the easiest of the explanations. The truth. Not *the* truth, but... close enough to keep the kelpie at bay.

"I'm not a siren," she said. Then, offered Kerr a small smile, which the male mirrored, albeit the look in his eyes told her everything she needed to know—that he didn't buy that one bit.

"Sure you aren't."

Cassandrea bit her lip.

"No, you know what I mean. I'm not a *true* siren."

She took a small breath. So far, she hadn't lied, but Kerr still raised his eyebrow and shrugged.

Nervous like a child trying to explain a broken mug, Cassandrea raised her hand and rubbed the back of her neck, suddenly very aware of the scars marring her beauty. Ruining it. Yet Kerr hadn't mentioned those. Neither did he stare at them like so many other people did.

"I didn't fit with the rest of them," she admitted. "Sirens hold their seers in high regard, and omens mean a whole lot to them. Tides, winds, and stars all have their meaning during a siren's birth."

Cassandrea gulped before she continued.

"I was a bad omen. A siren born with mostly human features. On a moonless, cloudy night, in the dead of winter, with the cold northern wind carrying ill warnings." There was some unveiled harshness in her words. But, as soon as she had finished that sentence, she looked up at Kerr and beamed the kelpie a smile warm enough to melt the snow mounds around them. "So I sought my worth elsewhere."

Cassandrea was so lost in her memories that she hadn't even noticed, until then, that her feet were finally walking on dry land. They'd crossed the marshland and continued towards the steep hillside, which was the overlook Kerr had told her about. Their last checkpoint before Renglow.

"And then the beloved king saw me," she continued, her voice warm when she spoke of Valderan. "Not as an omen. Not as a threat. But me."

Cassandrea had repeated those words to herself time and time again. It was those exact words echoing through her mind on the nights in which she felt terrible for doing the king's bidding and seducing yet another general or an informant or charming her way into the court of some influential nobleman in a distant land. She was useful to her king, and he cared for her. Not in a way a lover would, but in a way a father cared for his children. Hell, he saved her. Gave her a purpose. So she told herself again and again until those words became her second nature. She was useful. She had a purpose. She wasn't a tool. But one look into Kerr's eyes made her feel a little stupid about saying them aloud. The male certainly didn't seem convinced. But what did he know about any of that? About loyalty? About her life? And why did she tell him all that? He hadn't even asked.

"So," she blinked, deciding to change the subject, "what are *you* doing here? Shouldn't you be, I don't know, holding court or something like that, little kelpie?" she asked, forcing her tone back into a playful one. "Or should I call you 'my lord' instead?"

"I don't think I've agreed to another question, siren, but thank you for that answer, however honest it was." Kerr grinned and pointed to the far right end of the marshlands towards a hill currently obstructing their view. "That's where we are going. We'll see the city from there, and there is a small cave we can stay in for the night. Maybe I'll tell you something about my court when we get there."

"For the night!?" Cassandrea took a sharp inhale. "That will be cutting a full day from the time we have."

"Our journey is already cutting it short," Kerr shrugged, "and there is no way we're getting in tonight. I left almost a week ago when the gates were still open."

"And you still don't have a plan how to get back in?"

Kerr just shrugged again. However, there was something in that move that rubbed Cassandrea all the wrong way.

"You don't care if we get in, do you?" she accused him.

That casual expression on his face immediately turned into a hurt one.

"Of course I do! I wouldn't want your beloved king to love you any less for us failing this mission."

"You!" Cassandrea gasped for air. There were numerous insults she wanted to hurl his way, but none strong enough to actually make her feel better. So she just scoffed. "Now I am sorry I told you anything."

"Hey," Kerr's voice softened, and he even waited for her to catch up. "I didn't mean it that way. And two days are more than enough."

He offered her his hand once more, but she didn't take it; instead, she opted for making her own way towards the indicated hill.

"Besides, it is the truth!" Kerr called after her. "You don't care either whether we get into the city. Not for the fleet, and certainly not for the citizens. You just want the mission done to have your shoulder patted."

Cassandrea narrowly avoided a particularly wobbly heather bush and decided she had just had enough. He was right; she knew, but she wasn't going to admit it. Definitely not to him. So she spread her wings instead, ready to fly the rest of the way.

"I am going to get us some real information. Try not to take too long," she said.

To her surprise, Kerr laughed it off.

"Fly low, else they shoot you down," he even offered a warning.

Cassandrea didn't deem it worth a reply.

Chapter 5

The evening was cold. Not even Kerr's jacket was doing much against that, and Cassandrea wished they could make a fire. She had tried tucking herself under her wings, but her body was so cold and frozen that even the wings did nothing but make everything worse, as they, too, were cold and wet all the way to the hollow bones. Not to mention that the current lodgings were too small for her wings anyway. If she wanted to have them out, she would need to embrace the kelpie. Which was something she wasn't willing to do. Ever.

She was currently sitting in a very small and narrow cave, next to Kerr, and afraid that both her body and brain were frozen since the moment she had laid eyes on Renglow. It was easy to reach the hill. Easier to laugh at Kerr, who was left far behind. Much harder to look at the city and see its closed gates, and archers on the walls, ready to take down anything suspicious. Ever since then, she had been quiet, pondering their options. She didn't even speak up when Kerr finally arrived with two skinned rabbits and asked her if she liked raw meat. She didn't, but he apparently did. At the moment, he was sleeping, with his hands folded casually on his lap, his legs extended, and his head cocked toward her shoulder. She hated that he could sleep. Even more, she hated that he wasn't helping her to make a plan. And what she hated the most was that he wasn't cold at all. In times like these, Cassandrea really wished she had been born a full-blooded siren.

As if he could hear her thoughts, Kerr stirred and opened his eyes. Cassandrea half expected another witty remark about her past or her plan-making, but the male just smiled at her, mischievous sparks lighting up his red eyes.

"I want to hear your voice," he announced.

"What?"

"Your siren's voice," Kerr laughed, "you tried it on me earlier."

"Did it work that well?"

"No. Not at all. But I liked the sound of it. I bet you could sing a hell of a lullaby."

Cassandrea couldn't tell if he were telling the truth or making fun of her, and it was irking her beyond reason.

"Is that some Lord thing to do? Require a lullaby?"

"When the Lord is in a good mood... and in good company..."

"I think you were sleeping quite soundly even without a lullaby. We need to work on that plan, Kerr."

The male thought about it for a short while, and then nodded.

"Alright, a deal, if you would? I will make the plan with you; think of a way to get us both into the city, and *then* you will sing me a lullaby."

The audacity of that request made Cassandrea open her mouth.

"You're... bargaining about the plan?" she asked, stupefied. "You're my contact here. You're to help me get to the city!"

Kerr offered her a fiendish grin.

"Exactly. *To* the city. Not *into* the city. I've done my part."

Cassandrea was so shocked she forgot to close her mouth.

"Never trust a kelpie, I guess..." she scoffed.

Kerr's eyes flickered with something that looked like actual hurt.

"I am a male of my word. And I've kept it."

Cassandrea inclined her head with another infuriated huff. "You're making bargains over people's lives!"

Kerr quirked a brow, that roguish smile never leaving his lips. Cassandrea knew well enough she needed him. With a defeated, albeit very upset sigh, she leaned her back against the rocky wall again, pinched the bridge of her nose, and closed her eyes. She could still feel the red eyes watching her. She needed him, and he knew that. He probably would have helped her anyway, but he liked to play. That was it. The male liked to play. Gingerly, she opened her eyes and looked at Kerr.

"I will sing you a lullaby when you've helped me inside Renglow *and* answered a question of mine," she countered his offer. "I'll even sing you a lullaby that nobody outside the flocks has ever heard." She challenged Kerr. "Because I'm nice like that." Cassandrea knew the last words came out a little too pointedly, but she tried to make up for it with a smile.

"When I help you *make a plan* to get inside Renglow," Kerr specified, with a wild grin, "and answer your question. I am not waiting three days for my lullaby."

Cassandrea narrowed her eyes at Kerr. Clever, clever little kelpie...

"I want some kind of assurance that you will be joining me inside the walls, too."

Kerr's eyes flashed with something, and he let out a light laugh as he planted his palm on his chest.

"You have my word, Cassandrea."

And that was enough for her. Cassandrea nodded quietly, but then, a sudden shiver of cold shook her so violently she practically jolted from her seat. She stood up to warm herself, and started pacing back and forth.

"Alright, let's get this over with. What are we looking at?" she asked after a moment. "We know all the gates and entrances are closed. I can't fly in. They're not accepting any visitors?"

The summarisation sounded about as hopeless as Cassandrea felt. She stopped pacing and looked at Kerr. The kelpie's red eyes made her think of warm bonfires and neverending sunsets at midsummer peak. She missed summer dearly now, in this miserable, damp, cold cave.

"No, as far as I know, every entrance is sealed tight, and they're not going to open the gates until the anticipated attack."

Kerr's words sowed another level of deep desperation into the siren's heart. She groaned, rubbing her temples.

"Okay, and what do we know of... exits of the city?" Cassandrea's voice shuddered at the question, but this time, it wasn't because of the cold. The thought of the sewer systems gave her a physical, visceral gut feeling of illness and nausea.

"Stop," Kerr said quietly and opened his arms. "I am cold just looking at you."

"So?" Cassandrea crossed her arms on her chest in defiance.

"So sit down next to me. I know you are thinking about it."

"I am definitely *not* thinking about it."

"Heat," he corrected, utterly unfazed by her animosity, "you're thinking about heat. And that's what I am offering. Just that."

Kerr rested his hand over his heart.

"I promise."

Cassandrea took her time considering his offer. An entire three seconds of time before she sat down and leaned against his chest.

"Ok."

He was warm. Gods, he was warm. Like a proper furnace. Cassandrea shivered again, but this time, it was from the pleasure of feeling his warmth seeping into her body. Kerr wrapped his arm around her shoulders and pulled her closer. He smelled of sea and peat, and she found it oddly comforting.

"Ok," he murmured in that deep, soothing voice of his, "now we can do the planning.

"We've gotten nowhere so far," she sighed.

"Haven't we?"

Kerr laughed, and she felt that laughter rumbling through his chest.

"Do you really think I was sitting on my ass the past few weeks, and counting reeds? No, love. I've been busy making contacts in the city. And I did. Tomorrow morning, when the tide is high, we will swim to the west city walls. There is a sewer overflow carved into the rockface. It can't be accessed on a low tide, because both the rocks and the tunnel are smooth as your cheeks, but, when the tide rushes in, you can swim through. Underwater. There are iron bars covering the upper end, but my contact will open it for us."

Kerr looked down at the woman in his arms, and gave her a smug smile.

"Happy now?"

Cassandrea studied Kerr.

"You've had all this planned ahead. And you've made a bargain?" her eyes struck lightning, but she wasn't even entirely sure what for. She couldn't really blame him for it. It was clever. But, even though it saved her the trouble of planning, it also made her feel like an idiot for bargaining over something he had already done.

Kerr's smile didn't falter. Cassandrea wanted to punch him, just for that, but somehow, it made her grin instead.

"You are a massive-"

Kerr's barking laugh cut off the remainder of her insult.

"So, what's your question, love? I'd like to catch a few hours of sleep before we go."

Cassandrea looked at him. His body was unnaturally warm, and she could actually feel her own relaxing next to it, her fingers thawing, and her mind clearing up. She was almost cosy. If she could stay there for a little while longer, she would easily fall asleep. So easily... She slowly rested her head against Kerr's muscular shoulder, and closed her eyes.

"What happened to the human girl?" she asked.

"*That* story, really?" Kerr snorted. "You couldn't just ask me what my favourite drink is? Or colour? Or a sex position?"

Cassandrea growled, and nudged him with her elbow.

"Stop avoiding. I've asked my question."

"Mh," Kerr didn't laugh this time. He just shrugged. "She died. That's what humans do when they turn old. Haven't you noticed?"

"Still avoiding."

"Ugh," a resigned huff was the only answer she got. At first. Then, Kerr shifted a little and looked up into the darkness surrounding them. "Well, she left me. When she realised what kind of life we would have had. How short it would have felt for me. And how... unsatisfying for her, leaving me here to live for another hundreds of years."

His voice sounded somewhat melancholic for the first time since Cassandrea had met him. However, he quickly shook it off, adding, "she also may have thought I was a massive dick. A popular opinion among women, or so I've heard."

And he laughed.

Cassandrea listened carefully to every word. Even after Kerr finished speaking and laughed, she still listened—not to his words, but to the rhythm of his breath and the flowing tone of his voice. There was something immensely calming about it, like pressing a seashell to her ear and dreaming of rolling waves. Similarly, the strong, steady beat of his heart soothed her. Comforted her.

"I'm sorry," she said quietly, not entirely sure what else she could say to console the male, or if she should try to. It wasn't her place. Even if she were the reason he had to dig out those memories.

Kerr stirred and offered her one of those light laughs she now knew he threw around to lighten up the mood. Either for himself, or for others.

"For what it's worth," she continued, "you are a bit of an ass."

"Yeah—" Kerr started, but Cassandrea cut him off.

"But she missed out." She added quickly, a little softer than she had originally intended. "She really did."

Kerr fell silent, and Cassandrea could hear his heart slowing down. His hand moved over her shoulder, caressing her tenderly.

"Thanks, love."

Just that. No explanation. No protests. But there was gratitude in his voice, and something... something more real than what he had allowed her to see so far.

With a deep breath, Cassandrea leaned her head back against the warmth of Kerr's chest and closed her eyes. She was to sing him a lullaby. She had sung countless times. To people she loved, to people she hated, to people she didn't care about. She had sung to masses, to families; she had sung for the king himself. Most of the time, she sang to herself or the winds. But for some reason, she felt nervous now, almost as nervous as she had been when she revealed her voice for King Valderan. She shifted into the kelpie's embrace and wrapped her own arms around his waist. With another breath, she began to sing.

She kept her voice soft as summer rain, and the undulating words started echoing in the cave, as if her own ancestors had joined her on the song. The lyrics were not in the common tongue, but in a language long forgotten by the fae, and they carried a rhythm of the waves, as though her words were woven from the sea itself. A language she knew to be ancient, and born of wild magic of the north. A language that carried power in its words. The lullaby drifted from her lips as whispers of waves on a quiet shore, each word rounded and soft, lingering. It uplifted her, filled her with longing for the seas, and made her heart ache and tremble with joy. Cradling Kerr, she channelled the ancient, secret words that had been passed on for generations from mothers to daughters. Her gaze softened while she sang, her green eyes gained an otherworldly light, and with a gentle rustle, her wings sprouted out and folded around them both. She held the male tight as each note lilted into the next, and with every verse, the song curled around Kerr like some protective spell, soothing and gentle, as if the ocean itself was cradling him to sleep. This song was not just for comfort—it was a promise, a ritual of safety, an invocation of the strength of the tides and winds. As Cassandrea's voice faded into the final, breath-like note, the air itself seemed to sigh, heavy and drowsy with dreams and memories as old as the water.

Kerr hadn't moved the entire time. Or after. And when the final note stopped echoing through the cave, and he still didn't move, Cassandrea started thinking he had actually fallen asleep. But then, a light kiss landed on her hair. Just that. And she understood then that no words were needed.

Chapter 6

The following day started well. Cassandrea woke up in the warm embrace of a man smelling of sea and peat, and her clothes had dried over the night, leaving her feeling fairly comfortable. Her wings still draped around them, she yawned, content with the situation. Right until she peered out of the cave.

The weather outside was anything but nice. Heavy mist was rolling from the sea, the clouds were low, and the moisture in the air immediately wetted Cassandrea's blond hair, causing it to stick to her neck and forehead, making her want to crawl out of her own skin.

The rest of her good mood died when Kerr peered from the cave behind her and chimed with a voice full of optimism, "Well, isn't the weather lovely?"

"Somebody slept well."

"Like a baby in the arms of a beautiful lady."

He was definitely back to his usual annoyingly joyful self. Yet, Cassandrea felt somewhat relieved at that. She realised that the last evening had been anything but cheerful for him, and the fact that he was joking and happy again... It felt... good.

"Ok, lover boy," she decided to amuse his mood. "Where to?"

"Well, that depends," he grinned.

"On?"

"How good of a swimmer are you?"

*

Cassandrea understood why Kerr had asked that question about fifteen minutes later, when they were standing on a hidden black beach, carved deep into the hill's slope. The roaring tide grasped for her feet with every coming wave, and the mist was so heavy, the siren couldn't even see the end of the cliffs sheltering the bay.

"I hate you," she declared, looking mortified, as another cold rush took hold of her feet prematurely, and reminded her just how awful it had felt being in these icy waters.

"For a siren, you sure complain a lot," Kerr retorted with a beaming smile.

"I was born neither with wings, nor gills, nor a layer of blubber around me," Cassandrea protested, but bit back another complaint. Grumbling, she gave the kelpie a withering glance.

"For a kelpie, you sure-" Cassandrea never got to finish that sentence; her eyes went wide, and she looked up. Instinctively, her hand grasped from Kerr's shoulder to pull him down. The male didn't object, and he, too, looked up. The fog was too thick to reveal anything, but she held her eyes nailed to something far above. Something invisible. And terrifying. A full minute passed before she let go of Kerr's shoulder.

"That's odd..." Cassandrea breathed out as she straightened up. "The larger birds never migrate this early."

Suddenly, she had goosebumps, but the damp, cold air had nothing to do with it. Something was off in the air, in the unassuming winds. Something that she couldn't place, neither with a scent nor a feeling. Then her eyes widened.

"What manner of beasts has Terren subdued as his harbingers?" she asked, shuddering at the sole thought.

"I wouldn't know," Kerr shrugged. "I haven't seen anything extraordinary during my days in the city. Just the usual. Fae. Humans. Nymphs. An occasional selkie... None of those can fly."

"Well, whatever manner of fiends those were, I do not wish to find out. Let's go." Cassandrea said, but something heavy fell upon her heart. She had a feeling she was going to find out very soon just what it was that soared the sky, whether she wanted to or not. So to push those thoughts away, she walked into the water instead.

The sea was cold. It was so cold Cassandrea felt the icy grip in her bones. Wading waist-high in the waves, she followed Kerr's lead, and cursed the day she was born. This was beyond petty discomfort and the complaints of a pampered little siren. Her breath was misting with thick plumes, and every inhale she took was painful. Her skin was burning. Burning! And her muscles were refusing to obey.

"Dive with me," Kerr said, and even his voice rang with some discordant tone that Cassandrea only assumed to be discomfort.

However, the kelpie's body was exuding warmth, and with how easily he moved, one could swear he was taking a bath in a hot spring instead. Cassandrea didn't say anything; she merely nodded and took a plunge into the freezing waters. Her cheeks were instantly on fire, pierced by a thousand needles of the water sprays each wave hurled at her, and when the water hit her chest, it was like an icy fist punching all air out of her lungs. She cursed. The worst came once the water touched her head. It felt like something sharp had cut the crown of her head open and poured water so cold in it that it froze all of her muscles, nerves and thoughts. She had to kick herself back to the surface to breathe, as she had almost choked with the surprise. Her head was stinging and throbbing with a biting pain, her cheeks were burning, and she couldn't breathe properly.

The waters were relatively clear, albeit dark. The currents were rough. They tore and tugged on her clothes and hair, making it difficult to keep a consistent pace and direction, but she could still see enough to keep up with Kerr's pace, and even though she was a half-blood windborn, she could swim and she could do it well. She may have preferred the warmth of the southern seas, but she was a daughter of the tides. And no kelpie was going to get an upper hand on her in the sea.

Or... take her hand?

Kerr's fingers closed around her wrist, and he pulled her with him into the rough waves. Suddenly, it felt easy to follow. As if he were being propelled by some invisible force, a current of his own making. Or if he were just that strong.

"What are you doing?!" Cassandrea demanded.

"Making it a little easier for you, love."

The male laughed.

"No need," she sneered, "I can manage just fine on my own. Thank you very much."

She expected him to protest, but he let go almost immediately.

"Ok. Try to dive in, then, and only come to the surface to take a breath. The fog is thick, but they can still see us once we get close."

And he disappeared beneath the waves.

Cassandrea cursed again. This was going to be a nightmare. It was more than a mile to swim all the way around the cliff and into the city, and the tide was rough, mercilessly roaring in its desire to crush them both against the rocks. On top of that, the siren could still feel that earlier dark presence lurking above the clouds. It wasn't a messenger, she realised; it was a guardian. A watch. But what was it? How sharp were its senses? Had it spotted them already?

Cassandrea finally made it around the cliff, and the swimming became easier. Now, the waves were just cradling her, not trying to throw her on the rocks. Although she knew that was to be a short-lived relief. Right above the water surface, where the fog wasn't as heavy, she could already see the base of the cliffs protecting Renglow. And they were smooth, just as Kerr had said, with nothing to grip or stand on.

"We will have to dive again," the kelpie's voice whispered next to her, "follow me. Quietly."

Cassandrea did, and only when her lungs were aching and tearing apart, she pushed herself back to the surface to take a deep breath. From what she could see in that brief moment, they were closing in on the tunnel and its iron grate. She tried to make as few stops as possible, which had caused her lungs to ache even more. Still, that ache was better than risking getting the attention of whatever that thing in the sky was. For what she had felt in that wind was a terrifying force—something ancient, and primal, and cunning, and foreign. She was instinctively unnerved by it.

As she took in another breath of air, the smell of the sewer hit her with full force. She didn't even want to know what swam all around her in the stinking waters. Or how long she would have to stay in it.

Kerr beckoned her closer towards the wall and disappeared below the surface. Cassandrea followed. The tide was already quite high, so they had to dive to the entrance and swim the full length through the sewer in one breath. Something that would have been much easier should she know how long the tunnel was and whether the bars on the other side would be open or not.

The walls of the sewer were slick, and moss and grime coated every crevice. There was nothing to hold onto. Nothing to propel her forward except for her own legs and arms. Just a few more strokes, she told herself. A few more, and they would be through. For sure...

Cassandrea's shoulder hit Kerr's feet, and she had to try hard to squeeze into the space next to him. But she did. And her head was finally above the water.

Only an inch from closed iron bars.

"Kerr!"

"I know," the male muttered.

"What if he's not coming?" Cassandrea asked, trying hard to suppress the rising panic. She knew that the tide would soon roll back, and they would slide down into their deaths on the rocky shore. Or worse, the tide wasn't at its peak yet, and they would just drown there by the bars.

"She'll be here," Kerr said firmly. "Any minute now."

Cassandrea could do nothing but put her faith in the kelpie's word. Though at that point, there was not much of it in her heart. Maybe he had planned it all along. Wasn't it what the kelpies always did? Drown young women? But she was a siren! A siren... She reached up to take a hold of one of the bars to save her strength. She hated to admit it, but she was exhausted. Her arms felt weak, her legs were burning and her chest was heaving from the exertion. Next to her, Kerr extended his arm toward the bars, grasping onto them as well.

"She'll be here," he said again.

Cassandrea's teeth were chattering, but she nodded at the male. She was so exhausted she didn't know if she had any energy left to talk. Something slimy slid into the water between them and made the kelpie shudder.

"Gross."

A few minutes passed. Then a few minutes more. The tide was rocking them up and down, rising a bit higher with each round.

"She'll be here," Kerr said for the third time before Cassandrea had the chance to question his contacts. But the siren could swear she saw a sliver of something in his eyes. Worry. Nevertheless, it vanished with a relieved breath as silent footsteps suddenly echoed through the tunnel above the grates. Then, a slim gloved hand grabbed the bars, a key rattled in a lock, and the grate slid up.

Cassandrea decided she wasn't going to be a gentleman this time and used Kerr's shoulder to pull herself out of the water and onto a narrow sidewalk running along the sewer. Now that she wasn't in mortal danger, the stench of the sewers hit her in full, and she had to fight hard against the sudden urge to vomit.

"For the record? I am not sure I am letting you devise another plan. Ever. Again."

Kerr followed her up on the sidewalk with a wet splash.

"We are inside the city, aren't we? Even though you've shown so little faith in our daring rescuer."

But said daring rescuer didn't seem to care about Kerr's flattery.

"You stink, Kerr," the woman said in a rather haughty voice, "terribly so."

"I am aware," the male said apologetically. "But that is a temporary state easily fixed by a bath and some extra clothes."

Cassandrea finally looked up to see who came so late to save them. The person was a woman; there was no doubt about that. A fairly thin woman. But that was all the details Cassandrea was able to gather as the person wore a long hooded cape, and all that one could really see from her form was white hair peeking out of the hood. She must have been old then. Strange. Her voice didn't match that. It was melodic and pleasant. But maybe her senses deceived her. Due to the abhorrent stench of the sewers, Cassandrea couldn't even determine whether the female was fae or human.

"I can't wait," the woman said, and the hooded face turned towards Cassandrea. Then she sniffed. And the siren got a distinctive feeling that whatever the woman smelled, she didn't like it, for she just turned her back on them both. "You know the way out."

And the next moment, she was gone, her steps still echoing through the tunnel when Cassandrea turned towards Kerr.

"Your contact is... charming," she said dryly.

"Well," the male pulled off his shirt and started wringing it, "she did show up. At this point, I am not going to ask for more."

"Is she going to be helping us with the mission?"

Kerr raised his head and glanced towards the gloom on the far side of the corridor, which the woman disappeared off to.

"I don't think so."

"Small blessings," Cassandrea grinned, and it made Kerr laugh.

"In this case? Yes. I tend to agree. But don't worry. I have rented a small flat not far from here. We can take a bath there and change. I even have some female clothes. Although they might not be your size."

Cassandrea turned her back on him in order to keep some dignity while wringing her own clothes and to his credit, Kerr took the hint and turned as well before he pulled off his pants. For a moment, the corridor was filled with nothing but water dripping on the sidewalk and then pouring into the sewer. But a tiny curious bug was sitting on Cassandrea's brain, urging her to ask about where exactly Kerr had come across female clothing.

"Her clothes?" she prodded.

"Oh gods, no," he laughed.

Cassandrea pulled the trousers back on, and by the sounds of it, Kerr was doing the same. She hated how sticky and cold the fabric was.

"Another lover then? Smaller or bigger size than mine? Taller?"

Kerr chuckled.

"Curiosity killed the selkie."

"Good that I am a siren then."

Another chuckle.

"Who is she? Your contact?" Cassandrea continued prodding.

Kerr sighed.

"Don't you think that if I wanted to tell you, I would have?"

Cassandrea turned.

"I swear I should throw you right back into that sewer."

"Then you won't know where my flat is. Or the clean clothes. Or the bath... But be my guest."

"Touché," Cassandrea admitted gingerly, but Kerr could hear the smile in her voice, and it made him laugh.

"Come on, love, time to get civilised."

*

The city was still drowsy as the mists started to disperse in the morning sun. Drowsy, but not quiet. Bakers and fishmongers were wheeling their goods to the marketplace; wine peddlers and other merchants were opening up stalls next to the large awnings that must've belonged to the farmers. Farmers that were nowhere to be seen as they hadn't been able to neither enter nor exit the city since the lockdown. Because of that, the fresh food production was practically nonexistent. And even the fishmongers seemed to only sell heavily salted and cured wares.

Cassandrea and Kerr had snuck through a sewer grate from behind one of the town's two brothels, and it had provided them enough cover as the other vagrants and unwanted people started to mill about, not really smelling that much better than the two.

Sneaking into Kerr's apartment wasn't much of a challenge, now that they were already inside the city. However, there was still a nagging feeling in the back of Cassandrea's brain that she couldn't quite shake. An itch she couldn't scratch. Nervosity.

Only when she was standing at the very door to the flat did she feel the true warm rush of relief bubbling in her gut. Kerr unlocked the door and gestured for her to step in, and as the siren took in the humble abode, she was so relieved she could've dropped on her knees and sob. The flat was a small room with an even smaller bathroom but a large bed, a wooden locker, a basin for washing up, and a small table at the side, with two chairs opposite one another. It was ascetic and bare. But it was clean. And dry.

Cassandrea let her belongings drop on the ground and proceeded to peel off every layer of clothing she could while remaining somewhat decent. Then she rushed to the bathroom and began preparing a bath. Kerr helped as best as he could, lighting up a fire in the hearth and heating up big pots of water as fast as he could, but Cassandrea still felt it wasn't fast enough. Nothing would have been. And even though the warmth of the hearth radiating through the room felt good on its own, Cassandrea hardly spoke while they were filling the bathtub. But finally, finally, the bath was full, and she didn't intend to wait any longer.

"Thank you!" she called at the male, who was currently in the main room, and she shut the door. She was starving, but more than food, she needed to scrub off the filth off her skin. Hell, she would flay herself had it reduced the smell. Luckily enough, Kerr didn't protest against her going first, and she was eternally grateful for that.

Not that she would allow it to be in any other way, anyway.

*

An hour later, when they refilled the bath and switched, Kerr had left a neat package of clean female clothes waiting for her on the bed. It included a blouse, a corset, and a thick, layered skirt. None of it was fancy, but all the pieces were simple and practical, and the fabric of the blouse was soft. Cassandrea unwrapped the towel she was covering her form with, and changed into this new, dry attire with a hard-to-describe feeling of cosiness. Even the fit wasn't as bad as Kerr had suggested. Everything was about a size bigger than what she would have chosen for herself, but the corset and her belt fixed that easily.

Dressed up and with her hair slowly drying into big flowing waves, Cassandrea decided to snoop around the room while the kelpie was still out of the picture. To her disappointment, there wasn't much to discover. The wooden locker was almost empty, bar several bags of dried meat, a pouch of dried fruit, and some spare shirts and trousers. And that was all. No more equipment, no weapons, no notes, no food. Nothing that would help her discover anything about the kelpie's personality or intentions.

Cassandrea took some of that dried meat and sat down on Kerr's bed, fully intending to rest. However, the room still smelled of the dirty clothes, now lying on the floor, and it kept ruining her snack. Forced to get up, again, by that stench, Cassandrea sighed and started washing the clothes in the basin.

She was almost done when Kerr walked out of the bathroom wearing nothing but a small towel slapped at the front of his body. Cassandrea cackled. She didn't realise that when she had taken that big towel earlier, it had left him with nothing but this tiny sad excuse of a handkerchief.

"I am sorry," she muttered, having the decency to actually feel a bit bad about that.

"It is fine," Kerr laughed and walked over to the locker, dripping water all over the floor. "I should have taken some clothes with me."

Cassandrea closed her eyes, resisting the urge to turn around and take a look at his completely naked backside.

"I ate some of your dried meat," she admitted while her thoughts were circling around that impossibly shaped, muscular chest behind her.

"It was there for that. We can buy some more on the market later."

"You don't have much of... anything really."

"I wasn't planning on staying after the city is sacked."

"Right."

It made sense. It made a lot of sense. Still, it was weird. Seeing the apartment empty as it was.

"I am decent now. You can open your eyes, hypocrite."

"Excuse me?" Cassandrea turned around and blinked.

Kerr was indeed decent, wearing another set of grey trousers and a misty white shirt, but his eyes were twinkling with mischief.

"You liked what you saw. And yet you didn't dare to look."

"Fine," Cassandrea raised her head and crossed her arms on

her chest. "I am looking now."

Kerr raised his eyebrow.

"At?"

"You," she decided not to back off this time. Not until *he* felt uncomfortable for once. "Take that shirt off."

And to her great satisfaction, he hesitated. For a breath. A second. Then, suddenly, something shifted in his eyes, and the mischievous sparks flared up into a fire.

"As you wish," he said with a wry smile and his voice... Gods, his voice. It was even deeper now. Rougher. There was something in it that made her skin prickle.

With slow, methodical motions, Kerr removed his shirt and threw it onto the bed. He didn't give Cassandrea any time to admire his chest. Not then. For he cut the distance between them with two quick steps, strolling right into her personal space. There he stopped, and looked into her eyes, his own red ones burning like a furnace. No. Not just the eyes. His whole body was burning. Cassandrea could feel the heat of the recent bath radiating from it. Tempting her to touch it. Touch that stupidly perfect body that was designed to seduce and kill.

Some primal instinct kicked in, and while a coy smile spread across her lips and her eyes began to take in the kelpie's features, she nicked her head slightly back.

"Well," he challenged, "do you like what you see?"

"You should give a little twirl so I can take a proper look," Cassandrea replied, and every part of her brain screamed at her to stop playing. This was dangerous. On so many levels. For so many reasons. But the playful side of her suffocated those screams faster than an avalanche. She was born to tease. And she loved playing this game. Delighted by the surge of energy that took hold of her body, she relished the sensation of excitement, possible danger, and challenge. Because Kerr was a challenge. Her equal in this game.

Her heart was suddenly thundering in her ears, and she could only watch as he gave her a mean smirk. She tried to remind herself not to get too distracted, to not forget the reason the two of them were here, but Kerr had already started turning around... slowly. He was taunting her with every deliberate move, and she could see his lips curling up. Feeling the flush of excitement, Cassandrea inhaled sharply. Kerr was more than just a challenge. He was playing the game like she had never seen it being played.

Angling her head, she let a playful smile spread on her lips.

"I've seen worse," she said softly.

Her voice had dropped a bit, and it was coated with honey as she finally let her eyes take in the kelpie's body.

And what a body it was. Each muscle was beautifully defined under the taut skin, shifting subtly with Kerr's every motion. Cassandrea could swear she saw the heat glowing about him, and as he turned back to face her, his devilish grin spreading further, he was suddenly standing even closer than before. Trapped by his body on one side and the basin on the other, Cassandrea shifted sideways to escape. But Kerr moved again, and before she blinked, his left hand was already planted on the wall next to her head. He didn't touch her. Didn't need to. His face was close to hers, so close she could feel his breath hitting the side of her neck. The kelpie's eyes were smouldering.

"This is the part where I tell you it's not the body, as much as the ability to use it." Cassandrea met his gaze, sensual and inviting. She knew she shouldn't do that. But it had been years since she had played this game the last time, and studying the handsome features of Kerr's face, she allowed herself this moment. This reprieve.

"Would you like me to demonstrate?" Kerr's voice was rough. Too rough. As if he were actually holding back.

Cassandrea gave him a sultry look, lifting her chin up, knowingly leaving her neck open for him, almost like an invitation. The smooth, unscarred side of her neck. The one she didn't mind him seeing.

"Are you trying to distract me, Kerr?" she asked softly.

Kerr didn't reply. He lowered his head, and his lips met her neck, tracing a line from her shoulder up towards her ear. Slowly. Cassandrea closed her eyes, and despite the initial, knee-jerk reaction to flee when the male's face neared her throat, she was relieved to feel a wave of heat spreading through her body instead of a cold grip of panic.

With a pleased hum, she pushed aside that initial fear, and found her palms aching to move. She was tempted to touch him.

"I could ask you the same question," Kerr whispered, and his nose nudged her earlobe right before he took it between his teeth and pulled. "I know we should be out there seducing our way to the gates of Renglow. But I'd much rather be here with you."

"That's not-"

That was not what they were there for, Cassandrea reminded herself. But a not-so-small part of her wanted exactly the same. She exhaled softly, and Kerr's teeth grazed her neck just below her ear. Yes. She wanted this. This game. Or whatever it was. Him.

"Don't tell me you're not tired of sleeping with whoever they tell you to," the male continued. "Charming people who disgust you. Seeing the fear in their eyes when they find out who you are."

"I-"

Kerr's right hand moved to her side, and the back of his fingers caressed her curves. Gentle. Demanding attention. Silencing all the protests her mind was trying to form.

"I am not afraid of you, Cassandrea," Kerr growled into her ear. "Nor of your gifts. I am imagining what will happen when we both use them."

It was like the air itself had been sucked out of the room in that very instant, and Cassandrea could no longer breathe properly, only in shallow huffs. Kerr's voice was deep and primal, and it rumbled straight into her, leaving her taut like a too-tight string on a lute. She felt a surge of delight, knowing well enough her body was more than eager to play a round or two with the kelpie. *She* was more than ready for that. And the stars and the moon above knew she needed someone to hold her and make her happy. If only for a few moments. To make her forget.

"That's a dangerous thought," she whispered.

"You like it."

Kerr grinned, and Cassandrea leaned in and brought her own lips dangerously close to his ear.

"I do," she whispered, and her lips brushed against the lobe of his ear, repaying his earlier tease. When she continued, her smile was audible in every word.

"Work before play," she nipped at his ear before she casually dove from under the arm that was barring her move and strolled towards the table. She turned to look at the male, who hadn't moved. Only his eyes followed her around the room, and he was still grinning. Cassandrea leaned her rear against the edge of the table and crossed her arms. She knew the expression Kerr had on his face. That wild, greedy smile. Her own was a mirror image of it.

"It's a deal."

A corner of his lips curled up, and Kerr slowly turned around, stuffing his hands into his pockets only to... make the fabric strain even more around his crotch. Cassandrea looked at the male, then slowly her eyes descended down his body to his hips. She was absolutely sure he did that on purpose. For the sight... Well, she could see why he was so comfortable in his own body. So confident. She quietly wondered if kelpies elected their lords based on the number of women hunted down, because she was rather sure Kerr was on the very top of that ladder.

As if the male was happy enough with the chaos he sowed, his mischievous grin slowly softened into something lighter and more approachable. He even reached for his shirt and pulled it on.

"Well, what are you waiting for, love? We have work to do."

That made Cassandrea cackle.

"Why do I have the feeling that this sudden rush has absolutely nothing to do with your desire to win this war?"

Kerr shrugged and opened the door for her, staying in the door frame so that she would have to sneak around him.

"Can you blame me?" he winked.

"No," Cassandrea winked right back, and when she sneaked past him, she rose onto her toes and brushed her lips against his chin, "but it makes you rather defenceless, doesn't it?"

Kerr was still laughing when they walked into the streets of Renglow.

Chapter 7

Cassandrea was smiling as they walked, and she felt that the weather had improved rapidly along with her mood. There was no sign of the earlier gloomy morning mist or the dreary overcast. The day was bright and beautiful, with a crisp air that smelled of spring willows and fresh mud and tilled soil. The townsfolk were milling, going about their business, carefree and relaxed. Cassandrea looked at the curtain wall, taking note of the placement of the cannons and the nearby gatehouses that would be her way up to the platforms.

"I will need a distraction," she murmured quietly to Kerr.

She had asked to take his arm, posing as a young girl on a stroll with her sweetheart. She was grasping it firmly, and occasionally leaned in and giggled with the male, whispering hushed words of mischief, as if to hide her cheekiness from those who would take a second look at the pair.

"What's your plan?" Kerr's voice was equally soft, as the male gave her a playful glance. The kelpie was in on the act as much as she was. Far better than she had expected.

Cassandrea smiled softly, planted her hand on top of the one holding the arm, and leaned in.

"I will go and destroy the powderkegs by wetting them. But I need you to make sure nobody sees me going in."

"Consider it done," Kerr said, with the insufferable confidence Cassandrea was actually slowly getting used to. Which didn't mean she wasn't about to challenge it.

"How?" she asked.

Kerr stopped by a stall with salted fish in barrels.

"What do you want for dinner? Fish or more dried meat?"

"Fish for lunch, and meat for dinner. Some of us actually have to eat properly."

Kerr stepped away and took his time taking her body in from head to toe, as if he were actually evaluating that statement.

"Mhm. I can see these curves need some love. Both it is."

"Are you calling me flat?" she almost choked on those words.

"Quite the contrary. I am recognising that such gorgeous curves couldn't be built on air alone."

The kelpie smirked at Cassandrea and paid for three pieces of fish, handing the disgusting package over to her right away. Only when they were on their way again, and Cassandrea was munching on the food, did he oblige her earlier question.

"There are six cannons protecting the city. Each is ready to be used with its own supply of gunpowder and cannon balls. So you will have to take care of each keg separately. Plus the main gunpowder storage, right?"

"Something like that."

"And I doubt you feel like seducing seven watches while I am doing the work. So! We bring the soldiers some food," Kerr suggested, "this whole city is running on cooperation. Terren's army loves that crap. So they won't find it weird if we bring them warm tea and dried meat. Or wine to explain the extra waterskins that you will need to take care of the gunpowder. How does that sound?"

Cassandrea had to admit that it was a good plan. She nodded, tearing the fish in half with her teeth. She ate in silence. Thought about it.

"I like the way you think," she admitted.

"And?" Kerr's eyes twinkled. They were brown now, Cassandrea noticed. They had been that way ever since they left the apartment. Apparently, she wasn't the only one who could use magic to hide her distinctive features.

"The way you can treat a lady," she admitted further, repaying that mischievous smile.

"And?" he coaxed.

"And that you know a lot more than you let out. What do you know of Terren's methods?"

Kerr's response was a light-hearted laugh. He shook his head and gave her side a gentle nudge with his arm.

"Come on, give me something," Cassandrea insisted. "I'll make it worth your while. One for one, no?" She offered him an impish grin and nudged him right back.

She was curious, and while she had already started forming some plans on how to reach each of those six points in swift succession, that small detail had piqued her interest.

"Cooperation, as in... how?"

Kerr sighed, pretending to be in some terrible pain from that question alone.

"The social cohesion of the army, and his forces in general, is where Terren's strength lies." He beckoned towards the city. "They are patriots. All of them. But not in the same way our forces are. You know Valderan's army. It's based on obedience and strength. On how effective we are. How willingly we march into battle. How daringly we milk the farmers for supplies. How many slaves can be put to work when we need roads, bridges, and materials. It is what people usually call ruthless. Terren doesn't need to do any of that. He is working with idealists, who will still work as hard as slaves, still march into a suicide mission, and still provide all their resources for his war effort, but they do it willingly. They do it because they want to. Because they believe their cause is just. As naive as that is."

"You almost make it sound like our cause is not one to believe in." Cassandrea shook her head in disbelief.

Kerr shrugged.

"What is our cause exactly?" he asked.

The siren blinked. What an odd question.

"We are defending Entirie. And the king."

"From what?"

Her eyebrow rose higher.

"From the invading army, of course."

"Army of our own people," the kelpie countered, and Cassandrea noted that it had a sad tone to it. So that was what bothered him? That Entirie was fighting itself? Did he have friends on the other side? Did he have to make tough decisions, like she did with Ryker? Suddenly, his words made a lot more sense.

"That wasn't our choice, Kerr," she tried to comfort him. "They attacked us."

"Oh yeah. They did." Kerr's voice was bitter, and it made Cassandrea halt and look at him, but he changed the subject before she managed to ask.

"Anyway," he added in his typically upbeat tone, as though the previous discussion had been nothing more than a small talk. "We should buy some wine bottles."

Cassandrea decided not to question it this time.

*

Finding shops that would sell them wine and dried meat was easy. Kerr knew exactly where all the points of interest were, and he paid for the food as well, so Cassandrea had all her work done for her. Which felt odd and unsatisfying on one hand, but good and relaxing on the other. She had never had a partner who was this easy to work with, and she thought she could get used to it. Maybe if Renglow became an easy claim, the king would let her work with this kelpie lord again. And that thought didn't bother her as much as she had expected. It didn't bother her at all, in fact. During her marriage to Ryker, she often pondered what it would have been like had he worked in tandem with her instead of being her enemy. How it would have felt—not being alone. To have someone who knew what it was like, what this line of work demanded, how crucial and dangerous it was, and just how much the war effort depended on their contribution. Someone who understood what kind of sacrifices it took. And suddenly, she had a chance to find out. With Kerr.

The subject of her thoughts was lying on a low wall, enjoying the afternoon sun and waiting for it to set so that they could get on with their mission. He looked lazy and comfortable, like a cat basking in the sun. One of his legs was hanging down, swinging, and his eyes were closed. He seemed relaxed and sleepy, but Cassandrea knew that was all but a ruse, and he was well aware of everything that was going on around him. For example, when she sat beside him.

Yet he didn't stir.

Behind the wall, several snowdrops and cowslips were peeking through white mounds of snow in a small garden. One surrounding the city's bell tower. Cassandrea had no doubt that the bell was the one she had heard back on Ebongale—ringing to warn all ships of the invisible cliffs hidden in the fog. Not

Torquil's ships though, she realised with some unease. Nor Terren's ships either—the city was locked down. And it wasn't ringing in the afternoon nor in the morning, even though the fog remained thick. Cassandrea frowned. Why did it ring then? She looked at the tower, as if it could get her some answers regarding its strange behaviour, but the stone building remained silent. Dormant.

Kerr opened his eyes and poked Cassandrea's thigh with two fingers.

"A coin for your thoughts?"

Cassandrea bit her lip and looked at Kerr.

"Something weird about that bell," she said.

Kerr's eyes were full of questions as he turned his head ever-so-slightly towards her, then followed her gaze to the tower.

"What do you mean?"

"I heard it ringing yesterday. In the mists, when the ships were arriving. But it was... strange. It didn't sound urgent. It was slow and haunting, and... lonely."

Kerr's brow hiked up as the kelpie turned his gaze back to her.

"The bell sounded lonely?" he didn't mock her with his question or his tone, even though his expression was dubious.

Cassandrea nodded. "Don't ask me how I know. I just... do."

"I didn't hear it ringing yesterday."

Cassandrea finally looked at him. The male's face seemed genuinely confused. Concerned.

"I'm not going crazy," she said with a little sharper tone than she intended, and it made Kerr stir enough to lift his head.

"I'm not saying you are," he countered gently and looked towards the belltower. "I'm just saying I didn't hear it."

Cassandrea didn't feel like contesting that. She picked up a chipped piece of the wall, a thin sliver of stone she rotated between her fingers. Kerr's earlier words were still gnawing her insides, and the siren took another look at Renglow and its people. The city went on about its life, breathing with slow, calm breaths, oblivious to the incoming threat. Threat of an army that consisted of her own people. Entirie's people. Neighbours had turned to enemies overnight; brothers and sisters that had once shared lands no longer tolerated one another, and sought to drive the other away by force, by any means necessary. The thought stung her. Entirie's own people were brutally massacring each other for a cause she couldn't understand. Didn't want to. But she could only imagine her king's disappointment and hurt when the betrayal came. His own protégé. Terren. The Emerald Dragon Prince. Once the heir to the throne, and now their worst enemy. Cassandrea had met him once in his human form, almost two decades ago. She didn't remember much of him, just that he seemed sad and distant, and he didn't talk much. Was he already planning it back then? The treason? On his own liege... What could've been the reason for that? For this much chaos? Pain? Hatred? What was worth destroying the very land and people they were fighting over?

"Where did you go?" Kerr interrupted her thoughts, his eyes carefully studying her own.

Cassandrea realised she had been staring.

"How do you do that?" she asked. Her voice was strangely stifled, distant. Somehow, she found it difficult to look at the kelpie.

Kerr clearly found the question interesting, as he propped himself to his elbows and gave her a long, studious look back.

"Do what?" he asked.

"Despite all... this," she gestured vaguely at the city, "you still see the colours instead of darkness?"

Kerr followed her gaze towards the city, and a shadow passed through his eyes.

"I like life," he mused. "And if the priests are right, and beasts like us don't have souls, it will be the only one I'll have. So I might as well enjoy it."

Once more, Cassandrea couldn't tell whether he was joking or being serious.

"Really, now?" she doubted.

Kerr laughed and let his body drop down again, shamelessly using Cassandrea's thigh as a pillow.

"Why do you care, Cass? You were born a predator, not a saviour."

"Is that what you tell yourself?"

"Sometimes," Kerr was back to his cheerful self, laughing with his every word. "Most of the time, I have a beautiful woman in my arms, and that kind of takes the thoughts in a different direction."

"So you are screwing your way through life. Is that what you are saying?"

"I would not... put it in those exact words."

Kerr's head was heavy on her thigh, but Cassandrea found it oddly sweet. Oddly satisfying. Devoted. And tempting. She wanted to touch his hair. Badly so. And why the hell shouldn't she? He would have done it, and he wouldn't even ask. So, she reached down to touch his dark mane, and it was pure silk, soft, messy, and tangled like seaweed. It made her smile as she started untangling those short locks, caressing the skin of his head in the process.

She bit her lips and looked down at the male, only to find him watching her. There wasn't a shred of laughter left in his expression. It all vanished, replaced by an intense and thoughtful look, a curious one. One she hadn't seen on him yet.

"What?" she asked.

"I like you," Kerr admitted and it made Cassandrea's hand halt. "And no, Cass, I don't always see the colours. I don't wish for this city to fall. And I do not wish for its citizens to die during the attack. I do not wish for the people in Torquil's army to die either, but it is going to happen whether I want it or not."

His voice was so very quiet.

"I am good at what I do," he continued, "I am really bloody good at it. So where else would I be? What else should I do? I enjoy this job; I enjoy doing it. And I think you know exactly how that feels. So the question really is—why don't *you* see the colours?"

Cassandrea slowly resumed the caress, her fingers making idle paths through the dark waves of his hair. She didn't even notice that her stare went vacant as she thought about that question. It echoed in her head, burrowing deep into the depths of her soul, which she had hoped never to explore again. She wasn't even sure how to answer that question. How to explain that emptiness in her that Ryker had left in her heart. So she bought herself more time by taking a deep breath and looking away at the city, even though she didn't really see it.

"I don't want to see them dying either, Kerr," she finally said, easing herself into the topic. Somehow the feeling of his sable hair between her fingers was soothing her. Making the thoughts less painful. Perhaps that was Kerr's gift and curse as a kelpie. To make people talk, even if unwittingly. The thought stung her as it dawned on her; it horrified her. She cleared her throat, feeling uneasy once more.

"I do my job well. Always have. Always will." She barely recognised her voice. It was strained, pained. "And in our line of work, there's little light to be seen, little colour to be cherished."

Kerr's eyes were drilling a hole into her head, as if he were trying to see right through her, through the walls she had built for herself, looking for a window to peek in. Cassandrea made a mistake, glancing at him, and the cursed expression on his face, the look of sympathy and pity, made her pull a curtain in front of any window he might have glimpsed at. She gritted her teeth and looked away. She had said enough. She had done enough. She couldn't bring herself to hope, to dream that she could ever share that pain. She hadn't spoken a word to anybody about that night that had snuffed out all the light and colour from her world, and she wasn't going to tell this male about it either.

"And I think you know that, too," she said instead, as if to conclude the topic.

"There's little light or colour," Kerr replied gently. His hand moved, and he brushed her wrist with his fingers. "But it doesn't mean there isn't *any* left."

Cassandrea's throat tightened. She looked sharply up and away, letting a small gust of wind kiss her cheeks and dry out the tears that had tried to line her eyes. Swallowing, she breathed in deep.

"It's getting late," she said by way of changing the subject.

"And you look lovely in the setting sun."

Against her will, those words painted a smile on Cassandrea's lips.

"Stop it," she pulled at a strand of his hair.

"What?!" Kerr laughed. "I can imagine it. You. Sitting on a sharp rock above the roaring waves. Singing to lure the sailors in. Naked..."

Cassandrea yanked at his hair hard enough to make the kelpie yelp.

"And what should I imagine *you* as?" she teased. "Lord of the Moonlit Mire? Sitting under the starry sky among heather, barefoot, dipping your feet in the bog and waiting for a fair maiden to join you and get her skirts soaked?"

Kerr winked at her.

"We only eat those who don't like getting wet. The rest is too much fun."

Cassandrea chuckled.

"You're bad."

"Don't tell me you would drown a handsome muscular warrior, who-"

But Kerr didn't manage to finish that sentence, for something moved on the other side of the square. A group of soldiers walked out of a narrow street. Seven of them in total. Six of them looked human, although four were a little bit too stunning for that. Half-bloods maybe. One of them, a handsome blond man, looked at Kerr and smiled as if he liked what he saw. They didn't head in their direction, but Cassandrea's blood froze anyway. For the seventh male, the one leading the group, was over seven feet tall, and he had two giant twirled horns decorating the sides of his head. General T'aar.

Cassandrea had never felt this much fearful respect towards another creature. The male was abnormally large, even by fae standards, and the scarred, brutal face made her guts shrivel. Terren was using beasts like him to keep people in check. Despite what Kerr had said, she couldn't believe someone like this fomori general would really care much for 'cooperation' or unity. No. Cassandrea turned her head away, even though her eyes remained on the hulking male. She struggled to swallow, trying her best to hide her utter terror from the general and his men. And Kerr.

"Ugly bastard, isn't he?" Kerr muttered, his voice amused, even in the face of the terrifying beast across the square. "Especially the braided beard and hair. I think he should cut it.

Just a little bit."

Cassandrea didn't answer. Her eyes dotted at the broad back of the general. There was a green emblem embroidered on the black wool cape, fashioned very closely to King Valderan's sigil. But instead of the borders threaded with gold metal wire, the rim of the crest was stitched with silver, and instead of the proud black dragon, a green one was opening its maw in a mighty roar. As always, when she saw that sigil, Cassandrea felt a rush of fury rising in her guts. Everything about the emblem was an insult to her king.

"He's... terrifying," she admitted, in all honesty.

Kerr had already seen the horror in her eyes. Sensed it. Probably smelled it on her. So she tore her eyes off of the general and looked down. Embarrassed. Furious. Both at the general and at herself for feeling this way. For showing it to the kelpie. But Kerr wasn't laughing. He studied her with those unreadable brown eyes and said nothing of the matter. His voice was actually soft and soothing when he spoke up.

"Come on. We better start moving," he said.

Cassandrea hesitated. For the first time, she wasn't entirely sure whether she could finish this mission. If she had to actually be in the vicinity of that fomori general, she would probably die out of sheer terror. Or try to claw his eyes out. She wasn't sure which. For now, she just needed to be as far away from the beast as possible.

"Yeah," she nodded, "let's get out of here."

*

However, it wasn't until much later that they got the chance to charm the cannon crews. As it turned out, General T'aar was on his way to inspect them when they crossed his path, and after he had done that, all the soldiers were temporarily on high alert. Cassandrea wasn't happy about it, but she understood it. She would have done the same if the monster of a male decided to visit her station.

Fortunately, after a few hours, the night took its toll, and even the spooked soldiers calmed down and started loitering, chatting, or nodding off. Close to midnight, they were ready to be approached.

Cassandrea took Kerr's arm and swung her hips, ready to become a young altruistic lady, concerned with the well-being of the poor soldiers who had to spend their time outside in a cold and dark environment. Kerr next to her took on the role of her daring and dashing date, unwilling to let the lady go alone and eager to protect her from all lurking dangers.

It was a bit ridiculous, given they were probably the only real danger in Renglow, preparing the way for... No. She did not want to think about that.

Clearing their way to the wall was as easy as breathing. The people in the gatehouse didn't look twice at her after she had smiled, offered them a bit of meat and wine and asked if she could go to the wall to do the same for the patrols that were freezing in the cold ocean breeze. Her friendly voice was thick with a veil, and soon the soldiers were practically fighting over who would escort her to the stairs.

The first gun crew they approached consisted of a man and a woman. The man was lying on the ground, wrapped in a blanket, and dozing off, whereas the woman was leaning on the bulwark and staring at the sea. She turned when she heard their steps and straightened up, but when she saw none of them were her superior, she relaxed again.

"Oh, hello," Cassandrea greeted the woman. "It's quite the cold evening tonight, isn't it?"

Her voice was soft and demure; she even added a little shyness into the mix as she lifted the large basket with meat and wine on top.

"I figured maybe you'd like something to keep your spirits up," she continued. Her voice had grown softer, far softer than it had been before, and it carried a featherlight veil of the siren's magic. The guards were both humans. They wouldn't even notice anything was amiss until the cannons were prepared. The woman's eyelids lulled a bit as she smiled at Cassandrea, and the siren knew that the man, who was trying to rest, would certainly be resting far better than he could have ever hoped for, soon enough. The siren felt something akin to a small poke in her soul when she saw how easily the woman's mind bent to her will. Oh, how she had revelled in it in the past. But now... Mairi's words pressed against her conscience. *It is not their fault, is it?* the red-haired fae had said.

"Oh, how kind of you," the woman thanked Cassandrea and

reached for a piece of pork jerky. She took a bite of it, and her smile widened once her gaze landed on Cassandrea's companion. Another "oh" was all she managed.

"Hello, love," the kelpie lord winked.

This time Cassandrea could swear there was a spell in his voice. It wasn't directed at her, but the way the girl melted when he addressed her... Or maybe it wasn't in his voice at all. Maybe... Maybe it was in his very essence. Was that why she hadn't noticed before? Had she been waiting for something that wouldn't come because it was already there? Cassandrea did a double take on the male. Sensed for the magic in the air. Yet she couldn't feel any. Nothing like the smokiness of her veil nor the iron of fae magic. Kerr was just... Kerr. Cassandrea briefly considered she was going crazy, but then remembered that Kerr was a full-fledged kelpie, whereas she was unfortunately born as she was. Incomplete, without the visible fae heritage. Still, if his magic was so good that she couldn't even sense it, the gap between their abilities must have been gargantuan. And that made the siren uneasy.

The soldier girl giggled and hid the jerky behind her back, as if it were impolite to eat in Kerr's presence. The move was stupid. And the way the girl laughed was awkward and embarrassing, and it made Cassandrea cringe. However, Kerr kept his smile on, and everything in his posture was inviting and approachable. He started opening the wine bottle, and the way he smiled, the way his brown eyes shone... Cassandrea could almost believe that the awkwardly giggling human was the only girl he had his eyes for, the only girl he would ever have eyes for. He was certainly nothing short of devouring her with his gaze. And for some reason, that actually annoyed Cassandrea more than she would have thought possible. She immediately pushed that thought away, not wanting to know whether it was jealousy over his abilities or the way he was looking at the girl.

"Join me for a drink or two?" Kerr offered the soldier, and the woman stepped closer toward him, forgetting about Cassandrea's presence altogether.

Given that the male soldier was still sleeping, overtaken by both his tiredness and Cassandrea's spell, there was nothing between the siren and the powder keg. So she took her chance. She worked swiftly and silently as a mouse as she stepped next to the keg and drew out her blade. For necessity's sake, the kegs were always sealed shut to keep the moisture at bay, but only with a lid that was quick enough to move in case of a sudden, urgent need. It required little more than the tip of her dagger to raise the lip of the wooden lid up to have the black powdered contents available to her. No more than a few seconds later, the entire water skin from the basket was drained into the powder. Then a second one. Two were enough. It'd take a few hours for the black powder to soak everything in, and with the lid left ever-so-slightly ajar from the side, it was about to look like someone forgot to close the barrel properly and the mist got in, ruining the batch. Eventually. If they ever looked into the barrel. However, the opening was so tiny that no one would notice it on a nighttime glance, and if someone noticed during the day, it would be already too late to take any action before Torquil's forces arrive.

Slipping away from the keg, she took a look around and gave Kerr a subtle nod when it was safe to do so. One down, five more to go. For Kerr as well, apparently, as her glance had found him with an arm around the soldier girl's waist and his mouth on her neck. Cassandrea knew he was just doing this job. As was she. And it worked perfectly because turning around and watching Cassandrea was the last thing on the girl's mind. Yet... something about seeing it done by someone else, by Kerr, irked the siren. Terribly. So she coughed. Loudly. And pointendly.

The woman in Kerr's arms twitched, his spell broken by Cassandrea's interruption. The soldier laughed awkwardly and muttered a quiet apology in the siren's way, her cheeks burning.

"It's alright, love," Kerr assured her, "I'll take the blame for this one."

"You sure will, *darling*." Cassandrea grabbed his arm and started pulling him away.

Kerr didn't fight that, but he glanced over his shoulder and winked at the soldier.

"Totally worth it."

The visits to the following cannons were practically identical. Cassandrea lulled the guards to sleep, and where she couldn't, Kerr took the reins and diverted their attention elsewhere. It was smooth as butter and so easy it made the siren ponder if she could get a partner like Kerr always working by her side. Eventually, she shook off that twang of jealousy over his seemingly impossible abilities and focused on marvelling at the male's sheer skill. He was right. He *was* damn good at what he did. And she loved watching him.

After pouring the water into the last barrel and walking to a safe distance from it, she gave Kerr a sign with another cough and watched the kelpie peel his lips off an older woman, who had not wasted a second of her time and already started feeling the kelpie with her hands. The fair-haired human gave Cassandrea a withering look. She obviously did not want to let go, and it required several promises of further adventures before she allowed Kerr to bid his goodbyes.

"Do you ever feel violated?" Cassandrea asked, as they were once again strolling the streets, towards the gunpowder storage.

"No, love," Kerr shook his head and wrapped his arm around the siren's waist. "I think of my body as a gift. One I choose to offer to these women or men to brighten their day. Most of these people have never had somebody handsome showing them attention and longing for them."

"That's a bit sad, isn't it?" Cassandrea frowned.

"Didn't seem sad when she smiled at me, did it?" Kerr winked at her, his voice as light as ever.

"So that's your secret. You aim low to-"

"Oh, I wouldn't say that," Kerr interrupted. "I could charm a beautiful princess just as easily."

"I doubt that."

Kerr pinched her side.

"That sounds like a challenge."

Cassandrea chuckled and elbowed his side.

"One you will sadly have to pass on. There are no princesses in Renglow."

"Yet!"

"Yet," she agreed and looked at the kelpie with a warm glow in her eyes. She was slowly starting to like him. Actually like him.

But Kerr leaned down to plant a gentle kiss on her cheek, and Cassandrea was surprised to find herself not recoiling from it but leaning into it. Yet, she couldn't afford to let him realise that.

"You reek of others," she snapped and nudged him away with her shoulder.

"Do *you* ever feel violated?" he returned her question as if nothing had happened. There was a smile tugging on the corner of his lips.

The siren shrugged. She did. More often than not. But she had no way of explaining that to him or the will to go into details about how deep the self-loathing sometimes struck. She wasn't ready to share such intimate things about herself. Maybe she would never be. But seeing she had little choice now that he had fired back, she deflected with a chuckle.

"It's not... violation," she started, her eyes scanning the darkened streets, "but rather... dissatisfaction?"

Kerr made a face, and Cassandrea shook her head.

"Stop that thought," she said firmly, but her lips curled to a coy smile. "I mean it in a way that I... more often than not, leave my work behind and never look back."

Kerr angled his head.

"Just look at this," she tried to explain, gesturing at the quiet street. It was dark, illuminated only by a couple of street lanterns that dangled over tall, young boughs curling around their handles. "We're leaving soon. Never to come back. Probably never to meet again, you and I. Never to see these people again."

"Isn't that a good thing?"

Cassandrea frowned, and Kerr immediately laughed.

"I don't mean you and I, love," he elaborated, "though that frown was cute. No, I mean us and the people. Most of them are going to die tomorrow, so they are not going to be our biggest fans."

Cassandrea looked around and nodded. She couldn't help but feel a bit sorry for Renglow. It was a nice city. Quiet and neat. And the people seemed alright. Most of them smiled at the pair when they passed, despite the impending doom of Torquil's attack. And there were no slaves. Cassandrea noticed that little fact a bit earlier. She knew that cancelling slavery was one of Terren's selling points, but actually seeing it was odd. There were slaves everywhere in Entirie. Both humans and fae and other magical creatures. Mostly humans from Ordeara, of course, but her king wasn't opposed to utilising those who had done wrong. Most people considered that a mercy. The siren wasn't sure she would call it that. Pragmatic. That's what it was, in her opinion. Pragmatic. They needed the workforce.

"You've gone quiet," Kerr noticed and halted.

Cassandrea wanted to ask him why he had stopped, but when

she looked up, she realised that while she was lost in her thoughts, they actually reached the right building. It was a tall tower, and if her knowledge of the army's habits was correct, the gunpowder was stored in the cellar. Which meant not only befriending the guards but also persuading them to let her in. She stepped forth and gave the young guard a charming smile.

"Good evening, soldier, how-"

And before she could finish her sentence, the door opened and let out a beast that was good two heads taller than Cassandrea herself. His two curly horns were decorating the sides of his head, their tips pointed towards the siren. The male's hazelnut hair was braided and tied at the back of his head, and his mighty long beard was stylised in the very same way. He had a massive scar on the left side of his cheek and numerous others that marred his face. His brown eyes had flecks of gold in them, and they were sitting deep in his skull, hidden in the shadows of his brows. He could be considered handsome by somebody who liked wild storms, monsters, and headstrong rams. Cassandrea wasn't that somebody. She didn't feel charmed. Or lucky. Or particularly brave. For she was standing face to chest with general T'aar.

The male stopped and slowly glanced down, regarding the small blond thing blocking his way.

"What is this?" he asked in a deep, rumbling voice, and for a moment, Cassandrea's mind was full of avalanches and storms that were breaking trees like grass. She felt Kerr's hand gently touching the small of her back, but it didn't help. Nothing would help.

Luckily, Kerr replied in her stead.

"Food for the soldiers, General T'aar. We thought it would be nice to reward their service to Renglow. And to us, its citizens."

The might of the general's gaze turned towards Kerr. Then towards the basket Cassandrea was carrying. The general reached for it and pulled out the first waterskin he would find. He opened it and sniffed it.

"My men don't drink wine on duty," he stated, and ripped the basket from Cassandrea's hand. Slowly he picked up one waterskin after another, sniffed them, and returned them until he found the few with the water. He offered them to Kerr.

"This. And this. And the meat."

He pulled out the dried meat from Cassandrea's basket as well and passed it over to Kerr.

"That's what you may offer them."

"Thank you," Kerr smiled and took the permitted supplies back from the general.

Cassandrea had no idea how his voice still sounded so light when they were so screwed. She offered the general the sweetest smile she could muster and reached for Kerr to take a hold of his arm once more. She needed some support. And it helped. Looking up at the frightful fomori, she reminded herself of the role she was playing.

"Careful, general, the cobblestones tend to get really slippery during the damp nights," she said, summoning a gentle-hearted voice. Naturally, she wasn't even dreaming of using her veil, in fear of being discovered.

The male's eyes snapped to Cassandrea, and the siren held his stare with that disarming noblewoman smile.

"I will make sure the supplies you've spent your money on are still going to be used by my soldiers. *After* the battle, milady."

Tides below, it was like his voice was coming from the very core of the Earth itself, so low and coarse it was. Cassandrea didn't falter, even though the size and commanding presence alone would have been enough to send people running the other way.

"When can we expect it to happen?" Cassandrea let her smile fade. "I still need to take my father and grandmother to safety. Will our basement be enough?"

She cast her eyes up to look at the general. He met her eyes with an intense stare from under his heavy brows, and Cassandrea's lips curled downwards with worry.

A blink later, T'aar's eyes turned to regard Kerr. As if he were considering if the male was enough to protect this tiny blonde in front of him.

"You have nothing to worry about," he finally assured her with the quiet confidence of a warrior who had done his preparations, "the enemy will never make it to the city."

"Oh," Cassandrea uttered, and she, too, looked at Kerr. She didn't appraise her companion but beamed him a smile that indicated the general had indeed reassured her.

"Well, I am certainly glad to hear that," she said as she craned her head up once more to look at T'aar, "thank you."

The general held her gaze for another few, long seconds, during which she forgot to breathe.

"Have a good night," T'aar said.

Even though his tone was polite enough, there was not an inkling of a smile on his lips. Cassandrea started pondering if the male knew how to smile at all. She decided to not wear her luck any thinner, so she simply bowed a little and held on to Kerr's arm, waiting for the general to move along. Her grip on the kelpie's arm was tight, and she only realised she was barely breathing when the broad back of the fomori male finally turned around the corner.

"Good night!" Kerr called after the general as if they had just become best friends, and Cassandrea silently cursed his audacity. But the kelpie just laughed, tugged her arm, and pulled her inside the armoury.

The tower was half-empty, but the people inside were on high alert, no doubt due to having the giant general visiting them a moment earlier. The pair stepped inside and was immediately greeted by a wall of warmth. Outside, the night was cold, damp, and windy, but here a small fire had been lit in the centre of the room, emanating such sweet warmth it could reach one's soul. Cassandrea's smile was entirely honest when she walked in, greeting the people inside. Four of them. One was tending the fire, one was heading up the stairs, one was leaning against a wall, and one halted his hands that were halfway in his pockets, looking for something. All four looked at the newcomers and visibly relaxed, realising it was not the general.

"Hello, brave soldiers!" Kerr chirped in the same cheery voice, with which he bid goodbye to the general, and raised his arms heavy with the waterskins and meat. "The mean general confiscated all the wine we have brought you to uplift the spirit, but there's still some meat left, and it is all on us!"

Smiles spread on the men's faces, and even the guy heading upstairs turned around and stayed to pick up his share of goods before the others ravaged the gifts.

Kerr tossed the meat on the table, only keeping one waterskin for himself, and pointed at the man with his hands in his pockets.

"Is that a flute in your pocket or..." he grinned with a devilish smile.

The male's cheeks turned red, but he laughed and pulled out the flute.

"It *is* a flute."

"And can you play it? My lady here is a hell of a singer," Kerr continued working on where he wanted the situation to go.

Three of the four soldiers turned to Cassandrea.

"Would you grace us with a song, milady?" one asked politely.

"Something about the sea," the second one wished.

"A shanty!" the fourth one joined in.

"Milady won't sing you a shanty, moron," the first one gave him a cuff on the head.

"I will play the *Wayfarer* if you know it, milady," the man with the flute suggested.

Wayfarer was an old ballad, which Cassandrea knew very well. Not because she would have sung it herself, but because it was a popular song sung by many bards visiting the king's castle. So she nodded and gave Kerr a small smile.

"For you," she agreed, replying to the soldier, but with her eyes set on the kelpie male. For him. For him, she would sing it. But Kerr had already moved towards the door leading deeper into the tower and leaned against the wall next to it, ready to use her song as a distraction to conclude their business there.

So Cassandrea began, cursing the need to go on with their mission. She wanted Kerr to hear this song. Wanted to hear his thoughts on it. But it was what it was. Maybe another time.

Oh wayfarer, where do you roam?
In a search of a place called home.
All the kind hearts you've left behind
For a dream you hope to find

Young had he wandered through misty moor
Heart full of plans and dreams
When the first fair maiden had claimed his soul
And promised to be his

Kerr's eyes gained a dreamy veil to them as the ballad continued. Cassandrea knew what he was thinking about. She was thinking about the same thing. But as expected, at the last line of the second strophe, the male had left his spot and slipped into the corridor. Cassandrea didn't know why it had made her so sad. Nevertheless, she silenced that sadness and turned towards the man playing the flute, flashing him a bright smile as she continued.

Oh wayfarer, where do you roam?
In a search of a place called home
All the kind hearts you've left behind
For a dream you hope to find

Across the mountains, he roamed so free
The best years of his life
He met a huntress below old tree
She was to be his wife

Cassandrea winked at the youngest man of the four, who totally forgot to eat, and stood there with a completely love-struck stare. Kerr was still gone, so she continued onto the third part of the song.

Oh wayfarer, where do you roam?
In a search of a place called home
All the kind hearts you've left behind
For a dream you hope to find

By the riverside, he sat one eve
At the dusk of all his days
When farmer's daughter offered him peace
In her arms, he quietly sang

Kerr silently slipped back to his place by the door and gave Cassandrea a nod. She acknowledged it with a bright smile and laid her heart into the last strophe of the ballad. From what she could see, none of the four had noticed that Kerr was gone; they had eyes only for her, and hearts opened for her melodic voice.

I am a wayfarer, I've always roamed
In a search of a place called home
All the kind hearts I've left behind
For a dream I'll never find

The last words died into a feathery breath, and Cassandrea gave the guards a sombre smile as she pressed her head to a bow. The men were quiet, all staring at her, including Kerr. Then, the youngest one broke into applause, and the others joined him. The man with the flute beamed her a smile, shaking his head.

"Well, I'll be damned, aren't you a pretty little thing?" he said with tenderness in his voice.

Cassandrea smiled at him and bent her knees to a small bow.

"Thank you," she said and beamed the musician another wide smile.

She looked at the young boy, who was still holding the piece of cured meat in between his fingers, staring at her, his mouth slightly ajar. It was a funny picture. The meat had never made it all the way into the boy's mouth and drooped in front of his lips. The man next to him, the one that had tended the fire, snatched the meat and ate it with a chuckle. The boy, finally snapping out of his infatuated stare, looked at his fingers and shouted his protest. The men laughed, but the boy awkwardly ran his hand through his hair and looked at the siren once more. Cassandrea winked at him and then glanced at Kerr. And for some reason, for him, her heart ached. But whatever the kelpie felt, he didn't show it. Not there and then at least. He was merely watching Cassandrea with a kind and warm fire in his eyes.

"I'm honoured to have men like you keeping us all safe," Cassandrea added softly, "thank you for your service."

She didn't want to admit it, but saying those words felt wrong. No, worse, it hurt. Yet, she pushed through that pain and offered the youngest man a smile that could melt an iceberg. Then she turned to look at Kerr once more.

"I think we should go before the winds pick up and freeze us to death on our way home."

There was a subtle wave of protest from the men. The one with the flute angled his head.

"One more song," he asked, or judging by the tone of his voice, pleaded.

"Please, miss," the young man joined in.

"Yes! Sing about Vargsoul."

"Oh yes, please. The ballad of Vargsoul. Do you know it?

Cassandrea chuckled. Of course she knew it. She glanced at Kerr, as if asking whether they would have time for one more song. The kelpie male shrugged and found himself a place by the window, sitting down on a large wooden chest.

"By all means, love," he said gently, "far for me to tell you not to sing when your voice is so heartbreakingly beautiful."

And Cassandrea could swear that in that moment there *was* sorrow in his eyes.

*

In the end, Cassandrea sang a lot more than one song. They stayed with the guards for an entire hour, and eventually the siren obliged their requests for a shanty. She invited the men to join her in on the song, and for a brief moment in her life, she truly enjoyed what her gift of voice and charm was able to bring to people: joy. Kerr laughed and sang with them and clapped for her even louder than the soldiers, and as the night progressed, his mood lightened up, and he started stomping his foot to the rhythm of her songs.

As he was sitting there with the men, for once not trying to charm anything and anybody, Cassandrea found the kelpie male even more charming than when he was actually trying to be. His laughter was cheerful and relaxed, and his eyes were gleaming with the wine they had drunk before coming to the armoury. And he was... breathtaking.

When she finally reached for his hand to take him home, she found it surprisingly easy to pretend she was his lady. Easy to wrap her arms around his and lean into his warmth. Easy to rest her head against his shoulder. And eventually... easy to snuggle to his side in their bed while the fire was crackling gently in the hearth and lulling their wine-affected minds into slumber.

Kerr, ever the gentleman, didn't try anything. He just wrapped his arm around the siren's side and rested his head against hers, breathing in the flowery scent of her hair.

"Thank you for the song," he whispered.

And Cassandrea smiled, as she realised she could actually get used to this.

Chapter 8

But the peace of that night quickly turned into chaos as they awoke a few hours later. Cassandrea had hoped that three days meant three full days, but for some unknown reason, Torquil had decided to test her skills earlier. Or whatever the hell he was doing. For when they threw on some clothes and rushed to the city walls to see what was going on, there was a single ship sailing on the sea in front of the city.

The guards on the wall remembered Cassandrea and Kerr from the day before, so they let them pass, but they also warned them it was dangerous to linger, for the ship could decide to attack at any given point. But so far it was just... there.

Cassandrea leaned on the battlements and took a deep breath.

"What is he doing?" she asked Kerr.

"I wish I could tell you," the kelpie muttered quietly so that only she could hear. "Testing if we disabled the cannons?"

"He is going to ruin everything," Cassandrea breathed out. "What if they check? What if they load them and find out?"

"Maybe he doesn't trust us? Or maybe it is not his ship at all?"

"Oh, it is one of his ships, alright. It's Stormreaver," Cassandrea frowned, "a ship with a particularly sturdy hull. He uses her as his juggernaut."

"Then he is testing the waters," Kerr nodded.

"He is going to ruin it!" Cassandrea cried out in frustration.

"I doubt it." Kerr rested his hand on her shoulder and squeezed it gently. "Even if they find out, we were thorough. But he better move fast. And we, too. For when they *do* find out, and when the mayhem starts? The last place where we want to be is here."

"What about your contact? The woman from the sewers?"

"Hah," Kerr snorted and waved his hand. "She'll take care of herself."

Cassandrea looked at the male, but his expression revealed nothing. He seemed sure enough, so she just shrugged and let it go. But as she turned away from the battlements to look back at the city, her heart skipped a beat. On one of the towers, she saw the youngest soldier from yesterday. But he looked different. Very different. Gone was the cheery young man with a bashful smile. In his stead, there was a boy with fear gripping his very soul, an ill-fitting helmet tilted on his head, holding a spear and a shield that was a little too large for him.

"His place is not on the battlefield," Cassandrea whispered quietly and felt Kerr's hand squeezing her shoulder again.

"I'm sure he volunteered," the kelpie replied.

"That only makes it worse," Cassandrea hissed. She hadn't intended to be so blunt, but she knew deep down that the young man's grim expression, which he was defying his fear with, would haunt her for the rest of her days.

"Let us go then," she said, if only to get away and not see the young man die. "The tide's not optimal to leave the way we came from-"

Her words were cut off, as a shudder in the air currents made her yelp, and she embraced the kelpie faster than a wind and tackled him on the stone floor. A mere second later, the whole section of the wall blew up with a deafening crash, in the wake of a cannonball that had been hurtled from the lone ship. And with that sole declaration of war, all hell broke loose.

The impact sent plumes of dust and shattered stone flying everywhere, tearing flesh and splintering the wooden walkways. Another shudder, followed by another thunderous crack, and the impact of another cannonball bit out a piece of the wall, causing a part of the stone crenellations to buckle inwards. Screams filled the air. Voices. Cries of terror and barked orders to refocus and retaliate. The guards posted on the quaking wall staggered to keep their footing, shielding their faces, their heads, and their friends. The bell started ringing. But the ring was nothing like she had heard before. This was an urgent call to arms.

Cassandrea lifted her head to look at Kerr. "Torquil is going to level the city, Kerr! We have to get out of here. We have to jump."

"It's too high."

They both got back up and looked down over the battlements. It was too high, Cassandrea had to admit.

"I could carry you," she suggested hastily, "not your full weight, but if I fly, it would slow us down enough to-"

Another cannonball wheezed through the air, and this time the wind didn't warn her. It hit the wall to the far left of them and eliminated a small group of soldiers that was trying to get their cannon working. Cassandrea gritted her teeth. This was her fault. Their fault.

A loud roar suddenly echoed through the city, and a massive shadow passed overhead at a dazzling speed. Cassandrea looked up and forgot to breathe. It was a dragon. Not Terren, no, for this one was smaller and red and had a different bone structure. It was sturdier with strong legs like tree stumps, a sharp crest of lethal spikes wreathing its neck and a deadly, powerful thorned tail. Cassandrea had never seen this dragon before. She didn't know which side it was on. Was it Terren's whelp? No. This dragon didn't look young despite its size. With its strong bones and big wings, it was more like an adult drake.

The beast was flying high above the sea where the cannons couldn't reach it, and from the wall Cassandrea could see the ship's archers rushing to the deck to bring it down. The drake veered to the left and suddenly tucked its wings tight against its body, plummeting from the sky, its shining red scales making it look like the flaming tip of a spear. Just before the impact, it unfurled its wings with a deafening boom and extended its hind legs to tear off the mast of the ship. The groan and wail of Stormreaver's hull could be heard all the way to the city walls, accompanied by the desperate screams of marines as their mast shattered and fell, making the dreadnought heave and almost sink below the waves.

There was that unpleasant feeling again. Cassandrea realised that the drake had to be what she had sensed the day before flying high above the mist. And that realisation sent her heart shrivelling up. A cold fist of nausea gripped her guts, reminding her how little she still knew about the hand Terren was playing with. Furthermore, these dark thoughts prevented her from sensing a presence, that had seemingly materialised out of thin air next to Kerr. A hooded woman of a familiar stature, watching the sea and the drake battling over it. Her hands were closed into fists as if she were angry about something. The dragon? The battle? Death? Cassandrea looked at Kerr and opened her mouth to ask about his friend, but she never got the chance to do so. Another cannonball was coming at them, and the siren had just enough time to brace herself against the crenellations when the wall shook again, so violently it forced her on one knee. More desperate cries of the men and women trying to arm the cannons rang out, and there was warning being sent from one platform to another that the powder wouldn't light up.

"We have to go!" Cassandrea looked at Kerr.

The drake took off again, a glinting rain of arrows following in its wake. Some arrows stuck, some bounced, gliding off its scales like water from a swan's feathered back. But then, there was a triumphant wave of horns, announcing the arrival of the remaining seven dreadnoughts emerging from the morning mists. At the tip of their formation sailed the mighty Ebongale, her cream-coloured sails billowing in the first rays of sunshine the day had offered.

Whatever relief and joy Cassandrea had felt after hearing the sound of those horns, it vanished with the boom of the red dragon's wings, and she had only a second to marvel at the terrifying speed and grace the beast moved with before it spun slowly to a halt, then turned around and dove again. This time, it plummeted right into the ship, claws and fangs digging into the timber, hunching over the bow like a predator that caught its prey. The ship tilted heavily from the drake's weight and momentum, and the archers on the deck flew off the railing as the ship gulped water. There was a crackling boom on the horizon, and all seven of the arriving dreadnoughts, now finally in their position, fired their cannons in tandem.

"NOW!"

Cassandrea didn't think. She sprouted her wings, and before Kerr had any chance to protest, she had wrapped her arms around his chest and took off the wall. He was heavy. Too heavy. But she didn't need to fly, only to glide down to break their fall. And less than a second later, more cannonballs tore into the wall, shattering a large section and turning it into nothing but a pile of smoking rubble. The battlements exploded right above Cassandrea's head, sending stone, wood, and metal reinforcements flying in every direction. The siren willed the wind currents to propel their glide further away, but she wasn't fast enough. A sharp pang of pain shot through her leg, and she could feel it aching even through the fervour of battle.

Then there was a roar—a terrible, primal roar as one of the ships managed to hit the red drake with a cannonball. Cassandrea glanced in its way, and from what she could see, its hind leg was badly misshapen from the impact and bleeding all over the deck. The previous rain of arrows had left its wings pricked with small holes, and it was a small wonder that it was still moving. Still crushing the ship. Then, another cannonball ripped off the bow, forcing the drake to let go and leaving the Stormreaver to its own devices. To sink. With another thunderous beat of its wings, the red drake soared high into the sky and vanished in the clouds.

"Are we... targeting our own ships?" Kerr asked; his voice strained.

"She's gone anyway."

And so were they, Cassandrea thought. Her wings were screaming from the exertion while she was desperately trying to keep their descent steady, but the sharp stone shards and wood splinters had shredded her back and torn her right wing. She could feel throbbing pain in her left thigh and was more than certain that there was something sticking through it. She didn't want to look. Not yet. She was terrified to think of how badly Kerr had been injured, despite her best attempts to keep him shielded. Her arms aching and trembling, she held onto the kelpie all the way until his feet were an arm's length away from the water's surface. Only then she would let go of him.

"Swim," she breathed out before they both plummeted into the water and disappeared beneath the surface.

Cassandrea couldn't retract her wings. Not both of them. The right side wing had been badly injured, and there was a piece of wood or something else piercing the muscle. She couldn't reach it. Couldn't pull it out. So she sputtered and coughed and tried to swim, desperate to reach Torquil's ship. The tide was merciless. Once more it was coming in, strong and angry, and the water was dark red. She couldn't see anything. Couldn't see where was up and where was down. Her leg was refusing to work, and her back was aching so badly it made her cry in pain. A pointless thing to do, of course, and stupid, too, as her mouth and lungs instantly filled with salt water and blood. Not just her blood from the taste of it. She could tell.

"Kerr!"

Cassandrea reached out and tried to call his name, but there was only water. Blood. Water. A brief gulp of air. Then water again. A large wave rolled her body, ruffled her aching wings, and sent such terrible pain through her that she blacked out. For a second. Or two. Enough to make her lungs burn and her brain lose all sense of direction. Tears of pain and desperation sprung out of her eyes, instantly washed away by the sea. *Help me.* She thought. *Somebody, help me.* But she was alone. Alone and slowly sinking to the bottom of the sea. To the darkness and quiet awaiting her there. Eternal darkness. Was Kerr right that creatures like her had no soul? It would have been nice if he were wrong. It would have been nice if he were with her. If his hand grabbed hers and the currents answered his nature and helped them up. Up towards the rising sun, sending glittering beams through the rolling waves. Up towards the light and warmth. Towards life. Up towards...

The sea split above Cassandrea's head and spat her out. A gentle spring breeze greeted her with a warm caress, air filled her lungs, and she coughed and coughed and coughed, aided in it by a strong male arm squeezing her ribcage.

"It's alright," Kerr whispered into her ear. "I've got you."

It was the most beautiful thing she had ever heard. She could have kissed him for it if she wasn't still trying to cough out the entire sea and if her senses weren't darkened by the pain of her injuries. However, Kerr didn't care for what she did or said. He laid back into the waves and started pulling her broken body towards the closest ship, navigating through the currents with the ease of a creature in its natural habitat.

Cassandrea closed her eyes and let him do it. With a smile as she realised that she trusted him to do it.

Not that her current state would have allowed her anything else anyway.

And with another thunderous crackle of cannons, Renglow's wall crumbled behind them. And fell into the sea.

Chapter 9

Cassandrea woke up to dim lights and silence. Her body was still aching, but it was the pain of healing. Her muscles were sore and tingling with magic while her own powers were working on mending them. Her wings were out and bandaged, and so were her torso and leg. She was lying flat on her stomach on a bed, alone in a cabin, and from the gentle sway of the floor, she could tell the ship wasn't moving anywhere. It was anchored.

With a pained exhale, the siren tried to move the toes of her left foot and found it attainable. That was a good sign. Her leg was sore, but it worked. Then came the wings. Whoever had bandaged them had tucked them into neat bundles behind her back, and moving them was not possible. Not much, anyway.

With a withering wail, Cassandrea crawled to the edge of the bed and heaved herself up. She couldn't hear anything beyond the gentle rush of the waves and the soft groans of the ship. With some displeasure, she realised she had some new clothes on—a simple, pale linen tunic and matching trousers—a typical patient's garb. Judging by the cool breeze at her back, someone had cut a slit or two to fit the wings while dressing her up. Dressing her up! Like some limp doll. Cassandrea growled at the image, took a few staggering steps towards the door, and paused. She couldn't see Kerr anywhere, and suddenly there was a new kind of urgency filling her mind as she stumbled through the door into the corridor.

"Kerr?" she called out, continuing her hobble towards the door leading to the upper deck.

"Kerr?!" she shouted and threw the thick wooden door open.

Immediately, a smoke-filled gust of wind hit her like a punch to the gut and forced her to blink when her eyes started tearing up. The sun was shining bright, but it was hidden behind a thick veil of fumes rising from the burning city on the portside. Renglow...

"KERR?!" Cassandrea's voice had grown frantic now, and she turned on her heel and winced when the sudden motion strained the muscles on her side and sent a surge of pain through her body. But the kelpie was nowhere to be seen.

The ship had been docked at the port of Renglow and the harbour was crowded. Humble rowboats and fishermen's ships had been reeled off to make space for the remaining dreadnoughts. All seven except for Stormreaver had survived and were in the process of undergoing some minor repairs.

Cassandrea took in the gaping hole in the Renglow's seafront side where its wall had been entirely obliterated, leaving the city wide open to the sea, and a tight fist clenched her gut. Thick, dark smoke was rising in plumes from where the nice little houses had once been. From the market area, from... everywhere really. The city had been razed.

Feeling her heart suddenly pounding in her chest, Cassandrea let out a desperate, mournful cry.

"KE-"

"Missed me?" Kerr's voice chimed in from behind her, filled with that stupid, insufferable, self-absorbed... absolutely fantastic and incredible amusement that sent her heart aflight.

"Yes," Cassandrea sobbed and threw herself into his arms, uncaring whether anybody saw that or not. "Yes, you stupid swamp horse, I missed you!"

Kerr laughed and wrapped his arms around her body with care and carefulness that spoke volumes about how bad she must have looked. To her defence, Kerr didn't look much better. He had a bandage around his head and another one around his abdomen peeking from under his open shirt.

"You were the one who scared me, love," he whispered. "When I pulled you out of the sea, you nearly bled out on us. And then you were sleeping for days."

"Don't," Cassandrea squeezed the male in her arms, shedding a tear of relief. "I am sure you've found at least two girls to comfort you while I was unconscious."

"One." Kerr laughed and planted a small kiss on the top of her head. "But she wasn't much fun. She wouldn't get out of bed."

Cassandrea chuckled at his joke, and something warm found its way into her heart when she realised who he was talking about.

"Isn't that generally considered a good thing?" she teased.

"If only I were in that bed with her."

"Poor little kelpie. What torture it must have been."

Kerr laughed and canted his head, trying to get a glimpse of her smile.

"How are you, Cass?" he asked.

"I've been better," she answered honestly, "but we are both alive, aren't we? So that's a good thing. How long was I out?"

"Two days. We were starting to worry."

"My wings...?" Cassandrea asked with a sudden lump in her throat.

"They will be fine." Kerr raised his hand towards her cheek and caressed it in an effort to comfort her. "Give it a few days and you can fly again."

"And the city?"

"Ours," he confirmed what she already knew. "General Torquil will want to talk to you about the dragon. He was fairly unhappy that we hadn't warned him about it. But I told him there was no sign of it anywhere until Stormreaver decided to show up. It was unsanctioned, by the way. Captain Laster decided he wasn't going to wait for the right moment any longer.

He is dead now. Torquil fished him out of the sea just to impale him on his sword and throw him back an hour later."

Cassandrea nodded. She didn't know what else to say. She was glad Torquil was fine. Hoping Mairi was, too. But in her heart, she felt this indescribable ache that was gnawing it hollow. Her eyes moved back to the smouldering city. Kerr must have picked up on that ache, as she soon felt his thumb brushing over her cheek. Not wanting to show weakness or faintness of heart, she inhaled sharply and met the kelpie's gaze. And there was something in the male's red eyes that she couldn't quite place. She didn't dare to guess, but it was intense—so intense that Cassandrea almost broke down in tears. She thanked every star in the sky that he didn't speak. He just pulled her into another embrace and held her tight. Perhaps he did it for her so that she could quietly let out those tears into his shirt. Perhaps he didn't. But she was grateful for it either way.

"How touching," a cold voice, sharp as a dagger, lashed at the two.

Cassandrea took the last shuddering breath before she willed her face to neutrality and peeled herself off of Kerr's chest and looked at the male who had entered the top deck. It wasn't Torquil. Not that the general would be that much more of a welcomed sight; it was just that this one was far, far worse.

Ronan was a fae male Cassandrea wished she had never met. A half-breed changeling, but unlike most, he wasn't half human. No. There were wild stories about his origins, every one of them more gruesome and brutal than the previous, and the male had never seen it fit to correct any of them. He was lean and agile, a perfect balance of lethal precision, honed muscles and an absolutely remorseless, merciless heart. What he lacked in his appearance, he made up for with brutal efficiency. For he was not a pretty sight to look at, no. Ronan's face, due to his half-breed blood, was constantly shifting, ever-changing like the surface of a rippling pool. His hair colour was oscillating between dark muddy brown and bright amber. Just looking at him made people uneasy, and Cassandrea herself didn't particularly care to study the constantly changing features any longer than necessary. But that exact trait had made Ronan perfect for the king's purposes as his master spy and assassin, and Ronan had picked up that mantle proudly. It became very clear very fast to anyone working under him just how much the male enjoyed his work. Especially the more gruesome aspects of it.

"And here I thought you'd given up already."

Ronan's voice was dripping with venom.

"Sorry to disappoint you, Ronan, but I have work to do, places to be. Missions to complete. Kings to meet," Cassandrea winked at the male, trying to pretend she wasn't bothered by his presence.

Ronan frowned. He always hated how the siren came to be one of the king's most popular spies. He considered Cassandrea weak. Useless. A parlour trick at best, dead weight at worst.

"Due to your inability to relay accurate information, siren, we've lost a ship and four hundred and ninety-six good soldiers. On top of the sailors who operated Stormreaver," Ronan's voice was dangerously calm as the words cut through the air like lashes from a whip.

"There was no dragon in the city-" Cassandrea started her protest, but Ronan interrupted her.

"Torquil is waiting for you. And when he's done with you? You're coming with me."

Kerr slowly let go of Cassandrea to turn towards Ronan. He measured the male with a slow, unimpressed gaze.

"No wonder you are not the face of the operations," he evaluated calmly.

Ronan's attention snapped from the siren to the kelpie and the male let out a loud hiss that made Cassandrea unsure whether she should laugh or fear for Kerr's life.

"I've been working for the king for decades, horse. Show some respect." Ronan said with a poorly suppressed temper. "If you want to make it through your first year."

Kerr laughed, his beautiful red eyes sparking with amusement.

"One joke, and you are already resorting to pulling ranks? Very well, if that is the best you can offer... "

At that moment, Ronan looked like a cauldron full of boiling hot water, just ready to explode. Cassandrea didn't want to wait for whatever fell out of the man next. Be it some really nasty words or a dagger, she was sure she wouldn't like it. She quickly tugged at Kerr's arm and pulled him towards the general's cabin.

"General Torquil is waiting for us," she muttered urgently.

"Mhm," the kelpie nodded and allowed her to pull him away.

Yet he couldn't resist sending one last jab in Ronan's direction. "I talked to him earlier today, and he mentioned how impressed he was with our work on the gunpowder."

"Kerr, please," the siren whispered, trying to pull him away faster from the fuming changeling.

"Don't tell me that's your superior."

"In a way. Most of the time I work directly for the king. Most of the time," she pushed Kerr below deck and closed the door behind them. "That was foolish. Provoking him. He is dangerous."

The kelpie remained unimpressed.

"What happened to his face? He looks like something between a jellyfish and a chameleon."

"He is a changeling. Sort of. Half-breed. Pay attention, ok? He is dangerous." Cassandrea squeezed Kerr's arm a little too hard, frustrated by the male's daring ignorance.

"I recognise a piece of trash when I see one, Cass."

"Dangerous trash. Would it kill you not to provoke him?"

Kerr sighed.

"I will consider it. For you. Although I really don't understand why you are so scared of him. I thought you were devouring men for breakfast."

Now it was Cassandrea's turn to sigh.

"Not this one. If I could help it, I would rather exist on an entirely different continent than him," she grunted her response, still gripping Kerr's arm as she barged through the second door, towards the general's cabin.

Kerr didn't reply, but his eyes were now intently fixed on her face in a careful, studious gaze.

"What will he do to you when we're done with Torquil?"

Cassandrea didn't answer, not at first. Kerr halted in front of the general's door and turned to face her. And under the full weight of those inquisitive ruby eyes, the siren sighed.

"Honestly, I don't know. It could be anything," she started and splayed her hands wide, regretting the move immediately when pain shot through her brain—a punishment for such brash actions, "and I mean *anything*. He could take me to interrogate a prisoner; he could interrogate me instead. His mind is as fickle as his face. And I can tell you, *neither* of those options are pleasant."

Kerr narrowed his eyes at her. Or... no. Not at her.

"Is he going to hurt you?"

Cassandrea shrugged and stepped forward. She found it easier to push open the general's door and avoid any further questioning altogether. Although Kerr's questioning was likely the most pleasant one out of the three she was going to have to endure.

Torquil was poring over a heavy tome filled with dense handwritten text and some long list that Cassandrea assumed to be a tax ledger or something similarly interesting and helping the man with figuring out the possible income and current wealth of the now ruined city. He didn't stop his work but gave the two a long look from under his brows. The pale blue-grey eyes snapped to the bandaged wings, then slowly took in the rest of her. Cassandrea couldn't decipher what the expression on his face was, but whatever the general had seen in her, it was enough to make him push himself away from the table and straighten his back.

"You woke up," he said, by way of greeting her.

"Figured I'd napped enough," she grinned, but the usual edge of her voice was gone. Ruffled by Ronan. Still sore from the wounds. Tired.

"Glad to see you haven't lost your brazen spirit, siren." Torquil's last word was acid on his tongue, dripping with disdain.

"Glad to see you haven't lost your sense of humour, *general.*" Cassandrea smiled sweetly.

The general scoffed and crossed his arms over his chest. His eyes darted suspiciously between Cassandrea and Kerr, as if he expected some foul magic or spell to erupt at any second.

"Give me the full report of every encounter, every sighting, and every action you took. Furthermore, I want a damn good explanation for why there was a drake defending the city and we did not hear a thing about it."

Cassandrea commanded her voice to be calm and polite when she responded.

"I will write you a full report as soon as I can get my hands on a quill and paper, general, but-"

"Today, if you will," Torquil said firmly, "I am sending Mairi and that Valderan's badger dog Ronan back to Ithyren tomorrow. And I want them to have all the information we can gather to deliver to the king."

"I will write it today then," Cassandrea nodded, "but as for the drake, you know about it as much as we do, general. There was no drake in the city when we arrived. Nor anywhere near it. Nobody spoke of it, though nobody seemed surprised when it appeared. Is that weird?"

She had just realised that last bit of information, recalling that people did not scream when the drake flew over the city.

"It meant they knew it," Torquil gritted his teeth, "something for you to find out when you interrogate our prisoners. Also today."

Cassandrea sighed. This day was getting worse by the minute.

"I am sure that Ronan will be eager to-"

"Not him," Torquil didn't let her finish. "I want somebody who wants information, not his own pleasure. And that is not negotiable."

Cassandrea bit her lips. She knew it was pointless to argue, but the idea of interrogating the citizens of Renglow—those citizens of Renglow that they dined and laughed with—that idea was utterly abhorrent. She would do it, of course. She just wished she didn't have to. But she didn't say that. She could never say that.

"So, I want to know what that drake was. There haven't been any rumours about anything like that serving Terren. Is it his pet? Offspring? Soldier? Some experiment? Where did it go? Are there more? Can it do worse than roar and claw at things?"

Kerr twitched at that.

"Those claws have ripped apart your most durable ship,

general. I would say they are quite bad."

Torquil shot the kelpie a deathly stare.

"And I want to know," he continued as if Kerr hadn't spoken up at all, "where did General T'aar disappear off to and when."

Now it was Cassandrea's turn to twitch.

"You haven't caught him?"

"He wasn't in the city when we took it. If he was in there to begin with."

"He was," Kerr interjected.

"Rats abandoning the ship," Torquil said, disdain for the fomori general tangible in his voice. "When was the last time you saw him?"

"Last night around midnight," Cassandrea replied without thinking about it and then watched Torquil's eyebrows rise with surprise.

"She meant three days ago," Kerr corrected softly. "The night before the attack."

Cassandrea blushed and shot him a grateful look.

"Oh yes, that."

Torquil nodded.

"Well, what are you waiting for? You have work to do," he waved Cassandrea off and looked at Kerr. "You stay. I have a few more questions."

"As you wish, general." Kerr angled his head to look at Cassandrea. "I will meet you on the deck."

The siren gave him an encouraging smile and headed out.

She had indeed had a lot of work to do. Starting with...

bumping into Ronan, as the gods would have it. Or as Ronan would have it, for Cassandrea had no doubts he was waiting there for her.

She closed the door to the general's cabin and raised her chin to confront this particular bane.

"Spying on the general, Ronan?" she asked pointedly.

"Just waiting for you as promised."

"I would have found you."

"I am sure you would."

For a moment, they just stared at each other, and eventually it was Cassandrea who broke the silence.

"What do you want?"

"Where is that pretty kelpie of yours, Cassandrea? I wonder how much is left of him when Torquil will have had his fun."

Cassandrea bit her lips. She wouldn't let Ronan taunt her into anything silly, she promised herself. Not again.

"What. Do. You. Want?" she repeated very slowly.

"Or imagine how much fun *I* will have when I put his skills to use."

The siren chuckled. She had no idea what else she could do but throw her fear back at him with some gesture that he could take for insolence or a lack of interest.

"If you have nothing else, I will take my leave. *I* actually have real work to do." Cassandrea lifted her chin up as she tried to move past the changeling, but the male took a hold of her arm and spun her around.

"We're not done yet," he snarled, far too close to her face.

Her heart pounding in her throat, she narrowed her eyes.

"What do you want, Ronan?" Cassandrea asked for the last time, her tone clearly indicating she was tired of asking. And the male finally obliged her.

"I have use for your..." he paused, as if he were looking for the right word, "...abilities," he said finally, with such distaste for the word that Cassandrea thought he wanted to vomit it out.

"Oh?" Cassandrea mused as an unpleasant wave of cold washed over the back of her neck and poured right into her stomach.

"Oh indeed. You and I will visit the old seer that lives outside the city."

Cassandrea quirked a brow. "Why do you need *me?*" she asked.

"Because the seer is impaired. He cannot *feel* anything. Or see. So torturing the grandpa is not going to work," Ronan said, and Cassandrea saw he was disappointed, thoroughly so.

"What would you want from a blind seer?" she asked, and she regretted it instantly as Ronan shoved her against the wall, causing her to wince and gasp in agony as the pain shot through her torn wing.

"Do not question the king's command, witch. You will go with me, and you will make him talk. By *any* means necessary."

Cold shivers ran down her spine. She clenched her teeth but didn't protest. It was not so much a submission to Ronan as it was to her king. His orders, as long as she drew breath, she would never question.

"Meet me at sundown at the bridge just outside the city gates. Keep the kelpie out of it, or you'll regret it."

Cassandrea nodded.

Chapter 10

Renglow's keep had been turned into a prison. Each door locked and guarded, every window boarded up, and every side door barred. The mayor, Lord Beldran, was locked in his own council room like a bird in a gilded cage. All his serving noblemen were shoved into adjacent rooms, his vassals on the lower floor, and the further down the rooms went, the less important their prisoners were. The keep was completely full, yet not full enough. Somehow Cassandrea expected more prisoners to be there, more bodies in the streets to be buried. But maybe Torquil had already executed and buried them. That would explain it. After all, it had been three days.

The siren's face was a pale stone mask as she strode into the keep's dungeon. She figured they'd start with the people who had the least to offer when it came to title or status, but if Kerr was right, it was these people who had welcomed Terren's army with open arms and might hold the most interesting information.

Cassandrea's usually bright green eyes had dulled; there was no shine in them, no life. Kerr was unusually quiet, too. His bandages were gone, and there was a fresh, angry scar on his forehead. His eyes were still red, still bright, but the nonchalant, carefree smile was gone. And as their slow, assured footsteps echoed on the stone floor, Cassandrea spotted the townsmen and horribly mangled soldiers peering at her through the metal bars of their cells. Some recognised the pair, their mouths gaping at the wings. Cassandrea had kept them out but removed the bandages, even though her muscles were aching and throbbing with each move. However, she knew that the wings would incite fear, as much as her sharp canine teeth and the long, dark talons that she had slid out from her fingers—the razor-sharp weapons of a man-eating siren. She had buried her humanity deep within herself, hiding it from the world, in a desperate attempt to keep the sliver of goodness she still possessed alive.

Hushed voices and whispers of terror kept the pair company as they walked on, searching for the right target. And they found him. A stoic older man, someone the others would look up to. Someone they could rely on. With a wicked, brutal smile, Cassandrea ran one of her long, thin talons along the metal bars, causing them to clank coldly and slowly, like a funerary bell.

"Good evening," her voice was feral, and the way he looked at her while she tilted her head like a wild beast prowling for prey revealed the man's will, desperately trying to overcome his fear of the impending pain.

The man wasn't alone in his cell. There were four others with him: two men and two women chained up and tossed on the soggy straws, one woman so badly beaten and bruised Cassandrea could barely tell whether she was breathing or not. Two of the men were soldiers, injured. Dying. The last one, a young woman... No, just a girl. The man Cassandrea had chosen as her prey took a stance between the girl and her, as if to protect the child. Even with his chained hands. Even though he knew he couldn't do much. Cassandrea admired such defiance. The man gave her a firm stare, but soon his eyes shifted to Kerr. Holding his chained arms to the side as if to create a barrier between the kelpie and the girl, his chest heaving.

"Not her," his raspy voice croaked out.

"That depends entirely on you," Kerr replied with a shrug, "and your willingness to talk."

"I don't know anything, good lord."

Cassandrea chuckled and allowed her eyes to flash out with wildness she didn't really feel.

"Don't even try that," she hissed. "He is not good, and you are not just an innocent bystander. You all chose to fight for the usurper. Now you are paying for that lapse of judgement. All that is going to happen now? It's on you."

"Keep telling yourself that," the man said, his own eyes flashing with some unexpected bravery in the face of death.

Kerr sighed.

"What's your name, old man?"

"Rebidan. I am a seneschal in Lord Beldran's house."

"So you know everything about the mayor and his decisions," Cassandrea smiled. This was a lucky pick. The man was human, so an easy target. He was old. He had a girl, maybe his own daughter, to protect. Breaking him should be a piece of cake.

"I do not ask my lord for his reasons when he chooses to do something," Rebidan said slowly.

Cassandrea raised her eyebrow.

"When he chooses to support a traitor?"

"A liberator," one of the dying soldiers hawked.

"How sweet." Cassandrea stepped towards the bars and unlocked them. "I am afraid he is not here to liberate you right now."

Then she grabbed the soldier by the hair with one hand and cut his throat with the other's long talons.

Fear, Valderan had taught her, was the key to their souls. To anybody's soul. Besides, this soldier would have died anyway. It was mercy, or so she justified it to herself. With a heavy, unforgiving thud, the dead soldier collapsed on the straws.

Silence fell onto the small group, only interrupted by the young girl's uncontrollable sobbing. Cassandrea didn't say anything; she just stood up and moved towards the kid. The only thing she had to do for the old man to break.

"No!" he cried out and stepped into Cassandrea's way. "No! Please! Ask! Ask me! What do you want to know?"

The siren didn't dare to glance at Kerr. She didn't want to know what the male thought about her actions. She feared his thoughts. His judgement. But the kelpie spoke up on his own volition, and his voice was steady and undisturbed.

"Where is General T'aar?"

"I don't know," the old man spat out hastily. His eyes were wide and large as he shifted towards the girl, a living shield between her and the siren that had come to claim her.

Cassandrea tilted her head.

"How did he escape?" she asked, and as Rebidan opened his mouth, she turned towards the man, bringing one of those long talons under his chin, forcing him to look at her. "And before you say 'I don't know', remember that you are only one cut away from leaving that girl alone with me...," her eyes shifted to Kerr, "...and him."

The seneschal swallowed, and his eyes darted from Cassandrea to Kerr. He breathed out, then closed his eyes in a mournful, defeated manner.

"There is an old smuggler's tunnel that leads out of the city; it starts in the Rooster's Run inn."

Cassandrea let the vicious smile spread on her lips. The man snapped his gaze back to her.

"Please, not her-. Have mercy on her, she's just a child!"

"Oh," the siren purred and brought her hand to the man's cheek. Running the back of her fingers across his cheekbone, she chuckled.

"Are you going to beg?"

"No," the man shook his head ever-so-slightly. But something in Cassandrea's eyes made him quickly change that opinion. "Yes!"

The siren smirked.

"Bargain then."

Kerr's eyes shifted to Cassandrea but she didn't want to show him what her eyes held, so she kept her gaze firmly on the human. The old man breathed out hastily.

"I will trade anything I have for her safety. For her life. Unharmed."

"Anything?" Cassandrea asked.

"Anything I can give you, I will."

"And if we don't want anything from you?" Kerr's voice was silken as he, too, stepped closer.

"You want the girl to live. We want information that will be useful against Terren. Either from you or the others. I see a mutual, beneficial agreement here," Cassandrea's words came out as cold as ice.

"Don't-"

The protest from the second soldier, who was knocking on death's door, was cut when Kerr crouched near him, took a hold of his neck and brought a dagger to the man's throat.

"Did you know that a siren's song can imprison you into slumber for eternity?" he asked quietly from the soldier. The injured man shook his head.

"Imagine what it would be like to be stuck there forever, with all the pain and agony bestowed upon you? Forever..."

The old man and the soldier both looked at Cassandrea, who didn't flinch.

"The information," she growled.

"You're monsters," the soldier barked.

His words were still echoing through the dungeons when Kerr slashed his throat from ear to ear with a fluent and deathly beautiful move.

"I know," the kelpie male whispered, wiping his bloodied hands on the dead man's tunic. Then he turned towards Rebidan. "The girl will be next if you don't cooperate."

The old man gasped for air and shook his head violently. Then he began speaking at an extremely rapid pace.

"You will not harm her; you won't hurt her, imprison her, or inflict any terrible fate of a slave or a courtesan on her," the old man said firmly, "and in return, I will tell you everything I know. And in addition, I will tell you where you can find any information I was not privy to."

"Where?" Kerr asked.

"In the mayor's office. In a secret drawer of his desk. All the letters are there. Just below-"

"Unfortunately for you, the mayor's office was burnt down during the siege and there wasn't much paperwork left for us to work with. You will have to try harder."

The seneschal looked at Kerr and hesitated.

"But... You..."

It sounded like a protest, but Cassandrea wasn't able to tell what against. Or why.

"I may agree to your conditions," Kerr shrugged, "but only if the information is worth my time. Your daughter is very pretty."

The anger in Rebidan's gaze was strong enough to burn the kelpie alive.

"She is my niece. And she is just a child."

"Alright," Kerr tilted his head with a charming smile that didn't reach his eyes, "then persuade me. What do you know about the drake?"

Rebidan hesitated. His eyes found Kerr's and his expression grew even more desperate.

"Lord," he pleaded.

"It's alright," the male hushed him and stood up, resting his hand on the old man's shoulder. As if they were friends. "You can tell me."

Rebidan twitched, repulsed by the touch and the words. Repulsed by the kelpie's very presence.

"He was sent here by king Terren. To aid us," the old man dropped his gaze to the floor, unable to look at Kerr as if the male was the very embodiment of his shame. "His name is Elajas. Lord Elajas of the Ashfen Vale."

"King Terren..." Cassandrea almost spat those words out. She still hadn't let go of the man's chin and now the long claw dug into the soft flesh.

"Tell me, Rebidan, seneschal of Lord Beldran's house, where does that tunnel lead?"

The man swallowed. "To the eastern flatlands, just past the Ornis river."

"Hm. And when did the drake arrive and how come it wasn't here three days ago?" there was a tint of hurt pride in her voice. How could she have missed it?

"Lord Elajas was concealed as per the general's orders; he was hiding outside the city."

"Are there more drakes around?" she pressed the man.

"Not to our knowledge. We've only received word of one."

"From whom?"

The man's gaze began to wander once more. Between Cassandrea and Kerr. The girl. Cassandrea. Kerr. He hesitated. But Cassandrea took one look at his niece and Rebidan resumed immediately.

"General T'aar. He arrived two weeks ago and started making preparations for a siege. King Terren's forces were supposed to protect us from sea, sky, and land," the man said, and Cassandrea relished the sound of betrayal in his voice. However, there was that word again. King. King Terren. She hated that.

"And how did that pan out for you?" she mocked the man with a cruel grin. Then she glanced at Kerr, "Anything else?"

"No," the kelpie shook his head and his gaze briefly touched the young girl. "I doubt he knows anything else. I am surprised he even knew about the secret tunnel."

The old man looked away from him and Cassandrea could swear there was embarrassment in his expression.

"Nevertheless," Kerr continued, "it seems General T'aar indeed ran when we attacked. How pathetic for such a big male. Shall we?"

He beckoned towards the door, but Rebidan darted and grabbed his arm.

"And my girl?!" he demanded.

Kerr looked down at the old man and said surprisingly softly, "She will be released. You won't. But she will. After all, we shouldn't punish children for the sins of their fathers or uncles, isn't that correct?"

And he looked straight at Cassandrea, challenging her to dispute that. But she wouldn't. She was relieved that the girl was to emerge unscathed. Especially when Ronan was lurking nearby.

"It is correct," she confirmed. She felt tired. So tired. Her wing hurt. Her leg hurt. Her back hurt. Everything hurt. And she still had at least five more prisoners to interrogate to cross-check the information, write a report for the king and then meet Ronan and pretend she was all fresh and ready to talk to some blind seer. While all she wanted was to find a bottle of some good wine, drink it whole, and then fall onto the bed next to Kerr, snuggle up to him, and sleep and sleep and sleep.

*

The interrogations took longer than Cassandrea had anticipated. And it led to her being late with her report. Which led to her having almost no time to prepare for the rendezvous with Ronan. She had half an hour to gulp down a meal while still reviewing the report she had written down. She was sitting in the lounge of a building that had been vacated during the attack and later confiscated by one very hungry siren. By the looks of it, the previous owners must have been well off. Everything was tastefully decorated and well maintained. Thick rugs, expensive chandeliers, and even a whole collection of family portraits.

Over a thick, dark oaken table, Kerr was proofreading each page the siren had written, and Cassandrea couldn't have been more grateful for it. He added several footnotes and corrections, which she found extremely useful.

"Soon you're done, love, and we can go and get an ale or two at the Rooster's Run. Might as well go and check the tunnel," Kerr said as he put down the last paper she had offered him.

"I'm afraid I'm reserved for tonight," she replied, and once she saw the slight furrow in Kerr's brows, she canted her head and offered the kelpie a small, mischievous smile.

"For whom?" he asked.

"Are you jealous?" she shot back, the smirk of mischief spreading further.

Kerr rested both his palms against the table and leaned closer to her face, so close she could feel his breath hitting her lips. He stared at her, challenging her with every breath he drew.

"Maybe," he said softly. Way too softly. Something about the tone sent soft chills down her spine. "You want me to be," he added in that despicably desirable tone.

"Maybe," she responded, taking his bait and running with it. With a sly grin, she slowly began to rise, leaning in so close that their noses touched. Once.

"But Ronan needs me tonight."

"Would you choose him over me?"

Those sparking red eyes flared up and Kerr closed the final gap between their lips and brushed his mouth against hers. Cassandrea sighed, a wave of warmth pouring through her body.

"I am hurt," Kerr muttered into her lips, each word a reason for his hot skin to brush against hers.

"You don't sound hurt," Cassandrea whispered back, not pulling away from him. Not sure she could. Or wanted to.

"What do you know? My heart is bleeding."

Kerr's eyes flashed with mischief, and his lips left her mouth only to worship her jaw.

"You don't have one," Cassandrea mused, her eyelids fluttering.

Kerr's warm laughter rang through the room.

"That was a soul, love. I most certainly do have a heart."

He stole a small kiss from the corner of her lips, then drew back to look into her eyes and continued seriously, "You'll find out if Ronan dares to hurt you."

Cassandrea watched him retract and lean back, and only then, slowly, she stood up and crossed her arms over her chest.

"I'm a big girl," she said. "I can take care of myself."

"No doubt," his eyes sparked, "but you're afraid of him."

Kerr's eyes had something in them, something new as he studied Cassandrea's face. Then they suddenly stopped at the scar that ran down from the side of her mouth, all the way across her cheek and down to her neck, and narrowed as they followed the twisted and burnt pale patch that led to a gnarly scar that wreathed around her neck.

"Did he do that to you?" he asked.

Cassandrea had seen that question coming from a mile away, but nothing could have prepared her for that gnawing void it opened inside her chest.

"No," she said, "he didn't."

Kerr didn't take that for a satisfying answer, and his eyebrow rose while he was waiting for a better one.

"Though I'm sure he wished he did," Cassandrea added with a calculated, calm smile.

Deciding this was *not* the time to give him the full story, she offered Kerr another smile, warmer now, and buried the memories deep within her heart.

"But you should have seen the other guy," she offered, with a cocky wink and a light laugh.

Whether Kerr bought her evasion or not, he didn't show it. He chuckled in response, but his eyes were still busy studying her. Still pondering. He was about to say something when Cassandrea walked around the table, picking up the swords she had to abandon two days ago and found earlier that morning among the other spoils of war. Her twinblades, a masterfully crafted pair, were so sharp she swore they could cut air. She strapped the sheaths to her sides and turned to look at Kerr. He didn't move or say anything while she was arming herself. In fact, he looked a little too serious for his own good.

"Raincheck on that wine. I'm sure you can make yourself busy in the meantime, hm?"

The beautiful lips slowly spread into a grin that didn't reach his eyes.

"I will find some before you are back."

"Make it worthy of me."

"Always."

Cassandrea smiled.

"Cass? Be careful, alright?"

"Always."

There was something in those red eyes. Something that made her hesitate. Unsure whether she should leave after all. But Kerr didn't ask her to stay and there was a task from the king waiting for her. An important task. The kelpie could wait. So Cassandrea dipped her head and bid him a goodbye.

Chapter 11

Ronan was waiting on the bridge, visibly bored and impatient. Behind him, on the plains, Cassandrea could see Torquil's soldiers and three fae-seekers searching for the scent of general T'aar and the other cowards who ran away with him. The fae-seekers had always made her cringe. They were giant beasts; even when hunched, so thin, she wondered how they didn't break just by moving around. Their long tails were slashing behind their scrawny bodies, and their tongues were hanging towards the ground while they were using them to scent the escaped fae warriors. They had two long legs ended in hooves and two four-fingered hands with nails that reminded her of her own talons. There were few hairs on their bodies, mostly along their spines, and their tiny eyes, long maws full of sharp teeth and two horn-like ears were effectively making them creatures of nightmares. They prowled with uncanny grace, silent as the night, the long claws of their forelimbs dragging against the dirt. They may not have been the strongest beasts around, but the legends said that once they caught their prey's scent, they wouldn't stop until they tasted their blood.

"Impressive sweethearts, aren't they?" Ronan grinned.

"Oh, they are. So much, in fact, that I'd love to test their skills on a bigger challenge. Like something only half-fae, for example," Cassandrea offered him a sweet smile.

"You are in a good mood," Ronan canted his head with a wicked smirk. "Have you fucked the kelpie already? He seems to be rubbing off on you a little. I can almost smell him. Oh wait, no, I *can* smell him on you."

"Oh piss off, Ronan," Cassandrea swatted off the male that had brought his ever-shifting face closer to her. The genuine disgust in his eyes was burning with such acid she could almost taste it when he actually sniffed the air around her.

"Don't you have better things to do than shove your malformed weathervane of a nose into matters it doesn't belong in?"

Ronan's eyes narrowed, and the male let out a deep, low growl. A warning.

"Be careful, witch, for I don't think the king would care if I carved a few new scars on you."

Now it was her turn to narrow her eyes at him.

"But you would care if I tore your guts out and made you eat them."

She had no idea where she had garnered this kind of bravery to stand up to him. Ronan was the king's master spy, but he was also a ruthless butcher who enjoyed his work. She knew he wasn't just throwing his words around. Ronan bristled, moving towards her.

"Well, let's see about that, then-"

They were both interrupted by a long, bone-chilling howl that cut through the air and made them look towards the plains. Something that painted a grin on their faces despite the situation. A fiend had found a scent. And regardless of his earlier threats, Ronan turned and started walking.

Neither of them spoke. They crossed the bridge and headed east, across the flat, snow-covered plains. It was a long enough trek to make Cassandrea ponder why they hadn't taken horses to make it quicker. The sun was setting fast, and the temperature was plummeting. But they didn't stop, and they didn't talk. They walked until the sun was gone and replaced by the pallid moon that painted the scenery with silvery, cold light. Finally, they reached the edge of a dark, dense thicket. There was no road or animal trail to indicate an often travelled path, but Ronan seemed to know where he was heading. So Cassandrea followed. Her eyes keenly scanned the woods and she suddenly became very aware that the forest they entered was enchanted. She could taste magic in the air and see it sparkling in the small specks of light that were sifted through the leaves. She could smell it. And it was such a pleasant, wonderful smell. Full, rounded scent of spring flowers, sweet nectar fruits, and lilypads. Before she noticed, a smile had spread on her lips. A smile that fell off immediately when Ronan stopped and drew his blade. She moved her hands to the hilts of her own twin blades but couldn't hear or see a thing. Ronan's predatory eyes flashed in the darkening woods, and he dropped into a low prowl. His fingers drew a thin layer of dirt and moss from the ground and he sniffed it. Cassandrea knew, then, that it wasn't his brutality alone she should fear but how much he resembled the fae-seeker fiends.

"That way," his voice was so quiet she barely heard it.

With a silent nod, she let him lead her, and together they threaded through the thick, ancient trees that stood in silent vigil. Soon she noticed a faint smell of smoke and incense and a blink of a warm, dancing light between the trees.

They stopped at the edge of a clearing, from which they could see dilapidated ruins of some ancient temple with its pillars broken and fallen, stone and debris scattered around it. Everything was overgrown, decorated with ivy and vines and it seemed abandoned. However, on the last remaining intact surface stood a grand bronze brazier, in which a warm fire danced and licked the lip of a broken stone roof. In front of it sat a hunched figure in simple white robes, his head down, seemingly asleep.

"Find out what he knows," Ronan said as he stopped and shoved Cassandrea forward into the clearing.

"Know about what?" she snapped.

"What do you think? How to win the war, stupid."

Cassandrea growled. She had no idea why Ronan hadn't handled this himself. Was it dangerous? Would the seer demand a sacrifice? Had Ronan already tried to persuade the male and failed? With Ronan, anything was possible, so she had to stay careful.

"Hello," she started politely and waited for the seer to wake up and acknowledge her. Or just the first. The first would have been nice. But the seer hadn't moved an inch.

"Hello?" she tried again, a little louder.

The flames in the brazier stirred and shined a little brighter, but the man still showed no signs of being alive.

"Mister?" Cassandrea took a step forward, ready to shake the man's shoulder if necessary.

The first two steps went well. However, at the third one, something shifted in the air. The siren could sense it before it came, but she still had no means of stopping it. It was a blast of pure white energy, so fast and so mighty, it had thrown her on the ground and instantly the whole world disappeared.

Only to appear anew. Different. She was still there. Still on the same spot. But everything else had stopped moving. Ronan. The grass. The leaves. The wind. Only the brazier kept burning bright and the seer finally raised his head. His blind, milky eyes turned in her direction and the man spoke up with a melodic, thoughtful voice.

"You are here," the man stated, each word dragging like hot

wax, "yet you do not want to be."

Cassandrrea stood up and dusted her trousers, but she wasn't sure what to say. Or think. Ronan still hadn't moved, turned into a statue at the edge of the clearing, his mouth slightly ajar. For a moment she wondered what would happen if she sent a sword through his heart. Luckily for Ronan, the seer spoke up before she got a chance to do so.

"The answer you seek is not the one you want," he said.

Great, cryptic, Cassandrea thought. How the hell was she supposed to get any clear answer from this man? But if it was what Valderan wanted, she would find a way.

"I wish to know how to end the war," she said, "and how to defeat Terren."

"Is that so?" for whatever reason, the man suddenly sounded amused. "Then touch the fire, brightwing."

That sounded bad. And like the last thing she should do. Yet she stepped forth and reached towards the brazier. At the last moment, she hesitated and halted her hand.

"What will I see?" she asked.

"That's not up to me. Or you," the old man shrugged. "Nothing if you don't try."

Cassandrea snarled at him. She couldn't afford to see nothing. She had to see something. The answer. How to end the war. How to defeat Terren. She took a deep breath and touched the fire.

The next moment the world tilted forward, and she was plunging through splashes of colour, sounds, and smells shooting past her, as if she were travelling through pages of a book with blinding speed. Flashes after flashes, she tried to piece together what she saw, making sense of it all.

Overall, she didn't see much, for there were mists covering the landscape around her, but she could taste salt, ash, and blood burning in her mouth. The air was damp and strong; raging winds kept swirling around her. They weren't the usual friendly winds she could lean on and rest against. No, these were furious and whipping her sharply like the edge of a honed blade. Yet she felt warmth. Somebody was there with her. Standing tall and proud. A man. With black hair. Her king. She was sure of it. Her rock. Her saviour. Her ruler. When she looked at him, she felt her heart expanding in awe, in admiration. Yet something else blinked through the mists. Fire. A line of it. No. Not a line. It was a sword. A flaming sword. And a man holding it. A tall silhouette of a man. She couldn't see his face, but she saw an object in his other hand. A crown. The crown of Entirie. She could tell. She had seen it many times in the throne room. The man raised the flaming sword and one word filled the air, whispered by a cracked, rough voice. "Garoth." And in a blinding flash of white light, Cassandrea was ripped out of the vision and thrown back into reality. Back into the grass and forest. Back to the night and cold and Ronan's annoying voice demanding an answer.

"Well, are you going to do anything, or just sit there on your ass?"

Cassandrea heaved, still trying to get back to her senses and her thoughts. Her head was spinning. Foggy. She shuddered and braced her palms against the grass.

"Why don't you go and ask for it yourself?" she bit back as she lifted her hand to her temple to rub it, but immediately she pulled them away again as she felt something cold and wet touching her skin.

Her fingers had some soot on them. Slowly, curiously, she rubbed her fingers together, spreading the glittering dust, and then she looked towards the brazier. Nothing had changed. Then she realised it—she hadn't moved more than a few feet. She hadn't spoken to the old man. She was still at the edge of the clearing, where she landed after she took the third step.

"I don't need to explain myself to you, witch," Ronan hissed, and Cassandrea could swear she heard a tinge of shame behind Ronan's annoyed voice.

"Well, if you want to have answers, you better go get them, Ronan," she hissed right back at him.

Ronan's eyes flashed dangerously, and he took a step closer. He lunged for her. And stopped. Like he had hit some invisible wall. Cassandrea's breath caught as she watched Ronan's face twist in pain. She stood up slowly. Her heart was racing as she watched the man struggle against the invisible barrier separating them. Struggle to enter the place filled with magic...

"You're a nullsprite," she breathed out.

"Shut your foul mouth," Ronan barked.

It sufficed as confirmation.

A nullsprite. An unfortunate creature cursed by the gods. There was no legend explaining how the nullsprites came to be or why, but the children born as nulls were hated by magic. Repulsed by it.

Cassandrea blinked. *That* was why his face never settled. His own body was battling the magic in his fae blood. Or the magic in his body was battling him.

"Don't look at me like that, witch," Ronan snarled, but he backed off. The expression on Cassandrea's face must have triggered him. Even if she didn't want to, she pitied him. Felt bad for him. And he hated seeing that.

Cassandrea pushed herself up and looked around. The whole forest was likely enchanted. And the temple must have been carrying some ancient wards for keeping out uninvited visitors. Wards that let her in. But wouldn't let in a nullsprite. That's why he needed her.

"Shut your mouth and get to work or I will skin you alive," Ronan growled. His voice was dangerous now, and Cassandrea knew he meant it.

"I've already done your work," she shrugged, but stayed on the safe side of the wards. "I've been granted a vision of how to win this war. And I will tell the king all about it. Myself."

Ronan's face paled.

"You're making that up," he accused her.

"You know I am not," Cassandrea forced herself to look straight into those shifting eyes and hold his gaze. "I've seen what can win us this war, Ronan."

"And you would be so selfish to keep it for yourself? What if you die?"

"Well," Cassandrea gave him a sweet smile, "you'll just have to keep me alive, won't you?"

"Until we make it back to the king," he specified.

"Until then," she laughed at how angry he looked, saying it. "Can you do that?"

"Bitch."

Ronan was fuming, but Cassandrea knew she had the upper hand. He couldn't possibly do anything to her. Not then. Not while she was holding vital information for the king. A null like him wouldn't dare piss off a dragon. Ronan's eyes were shooting lightning when he spoke.

"Do not ever mention this to *anyone*, or I'll swear-"

"I take that as a yes. Now come on. We are going back. I have a dinner I am looking forward to."

Chapter 12

But the dinner had to wait.

A commotion, torches, soldiers, and fae-seekers, welcomed Ronan and Cassandrea outside of Renglow's city walls, and there was a scent of blood in the air. A thick one. Luckily, Cassandrea spotted her favourite kelpie in the crowd, so she left Ronan behind and headed toward Kerr. The male waved at her with a tired smile.

"What happened?" she asked.

"A murder," he answered quietly, reaching for her to pull her closer as he spoke in a low voice. "A messenger was killed. And not one heading out. This one was heading in. To Torquil. We don't know from where. There were no documents found on the body. But Torquil said he knew him and that he was definitely a runner."

Cassandrea instinctively shifted closer to the male.

"How?" she breathed.

"Stabbed. It was clean, so he probably didn't fight back. Much."

"Who found him?"

"I did," Kerr sighed. "I was outside; I wanted to make sure the fae-seekers wouldn't run into trouble with the kappas as their handlers informed us that the trace is leading into the swamps. And when I was coming back, I found him lying here, almost cold already."

Cassandrea let out a frustrated sigh.

"This day just... keeps getting better," she murmured, then took a look around.

"Did the runner have anything on him?"

Kerr shook his head.

"No messages, no tokens, nothing."

Cassandrea grunted a nod.

"Damn it," she breathed out, "damn it, damn it! Those sons of pigmen!"

Folding her arms crossed, she gritted her teeth and looked up at Kerr. The Kelpie looked distraught. The same way she felt. Desperation closed a cold grip around her heart and tried to squeeze the air out of her lungs. She gasped for air and only Kerr's hand on her shoulder shook her out of it. The red eyes looked tired, but he still tried to smile. She planted her own hand on top of his and squeezed it.

"What's that?" he asked as his eyes spotted the dark, soot-stained fingertips.

"Oh, that's... a long story."

She smiled, looking around. "For a different audience."

Kerr took the hint. He slipped the hand around her waist and nodded towards the gates.

"Please tell me you have wine," Cassandrea pleaded.

Kerr's lips curled upward. Such a coy smile, he had.

"Who do you take me for, love?" his voice finally eased into the well-known playful tone. "Of course I have wine. I had robbed a certain Lord's cellar before anybody else managed to find a key."

Kerr winked and canted his head toward Cassandrea's.

"I even have some food. Real food, I mean. Fresh fish, fruit, cheese, frogs from the swamps-"

Cassandrea gagged and Kerr chuckled.

"Just joking, love. But we do have cheese, fish, and fruit. I've found plenty in the mayor's stash. And some pretty clothes for you. Warm and classy. Even a nightgown I would love to see you in."

"Why are you so generous to me?" Cassandrea squinted at him, but there was no hiding the smile that lit up her eyes at the mention of fruits and cheese. And no denying that she appreciated the gesture. And the clothes.

"What's the catch?"

"Wow," Kerr chuckled and squeezed her waist, "now I need a

reason to be nice to you? I literally stole all that. We won a major battle, Cass. I want to celebrate it with you."

She smiled.

"Torquil is furious, isn't he? About the runner?"

"Yes, though he is hardly someone I want to talk about right now."

"Did you give him the report?"

"Right after you left," Kerr nudged her side with the fist of his other hand. "Seriously, do you ever let go? We've handed him the entire city; he can do his job for a while. You're injured; you need to heal, and you need to relax. And if you still require a reason for me to be nice... How about you saving my life?"

Cassandrea gave him a surprised look from under her brows, but seeing his smile, she closed her eyes and shrugged.

"You looked pretty banged up this morning," she stated. She didn't want to confirm it, but... she did save his life. And she was happy she had done so. When she opened her eyes, they were softer than before.

"Alright," she said, and the kelpie answered her with a gentle caress of her side.

While they were making their way back to the townhouse they had confiscated earlier, Kerr didn't ask further about her trip with Ronan, and she didn't ask about his trek either. Not until they stepped inside the house, and she dusted the rest of the forest's mud and foliage off her clothes.

"So... the hounds are heading south? Through the marsh?"

Kerr nodded. "Seems like General T'aar took a sharp turn

after exiting the tunnel and led his people there."

"Why?" Cassandrea asked as she peeled off her boots and unstrapped the sheathed blades. "Why south? Their forces are marching from the north."

Kerr looked at her and squinted. He thought about it. "It's possible they didn't make it past the marshes. The kappa didn't seem too keen on visitors." He took off his jacket and threw it over an arm of a couch, revealing the shirt underneath that he, of course, had left partly open.

Cassandrea frowned. "Maybe. But unlikely. Some of them had to make it through, or deep enough at least. The fiends wouldn't have sniffed their trail there otherwise."

"True enough," Kerr admitted. He gestured at the table that had a wide, shallow bowl on it filled with fruits and berries, with large chunks of beautifully aged cheeses teetering over them.

"How about you don't think about General T'aar, or the stinky marshes, or the kappas, or death, or gloom, or work for a few hours," Kerr said casually as he strode towards the table and opened one of the undoubtedly exquisite, and judging by the looks of the dust on the bottle, very old wine. "... and I'll promise to make it worth your while."

He poured the rich, dark red liquid into two glasses.

Cassandrea sighed. She was not sure if she could drop everything as easily as he did.

"Please?" Kerr added, offering one of the glasses to her.

"You *are* trying to distract me, Kerr," she said dryly as she looked at the glass, then took it and sat down by the table.

"I'm trying to distract you from *yourself*," Kerr countered. "The work we do is hard. You're going to burn out if you don't allow any fun into your life. So, let go. For one night? Just be here. With me."

And, his eyes still locked with hers, he dropped on his knees in front of her and rested his elbow on her leg. He was holding his glass in that hand, so the cup suddenly ended in between her knees. Still holding her gaze, the male took a slow sip, savouring the taste of the wine. His red eyes sparked with that beautiful mischief of his while he was waiting for her reaction.

So Cassandrea pretended she hadn't seen any of that. She glanced at her own wine, swirled it, then smelled it. She took her time doing so. It *was* exquisite. Her mouth already watering, she closed her eyes and enjoyed the scent for a long while, letting him wait. When she opened them again, she reached out and brushed a lock of Kerr's hair from the new scar on his forehead.

"You're so sure I will like it," she teased.

A bright, warm smile spread across his lips.

"Why wouldn't I be?"

"I am not your usual target," she said and raised her chin, "and you're not the first handsome male I've had on his knees."

Kerr laughed, and it was light and cheerful. She loved that laugh.

"That scar makes you look all roughed up and tough," she said softly, a playful tone filling her voice.

Kerr laughed again, and it made her smile brighten up.

"Oh yeah?" he asked.

"Oh yeah," Cassandrea confirmed, her eyes studying that scar. "You look like a mean hunter now," she purred.

"I do enjoy the hunt," he replied, flashing his teeth at her, "so by all means, keep making it harder."

Cassandrea grinned and was about to do just that, but the male rose to his feet and offered her his hand.

"Come."

Cassandrea hesitated.

"Where to?"

Kerr winked at her.

"Not the bedroom. Don't worry."

"No?" she asked, trying not to sound too disappointed. But truth be told, she was a little unsure where this was leading. Was he giving up the game already? And would that be a good or a bad thing?

But Kerr pulled her up and led her towards the cellar, never letting go of her hand. She followed, still holding onto her wine and growing slightly worried. However, the kelpie seemed to know what he was doing, and despite her brain protesting against every step, her heart was at peace. She wasn't afraid of Kerr.

The male opened the cellar door and stepped aside to let her pass. She did. And what she saw... This wasn't a cellar at all. It was a treasury.

Illuminated by a faint light of two torches, the small cellar was hiding riches she had never dreamt about before. Gold coins, necklaces, marble statues, paintings carefully wrapped in fine cloth, and yards and yards of silk and velvet wrapped in thick bolts.

Cassandrea opened her mouth.

"What is this?" she asked in a thin, quivering voice.

"Spoils of war," Kerr stepped behind her and rested his chin on her shoulder, his breath tickling her ear. "Everything you want. You could get out. Stop serving Valderan. Do whatever you like."

"Why... Why should I want that?"

There was a long pause as the male hesitated at her reply. He took a long, deep breath, and for some reason it sounded a bit disappointed. Or sad... Yet when he spoke up, he had his voice under control.

"What *would* you want?" he asked.

Cassandrea didn't answer. Not at first. Not because she didn't want to, but because she wasn't sure if she knew how to answer that. There were a lot of things she wanted in her life, but none of them tasted as sweet on her lips as seeing her king smile at her.

"I only want to do right by my king," she replied and spoke the truth. Yet before those words had even fully come out of her mouth, something dark and painful simmered in her heart. Like the last wink of a dying star. She didn't dare to study that pain. Didn't dare to name it. Not now. So she wore the smile she had learnt to wear and angled her face towards Kerr's. The kelpie's expression was unreadable. To his credit, he hadn't flinched at her words. Perhaps, he had expected that. But his eyes were studying her even more intensively now.

"But I won't lie," she started again, her voice gaining that silken softness once more, "playing a little with the spoils of war sounds like a world of fun."

She turned her head further, enough to have her nose nudge his cheek. "In the right company."

Cassandrea grabbed Kerr's hand and guided him closer to the shelves. She took a hold of a bolt of the lightest, finest silk, so soft and airy that touching it was like touching water itself. How it had been weaved, she couldn't fathom, for the fabric took a different colour when the light touched it, turning the deep wine red into a bronzed green hue. She breathed out in delight, forgetting all the pain she had felt before. Forgetting the work and her missions. Forgetting the world. She put down her wine and let out a happy little giggle. Not ever had she laid her hands on anything this luxurious. A single dress made of such material would have cost a small fortune, and one bolt could make for at least five such dresses. Cassandrea grinned and pulled out a yard of the silk, just to splay it out and watch it dance in the air.

"Have you ever seen anything this beautiful?" she asked and lifted the fabric and let it slowly float down. It was captivating. Like a waterfall made out of red and green light.

Cassandrea looked up to Kerr, beaming him a smile she had not shown in three years. A smile of genuine happiness.

"Why don't you try it on?" he suggested, drew a knife, and stepped towards the bolt. "Hold it tight."

She laughed, and nodded, and watched him work. He was

skilled with the blade. Extremely so. The knife was rapidly moving and flashing in his fingers, reflecting the torches' fire, and soon he was holding three long strips of silk in his hand. He offered them to Cassandrea with a confident smirk.

"For you, love."

"Let me guess, you want me to put it on right here?" she asked, snatching the fabric and pulling it closer to her body. It was soft. So soft.

A devilish smirk was Kerr's reply. "That was the hope."

"It's cold in here," she complained.

"Gods, I should have seen that one coming!" the male laughed loudly and grabbed the rest of the bolt together with a necklace with green emeralds.

"What's that for?" Cassandrea asked curiously.

Kerr raised his brow.

"You want to sleep in ordinary sheets when we have yards of silk? Come on."

"And the necklace?"

His devilish smirk grew wider.

"That's for when the silk is off."

*

Kerr had draped the silk over their linen sheets, and he was now sitting on the top of it, leaning against a pile of pillows with a lazy smile. One leg stretched, the other bent, his right arm resting on his knee, and a glass of wine in his left, he was the perfect portrait of nonchalance. He had the emerald necklace wrapped around his right wrist, and he was playing with the gems hanging between his fingers as if he were bored. But he wasn't. Not in the slightest. His ruby eyes were focused on the woman standing in front of him, her body wrapped in nothing but three strips of silk. The fire in the hearth was casting soft, dancing shadows around the room, and the light lent Cassandrea's skin the tone of honey. She was gorgeous in her improvised silky robe, her golden hair falling in rich waves over her shoulders and her chest rising and falling in soft breaths. Her skin was heated by anticipation and emanating a flowery scent that sent Kerr's mind into a hazy mist of desire.

The three silk stripes that had replaced her clothes were covering very little of her. Two of them were thrown over her shoulders, displaying the delicate arches of her breasts, before they met in the centre of her form, tied by the third strip. From there, all six of the loose ends were falling down along her thighs, revealing the skin of her legs and hips with every move. A crafty and refined design, no doubt created this way to torment him. He let out a low growl. Cassandrea was beautiful. No, not beautiful. She was more than that. She was perfect. And he wanted her. Badly. He wanted to play with that perfect body, feel it reacting to his touch, and have her scent all over him. Even the fresh wounds marring her skin were teasing him. Screaming about what he could do to her. With her. Touching their rough edges to soothe. To comfort. To probe. She could take it. This female wasn't a toy. She was a player. Like him. The most beautiful player of them all. And he would play. Until she would show him who she really was.

"It's missing something," he said and raised his hand with the necklace.

Cassandrea gave him a coy smile and sat on the bed, her back towards him. With one hand, she gathered the golden waterfall of her hair and moved it up, revealing her neck.

"Is that so?" she purred. "Why don't you fix it then?"

Kerr slowly set his wine on the bedside table and kneeled behind the siren. He didn't rush to put the necklace around her neck. Instead, he let his fingers wander down the bare skin of her back until a shiver of pleasure ran down her spine, making her body tremble beneath his fingertips.

"It matches your eyes," he whispered, and finally set the necklace around her neck.

It fit perfectly and even covered most of the scars ruining her smooth skin there. Scars Kerr had now touched.

"Who-" he started but never got to finish.

Cassandrea froze, and a second later, she reached up to pull his hand away.

"Not now," she said firmly, and he felt fear—actual fear—in her voice.

Not wanting to ruin the moment, he obeyed and caressed her arm instead. The siren immediately relaxed, although some stiffness remained even as she let down her hair and covered the scars with it.

"Sorry," she muttered, "I just..."

"Don't be," he whispered, "I won't touch them again. I promise."

She didn't want to tell him, and that was fine. Although, for some reason, it also hurt a bit. But maybe that was a good thing. The less she told him about herself, the better. Yet he wondered if he could make her forget. For a night at least. Or two. And as if she were thinking the same thing, she asked, "Can you play nice? If I ask you to?"

She was still facing away from him, but something in her voice broke a piece of Kerr's heart. That sadness. He knew that sadness. That need. Need to be held. Need to be gentle among all the shit the world kept throwing at them. Need to not be hurt. And the fear of the opposite. He knew that as well.

"You don't have to ask, love," he said softly, his arms already wrapping around her body and pulling her closer into a gentle embrace. "I'll play nice. For you."

*

Cassandrea woke up naked, with just the emerald necklace decorating her neck, her body caressed by silk fabric wrapped around it like the softest blanket. The first thing she realised, to a rather big surprise, was that Kerr was still in the bed with her. His body was warm, his chest rising in steady breaths, and his arm was wrapped around her waist, keeping her close. He was sleeping. Or pretending to. No. Actually sleeping. Because his face was... different. It was strained by a bad dream or some painful thoughts; his lips pressed tight and his expression more serious than she had ever seen before. It felt strangely intimate to see him so vulnerable. Unaware that somebody was watching him, seeing more than he was willing to show.

Then his brows twitched. Cassandrea couldn't tell if it was from anger or from pain. And she debated whether she should wake him up or not. She lifted her hand to do so, but when her fingers reached the kelpie's chest, she halted. Her skin was so pale compared to his rich hue. And somehow only now she had realised just how clear her mind suddenly turned to be. The constant static of anxiety and pressure she kept harbouring in her brain—to work, work, work—was gone. She had forgotten. Herself, her work, even her king, as much as she hated to admit that. But in the simmering heat of the dying embers in the hearth, she didn't feel bad at all. She felt at peace. And she hadn't expected that at all. For three years she hadn't been able to sleep soundly around another male. Especially not this close to one. Yet somehow, not one night in Kerr's presence had she felt the need to be on high alert. Or to be vigilant.

The muscles in Kerr's jaw tensed again, and Cassandrea decided to wake him up after all. She lifted herself on her elbows and reached out to gently kiss his cheek. He didn't deserve to be trapped in a nightmare like that. Not after last night. Not after all that he did for her. He was more thoughtful and attentive than anybody else she had ever been with. And not just physically. He was actually really, really sweet.

Kerr stirred at that same moment she leaned over him, and

their bodies crashed into each other like two waves meeting by the shore. Gods, he was gorgeous. His eyes opened, and he smirked, his lips immediately forming into that familiar smile he always wore. As if the shadows of his dreams were never there.

"Good morning, love," he purred.

Cassandrea breathed out a soft sigh. The deep voice resonated through his chest in a way that made her want to touch him. Have her palms wandering over the velvety iron of his muscles and feeling his warmth. So she pressed her lips on his and did exactly that.

Kerr laughed, but to her relief, it wasn't the confident, mocking sound that some men produced after realising the woman was infatuated with them. No, this was a happy, relaxed, and gentle sound. As gentle as his strong arms now wrapping around her body.

"You didn't use your gifts," she whispered into the kiss, a question in her voice.

Kerr pulled away to look at her, quiet amusement shining in his red eyes.

"Didn't I?"

Cassandrea hesitated, discomfort creeping into her heart, but the male raised his hand to cup her cheek and immediately continued.

"I'll let you in on a secret, love," he winked. "I don't have any."

"What?!"

Kerr shook his head and chuckled at the surprise displayed in her eyes.

"Not like you do. I can't magically force my way into people's hearts."

Cassandrea just stared at him, stupefied.

"Not a chance," she protested and leaned back, only enough to take in the kelpie in full. "You're telling me, all -this-," she continued, waving vaguely with her hand at him, his body, "is all just... just you?"

Someone could have taken her words as an insult. But Kerr just smirked and took hold of her splayed hand.

"Just me, love. You'd be surprised how far you can go with nothing but a smile and an open mind."

Cassandrea's mouth was left ajar, but then she scoffed into a chuckle.

"You are..." she tried to find the word. Nothing fit.

Kerr's smirk grew into a wide grin.

"Handsome? Yes. Wild? Oh absolutely. Blessed?" he gestured at his body. "Most certainly."

Cassandrea laughed.

"Insufferable? Perhaps. Modest? Definitely not."

It was Kerr's turn to laugh, and he turned to his side, pulling her into a tight embrace.

"Why should I be modest? I have no reason to be." The mischief was practically tangible in his voice.

Cassandrea laughed again. It was a free, airy, happy sound. One she thought she had lost all those years ago. She threw her leg over his thighs and curled up against him, burying her face into his chest, breathing in his scent.

"No, you really have no reason to be modest, Kerr. Quite honestly," she finally leaned back, if only to study those red eyes that seemed to glow in the dim room. "I think you're perfect the way you are."

His smile lit up his eyes, and he leaned over to plant a kiss in her hair.

"And," the siren continued, "thank you. For everything you've done. For me. For us. For Entirie, really," she said quietly.

Kerr's lips were still in her hair, and they stayed that way for a long while after her words, as if he weren't sure what to reply or do. Only after a moment, he cleared his throat and shrugged.

"I did what anyone would've done, Cass," he said.

Cassandrea shook her head.

"You did more," she objected, and the mischief sparked in her eyes as she swiftly glanced at her naked leg over his. "You were right, you know," she said. "I did need to let go for a bit."

His palm slid to her cheek, cradling it. Cassandrea tensed, for it was the cheek with the scar, but Kerr's fingers just slid over it.

"I loved every second of it," he whispered.

She believed him. She saw the reactions of his body. Real reactions. Not something caused by her veil. She looked down at his body, so shamelessly displayed in the silk sheets, and she touched the new red scar on his abdomen. She wondered if it would disappear soon, leaving no reminder of their time together. It made her a little sad. She wanted him to remember her. Wanted to work with him again. Be with him again. Maybe show him that she had a wilder side as well. She wondered if she could afford saying it. That this didn't have to be their last time. Yet, once more, as if he could read her mind, he beat her to it.

"I would love to work with you again," he said.

She looked up from the scar she was caressing and met his burning gaze. He was smiling, yet there was something in those eyes. A shadow. One she couldn't bear seeing. So she forced a grin, winking to chase it away.

"Just work?"

It worked like a charm. Kerr laughed, and his fingers tugged at her nipple and twisted it in a way that brought a tormented moan to her lips.

"Never."

"You scoundrel!" Cassandrea's cheeks flushed. She bit her lip and beamed at him. He was going to pay for that.

"Well, you're in luck, Kerr," she started slowly, accentuating the tender and satisfied tone of hers with moving her leg just a bit higher on his thigh. "I happen to find time spent with you extremely fun."

Her eyes sparked, and she trailed her long, delicate fingers from his collarbones down to his abdomen. The male in her arms just sighed and closed his eyes, submitting to the pleasure of her touch.

"I indeed feel quite lucky," he mused.

"So what happens now?" she asked. A part of her was scared to know the answer. A part of her knew he didn't want to think about it either.

But Kerr's chest seemed to shiver under her touch, and it

brought yet another smile to her lips. How could such a small thing make her feel so... happy?

"What happens now is that you and I are going to have a very slow, long morning," Kerr murmured and leaned into her lips, preventing her from objecting or protesting that it wasn't what she had asked. She didn't want to ruin the moment, so she just giggled and threw her arms over his shoulders and leaned tighter into that kiss.

"Maybe some leftover wine," he continued while exploring every corner of her curved lips.

She hummed. He tasted so good...

"Whatever is left from the fruit and cheese," he went on, nipping at her lips.

"That sounds like something we both deserve," she grinned.

"And finally, or maybe as the first thing..."

His eyes sparked up, and he moved, landing on top of her while he deepened the kiss, claiming her mouth all for himself. Cassandrea just sighed and wrapped her arms around his shoulders, holding him close. Gods. His body moved like a tidal wave. Strong. Unrelenting. Embracing every single part of her at once. She loved it. Loved his warmth, his smooth skin, and the way he was kissing her. Like he had all the time in the world to do so. It was easy to like him. So easy.

Cassandrea relaxed and took Kerr's head into her palms to look into his red eyes.

"I like you," she said.

Kerr's eyes smiled back at her, filled with the beautiful

warmth that had such a soothing effect on her.

"I like you too, Cass. I like you too."

But then he grinned, and nothing else about that morning could have been called *soothing* after that.

Chapter 13

Cassandrea took a long, lazy bath, and this time she allowed Kerr to go first. Not only because he deserved it, but also because she was hoping he would prepare some sort of breakfast before she washed herself.

And he did.

When she walked out, there were hot potatoes waiting for her on a plate, hot melted cheese poured over them, and a bunch of grapes smiling at her on the side. Kerr himself was standing by the hearth, one hand resting on its edge, the glints of flames dancing on his face and lighting up his eyes. Cassandrea beamed him a smile, and she was about to chirp him another good morning when she noticed the expression on his face. It wasn't a happy one. At all. With his lips pressed tightly together and his jaw tensed, he looked a lot like when he was sleeping. The same nightmare? Same memory? So Cassandrea slipped behind him and hugged the man. She didn't ask what was bothering him. She didn't want to talk about her own memories either. So instead, she had offered him a silent understanding. And a warm embrace.

Kerr's hand moved, and he rested it over hers on his chest and squeezed it gently in his palm.

"Breakfast is on the table," he said.

"I know," she smiled at him, "it looks beautiful."

"Thank you."

Silence fell over them, only interrupted by the cracking wood in the hearth.

"I still think you should take the riches from the basement and go spend them somewhere... Well, somewhere where they still have shops to spend them in."

He spoke so quietly, Cassandrea barely heard him, so she reached out, grabbed his hand, and turned him around. And watched how the melancholy on his face instantly turned into a smile.

"You bet your kelpie ass we will," she winked at him and tugged him towards the table. "As soon as we are back in Alanthys, we are going to spend all of it on fine clothes, wine, and apartments so luxurious we will feel like living in a king's palace. And I will get a dress made from this silk. It will be glorious."

That thought spread his smile a little wider.

"Like heather on peatbogs. Red, brown, and green," he said gently as they sat next to each other.

"Sun kissed," she laughed and shook the crown of her golden hair.

"Sun kissed," he repeated and leaned over to plant a kiss of his own on her cheek before they started eating. "Promise me one thing, Cass?"

She narrowed her eyes at him.

"What thing?"

"That you will always find something to laugh about," he said seriously and nudged her shoulder with his own, "smile suits you. You have no idea how much."

Cassanrea gladly granted him the smile he so admired, and she was about to reply when a loud knock on the front door interrupted their conversation. Kerr twitched.

"Let me," he muttered and stood up while Cassandrea just nodded and tried to stuff the potato into her mouth as fast as she could. There was no guarantee that they wouldn't be dragged out of that comfortable house in the next thirty seconds, and the breakfast was too good to be wasted.

One look at Kerr when he came back confirmed her suspicion.

"What now?" she asked, swallowing the last piece of cheese and picking up the grapes to take with her.

"Torquil," Kerr sighed, "he wants to talk to us."

"What about?"

"No idea," a sudden spark of mischief flashed through the kelpie's eyes. "I bet he sniffed our breakfast and wants a piece."

The siren chuckled.

"Well, tough luck for him; I just ate it all."

And she gave Kerr an innocent wink. One he returned with a grin of his own.

"It is guaranteed he will be in a foul mood then."

*

Kerr wasn't wrong about that. Cassandrea could sense the shift in the air as soon as they stepped on Ebongale. Gone was the cheerful optimism of the recent victory. The ship was quiet, and most of the soldiers stayed out of their way.

Cassandrea finished her grapes and tossed the now empty stem into the waves while she was counting the ships in the port. One less than the other day. Mairi and Ronan were already gone. That was a good thing. She had no desire to see Ronan's ugly mug. Not that Torquil's would have been that much better.

The general was waiting for them in his cabin, and there was nobody else with him. Not even captain Ualan. As if he wanted to keep whatever was about to be discussed as secret as possible. Ominous. Especially when he took the effort to actually check the door behind Cassandrea and make sure it was locked.

"What is it?" she asked impatiently, something about his behaviour making her terribly nervous.

"I won't sugarcoat it," Torquil said firmly and pointed towards a map on his table. "We've got played. While we were busy with Renglow, Terren managed to surround us. I suppose I should have suspected something was amiss when there were fewer defenders than what the reports had suggested. T'aar had planned for this. He must have gotten some of them out just before the attack."

"What?" Cassandrea couldn't believe what she was hearing, and Kerr seemed just as stupefied as she was. Her blood froze over, and for a second she just stared.

"Look. We are here," Torquil pointed out Renglow on the map.

"This is Achaross."

His finger moved south-east.

"They surrendered to Terren's forces three days ago."

He tapped onto another city's name to the east.

"Sidoria. Taken by general Rheon Nightshade. Also three days ago. And Finpool."

He finally pointed to a coastal city south of them.

"Taken by Terren himself. Also three bloody days ago. It was all planned. To trap us here. In Renglow."

"How do you know all that?" Kerr asked.

"A warning's just reached us. From our loyalists in Achaross. Funny thing is the runner said he was the third one they had sent. And none of the previous ones got to us."

"The dead one?" Kerr enquired.

"Must have been one of them," Torquil nodded. "T'aar must have left some of his people behind to take them down. But the fae-seekers weren't able to detect anything on the site."

"So," Cassandrea asked slowly, "what are we going to do?"

"That's the problem, isn't it? If Terren is guarding the sea and the east is taken by Nightshade and too close to the bulk of their forces anyway, the only way through their lines is through Achaross. That must be where General T'aar was headed over the marshes. To organise their offence from there. So we have to get there before he can do that. Or we can sit here and wait to be sieged. Or... we can risk sailing and trying to avoid the dragon on the sea. But I wouldn't bet on us getting past him."

Dragon. Scouting the sea. Cassandrea gasped for air.

"Oh gods, your cousin!"

Torquil's pale eyes flashed with anger and pain.

"Mairi will get through," he said in a tone that left no room for discussion.

Cassandrea swallowed down the worry she wanted to express. It wouldn't have changed anything. So she offered the general a nod. A firm nod of confirmation and belief.

"She will get through," she repeated, albeit far more quietly than Torquil had.

All three of them looked at the maps.

"I went through the marshes with Kerr," Cassandrea spoke up, then brought her finger over the map, her fingernail pointing to the dead centre of it.

Torquil's eyes snapped to the pale grey splotch on the map.

"I believe that the kappa's warning was for this exact moment," she said suddenly.

Both Kerr and Torquil looked at her as she brought her other hand on the map too, measuring the distances between the places.

"She said they'd be waiting. I think... this is what they were waiting for. If... if we're lucky, they might have taken out the brunt of T'aar's forces and drowned them."

Suddenly Cassandrea's speech flowed faster and more urgently. While she was furious over the situation, she was also trying to find some kernel of light in it.

"So you're suggesting we go through the marshes, too?" Kerr asked carefully.

"Yes. If T'aar went around them, we could be faster and cut them off before they get to Achaross. If he went through them, chances are, they were all eaten. But regardless, if we want to be quick about it, we need to go through the marshes and do it now."

She nodded to herself and looked up from the map. Torquil's eyes were studying her fingers that were still touching their two points of interest. Renglow and Acharon. And the marshes in between.

"What about the kappas? Won't they eat us too?" the general looked at the siren.

Cassandrea shook her head.

"They serve our king. No. If anything, we could obtain information about the dead party that passed through. Right?" she looked at Kerr for confirmation.

"They did pledge themselves to our king," the kelpie

supported her claim, "but I doubt they were collecting information while devouring their prey."

"T'aar has a three-day's headstart," Torquil said, contemplating, "and we have no horses. Only those they left behind in Renglow's stables."

"We better hurry then," Cassandrea insisted.

Torquil gave the map another glance, then looked around. With a deep, sharp breath he leaned back and crossed his arms. His expression was grim, calculating.

"Cassandrea, you're the fastest with your wings. So I want you to be our eyes in the air. Scout ahead and give us a warning if you sense as much as a whiff in the air from anything related to T'aar or his ilk."

"Of course," she said.

"Kerr," Torquil turned to the kelpie. "I want you to go with us. You went through the marshes before; you'll be our guide through it."

"Naturally," Kerr said. He looked at the marshes with a sliver of doubt in his eyes, but Cassandrea planted a hand on his shoulder.

"You know them better than anybody. Is there anything...?" she left the question open.

"No," Kerr shook his head, "but it will be unpleasant."

Cassandrea squeezed his shoulder and winked.

"Just... don't let her slobber you with a kiss or something. That was gross."

Kerr managed to smile at her.

"Enough chatter," Torquil's eyes pierced through the siren. "Get going. We will travel lightly. Switch on the horses when people get tired. One fiend and two hundred men per formation. We need to be fast but ready in case our enemies haven't been eaten. I will send the ships back to Ithyren with minimal crew. Hopefully some of them will get lucky and pass. Either way, it is better for them to be destroyed than taken."

Cassandrea nodded.

Torquil frowned at both of them. He didn't seem angry, but he was on the edge. Rightfully so for once.

"Now go. Get ready. I will start assembling the troops. By lunch, I want them on the way."

They were almost out when Torquil spoke up again.

"Oh, and stop by in the keep. Kill the traitors in the prison. Release the few that got caught in the middle."

Cassandrea froze on the spot, but before she could say anything, Kerr already nodded.

"I'll take care of it," he said.

Cassandrea would be lying if she said she was not relieved that she did not have to participate in that.

*

Three hours later, everything was ready. All horses were saddled, assigned and waiting for their riders. There were about forty of them, all from the mayor's stables, proud and beautiful beasts of various colours. Cassandrea patted one with a pale yellow mane, and the stallion looked at her with intelligent, proud eyes. She smiled and felt the velvety muzzle of the beast against her fingers. The mayor should have taken one of them and ran. Now he was dead. By Kerr's hand. She quickly suppressed that thought. He deserved it. He was a traitor. Same as the mayor of Achaross.

"Traitors. All of them," she told the horse and patted its neck again.

"You will get them," sounded a deep, warm voice behind her, and she turned around to find Kerr standing there, his hands in his pockets.

She smiled.

"One day. Yes. Soon if we are lucky."

"If we move quickly, it will take us a little more than a day to cross the marshes, but I believe we should rest at night. It won't do anybody any good if we arrive at the battlefield exhausted.

"How long would it take T'aar if he went around?"

"Roughly four days if he didn't sleep."

"So it will be tight."

"Hm. But it is difficult terrain. Not at the start, but there is a small mountain range between Achaross and Sidoria that he will have to cross."

"Is it possible he wants to meet Nightshade's forces there?"

"That depends on what their plan is. If they want to march towards us, Nightshade has it easier to avoid the range on its north side. There's a mountain pass a few miles above Sidoria. But if they want to squeeze us in Achaross? Then yes, it is possible."

"Hm," Cassandrea frowned, "it's not looking good for us, is it?"

"I'd trust Torquil," Kerr shrugged, "he knows what he is doing. And I am impressed that he tries to get everybody through, not leaving them to defend Renglow without him."

"He is not the worst commander," the siren admitted reluctantly, "but he can be a major ass."

"Oh, I am sure," Kerr laughed. "Either way, be careful. And if it gets dangerous, just fly away. Don't look back. Ok?"

Cassandrea frowned. She could feel the horse gently reaching for her hand, and she gave the massive head one more rub over its forehead before she turned towards Kerr.

"You be careful. You'll be on the ground with the brunt of our forces."

"I'll be fine."

Cassandrea nodded quietly. There were several unspoken things between them, but Cassandrea didn't want to address any of them. So she gave the kelpie a warm smile.

"Hey," she said quietly and walked closer to him, "this is not a goodbye, alright?"

Her voice was firm, and she did her best to not let it falter.

"I know it's not," Kerr replied.

"So stop looking so miserable, puddle pony; we'll be celebrating with another bottle of wine in a few days. I promise." Cassandrea said as she cut the distance between them and embraced the male warmly.

"Oh, about that," Kerr grinned and pressed something into

her hand. A pouch. Full of something heavy. Coins, by the size of it, and a few sharp objects. Jewellery? Oh, she knew what it was.

"Keep this. Just in case," the kelpie said, "I don't think we are coming back to Renglow any time soon, but at least you will have some spending money in Achaross."

Cassandrea beamed him a smile.

"I can't wait."

She pressed her face into his chest and breathed him in, feeling the kelpie resting his chin against her head. Behind her, the stallion huffed out and stomped on the ground. There were noises coming from the outside. The warband was gathering, and the horse sensed their restlessness. Cassandrea leaned back and kissed Kerr's lips.

"I'll talk to you when we camp."

Chapter 14

It was a sight to behold—their fully amassed force that marched from the gates of Renglow. The streets were swarming with locals as the army, three thousand strong, finally poured out, leaving the abandoned city to fend for itself. Cassandrea reminded herself that this was the price of insurrection. They had opened their gates to Terren's army and paid the price.

The ground thundered and shook in the wake of the army as it made its way across the bridge, then started its long march south-east, towards the marshlands. The rhythmic thuds of thousands of feet, the whooping calls of the fiends, and the clatter and jingle of armour filled the air. It was difficult not to feel joy and gratification swelling in one's heart when the proud cream banners flew tall and the might of the marching soldiers painted the landscape gold, white, and black.

Cassandrea let her wings out, and with a deep, thunderous whomp, they shot her up to the skies. The wind was picking up, and she spent a few moments just listening to its secrets. Sensing the shifts, the scents and the stories written in it. Something was eating at her conscience, something that she couldn't quite place. The wind was mournful and grim, and she knew it was because of the incoming battle. There were good people in Entirie. Good people, that were so disillusioned and misguided, to trust the vision of a whelp. And crown him king. A king. That word still burnt her tongue every time she heard it. She pushed the ire out of her mind and looked down at the slow-marching army trudging forth. An army led by two men she both knew. One with long red hair and one with short black mane. Kerr. The sight forced a smile on her lips.

She leaned forward, into a surge towards the marshlands. Normally, she would be much faster than them, but she had a much wider area to cover, as both flanks, despite their scouts, needed her sight. So she started first by flying over the ranks, keeping herself well above the treeline to see further ahead and to hear the subtle whispers of the wind. Despite her best efforts, her gaze remained drawn to Kerr, and she kept her eyes on the kelpie until she had flown so far that she could not look at him without turning around. Both he and Torquil were walking on foot, lost in some conversation that she was too far to overhear. But it was probably civil and friendly, as there were no hostile gestures going on between the pair. It made her wonder how it was possible that Kerr got along with the general so easily while she remained a persona non grata. Was he really that good? Or did he have some magic he didn't tell her about? Did Torquil know Kerr had no spell to charm him with, and therefore he thought it was safe? She sighed and turned her head away from the males. Sometimes, she wished she had no veil either. But then, she would be a lot less useful to Valderan. Then, looking at Kerr, maybe there were other ways to do her job without it. She would have to ask him once they were alone again.

*

The army below her reached the marshes, and their progress slowed down even more. Torquil made sure they had left the heaviest parts of their equipment behind, but the bogs were simply not made for heavy boots, stomping them with the force of three thousand feet. Humans struggled a lot more than Torquil's fae, but soon it was obvious the fae would have to slow down not to leave a significant part of their army behind.

There was still nothing to see, neither ahead nor on the sides of the marching force, and due to the lack of trees in the centre of the marshlands, Cassandrea could see miles in either direction. Yet there were no kappas and no soldiers walking either away or towards them. No dead bodies either. In fact, the swamps were deathly silent.

After another hour, her wings started to hurt, so she landed next to Kerr and decided to walk next to him for a bit.

Not much was said. Not much could be said. The air was heavy and gloomy, and evening fog started to gather around them while the sun was gracing the land with its last rays of warmth.

"We should rest, general," Kerr suggested as the sun finally set, leaving the land illuminated only by the dim light from their torches.

"We cannot," Torquil replied promptly. His sharp grey-blue eyes scanned the surrounding landscape as far as he could see, and what he saw made him curse.

"This damn fog is going to be the death of us. We could lose some of the troops," Kerr countered, "and not just to the poor visibility."

"We cannot afford the luxury of resting, boy," the general snarled as he ushered the soldiers to continue. "We march through the night and we will camp once we're outside the marshes."

And so the army slogged on. At nighttime, the marsh was an eerie place to be in. Dangerous and terrifying with its long, sinewy shadows of an occasional dead tree, its thin branch fingers reaching for the unfortunate souls passing by. The pungent smell of peat and decay accompanied their every step, and the unnaturally still air was quiet—too quiet. Even the constant churning, chirping, trilling, and croaking of bugs and whatever creatures lived in the bogs sounded muffled. The fog was truly rolling in now, and within an hour it had wrapped everything in its heavy velvety blanket that made their cheeks cold and clothes damp and heavy. Small blue pulsing lights could be seen in the distance, at the roots of low, rotting tree trunks, and yellow glowflies danced around mounds and tufts of heather, darting away from the heavy boots stomping down their homes. The air was so damp and thick with fog that it was difficult to breathe, and the entire army fell silent, the atmosphere weighing heavily on their spirits.

At Torquil's command, Cassandrea took flight once more, trying to make sure there was nothing waiting for them in the fog. Her heart was heavy as well, and she could not shake the feeling that something was seriously wrong. But she couldn't see anything. No enemies. No bodies. No monsters. The fog grew so thick that she could not see the ground, but she kept her vigil, her silent, unwavering watch over the army.

She had been flying for half an hour when a terrifying sound pierced through the muffled silence and stopped her heart. A scream of a dying man, so visceral and horrifying it couldn't have been from an accident or a soldier falling in the water... unless he was being dragged. Panic surged through her body, almost freezing her in place, as the scream was soon joined by another. And another. And another. Then the air was suddenly filled with them. Screams, cries, shouting, and something much, much worse. The sounds of torn flesh. There were dozens of them. Hundreds... The siren turned around and soared back as fast as she could.

Her heart in her throat, she forced her wings to work as hard as they could, commanding them to carry her faster. Faster than she would've ever flown. What was happening? Where was he? Was he still alive? The screams were everywhere now, echoing from left, right, down, and further away. They were mixing with other kinds of cries. Unnatural and ghastly. Feminine screeches that chilled her blood. The blue and yellow lights were dancing in the mists, easy to be confused with torches, and it took Cassandrea a while to find her way through the fog back to the ground. She drew Dusk and Dawn, and the moment she landed, she realised she was in the middle of pandemonium.

The smell of blood was what hit her first. It was everywhere. The reek of bodily fluids and gore and fear. The army was in chaos, fighting against what seemed like the marsh itself: large, ancient-looking lizards nobody had seen in ages were clamping their maws around soldiers' feet and dragging them into the dark waters. White gaunt feminine figures, clad in nothing but pale rags, were floating above the heather, their skeletal arms extended, screaming and tearing their long claws into whatever they could reach. And then there were the men—forty flawless-looking men who were slicing through the army like wheat. They were fighting with liquid grace, their blades slender and sleek, their moves near-perfect.

Cassandrea looked around, confused, feeling her world collapsing around her with each shriek, each earth-shattering gargle, and snap from a broken body. Her mouth formed a plea as she turned and tried to help the closest soldier, who was decapitated just as she reached him. The attacker, an impossibly beautiful blonde male, turned his blade and angled his strike at her. Then halted.

Cassandrea didn't notice it at first—why he had stopped. Then, as if something finally snapped inside her, it all started tumbling in. She recognised the male. He was one of the soldiers marching with T'aar back in Renglow. His eyes, those large, intelligent dark eyes that had glanced at her. Not in the city, but in the stables.

"No-..." she breathed out, stumbling back a step.

The male didn't say anything. He just lowered his weapon and smiled at her, only for a beat, before he vanished into the fog. There was a new, agonising scream where he had gone that tore Cassandrea's heart open. Kelpies. They were kelpies. Knowing she shouldn't let herself collapse, willing herself not to, she staggered a step forward, then two more.

"Torquil," she called out, but the word came out as nothing but a whisper.

There was a clicking sound close to her, and she barely had time to register it as one of the kappas lunged from the murky waters and its long claws swiped at her with inhuman speed. Cassandrea used Dawn to parry the claws and Dusk to stab the creature, but she missed. A horrendous maw of the blind thing opened up wide, and lines and lines of sharp teeth buried into her arm. Cassandrea screamed from the pain, both physical and mental, and struggled against the kappa trying to drag her into the waters.

"Not her!" a voice commanded. Deep, rich, and dark voice.

Enveloped by shadows.

Cassandrea knew that voice. Knew that male. But at the same time... A snap of his fingers was enough for the grip on her arm to loosen. The teeth pulled away, and the kappa retreated, obeying her master's order. Kerr's order.

Cassandrea staggered backwards, only to see the Lord of the Moonlit Mire standing there amidst the chaos, his silhouette a roiling shadow in the fog, eyes burning like vibrant red flaming rubies.

A tight fist of shock clenched around her heart and squeezed. Squeezed it so hard it nearly stopped beating.

"No," she whispered, shaking her head. Her throat was burning. The pain inside her chest was so bad it was threatening to shred the remaining slivers of her humanity. She took a step backward. Lifted her twinblades. She wanted to ask why. But it didn't matter. He was a traitor. Not just any traitor. He was the commander of these things. Their Lord. Everything suddenly started to make sense. Everything he had done... The distractions. The runners. Why everything was so easy. Was this how Ryker felt back then? When he learnt about her?

"Cassandrea," Kerr extended his hand as if he were inviting her to join him. Was he out of his mind?

"Please," he whispered.

But she couldn't join him. She didn't want to. He betrayed her. Worse. He had been betraying her for days, working behind her back even as he... As he... Her mind couldn't even finish that thought. She raised her eyes to him and saw... that he knew already. For there was sadness in his eyes. Regret. The same sadness she saw in him before. He knew. Even then he had known. That she would never join him. That it would come to this. The pain in her chest burst into an explosion so vicious that she just screamed at him. Screamed with all the agony and grievance tearing her apart. Screamed the feelings she couldn't put into words. That she could never put into words.

Kerr took a step closer, but Cassandrea lifted her chin and, in her fury, beat her wings once to rise up into the air, above him. She pointed her sword at the kelpie lord and stared him down with nothing but hatred so visceral it incinerated the air between them. Then, with one mighty flap of her wings, she shot into the skies and started her search for Torquil.

*

Kerr was left standing in the middle of a victory. His victory. Carefully orchestrated for months and executed with precision anybody would envy. Victory that removed seven ships and four thousand of Valderan's soldiers from the equation at a minimal cost. Minimal cost to everybody else, but him. He closed his eyes and clenched his hands into fists.

"Do you want me to look after her?" a teasing voice rang next to him. Cale. The blond kelpie with big smart eyes.

"You've almost ruined it," Kerr said, his eyelids still shut tight. "In the stables."

"*I* ruined it?" the male laughed. "She didn't see anything but you."

Kerr took a deep breath and opened his eyes to look across the marshes.

"Make sure she makes it out alive," he said.

Cale nodded and didn't wait for anything else before he disappeared in the fog.

Kerr stared after him for a good few seconds before he noticed that the screams around him started dying out. Only then he finally turned away and moved to survey the situation. The battle was almost over. All enemies dead or running, ready to be hunted across the marshes. A victory indeed. With a taste of a watery mass grave.

*

Cassandrea was flying above the foggy bogs, watching in horror as the monsters from Terren's army hunted down soldier after soldier, forgetting some of them only to feast on those who had already died. The scent of blood filled the air and her every pore, and she had to fight hard not to vomit. But she couldn't give up or fly away. Not yet. There was one man she had to find. One man who could maybe still do something for the soldiers around them.

"Torquil!" she screamed and swirled on the spot to look around.

However, there was no reply. Same as the six times before when she screamed that name. There was no Torquil and no fae magic blasting around the swamps. Cassandrea realised that the beasts must have targeted their fae forces first. Took them out. But how? Torquil would have been at the front of the army with Kerr when the attack came, but where did he go after that? Was he on horseback? On kelpie's back, she reminded herself with a violent shudder.

Suddenly, she spotted a pale woman approaching her. She was floating above the heather bushes and wailing, her arms extended towards the siren. Cassandrea had only a vague idea what *that* was, but she immediately steered higher to avoid the attack and then lower again not to lose sight of the ground. And there he was, lying in the peat, his legs in a rust-coloured pond, and his back covered in blood. Cassandrea couldn't see his face as it was buried deep in the heather, but luckily, his hair was unmistakable. She risked going lower and landed next to the general's bulky figure.

But Torquil wasn't going to help anybody. With a gaping wound in his side, he was barely breathing, slowly bleeding out into the pond. Kerr. Cassandrea grinded that name in between her teeth. He must have taken the general out as the first. The signal to attack. That's how she would have done it.

However, Torquil was still breathing. For whatever reason, Kerr hadn't finished him. Not that it meant much. They were still in the middle of the enemy army, with an endless number of monsters willing to finish the job.

Cassandrea looked at all the blood around the male and sighed. The magic was already working on the general's wounds, but he wasn't going anywhere any time soon. He was too heavy to be carried. Too big to be flown. Yet she had to try. For Entirie. For Valderan. In spite of Kerr. Even if the whole army was doomed, she wouldn't leave him this price. General Torquil. A wail sounded behind Cassandrea, and she barely managed to dodge as a ghostly-looking woman passed through where she stood before. Cassandrea lunged towards Torquil, her wings shielding the warrior under them. She held her blade up, hidden behind the wing, but to Cassandrea's surprise, the wailing banshee didn't attack; she just continued onwards as if the siren wasn't even there.

"Torquil," Cassandrea touched the general's shoulder. The man let out a pained, weak groan.

"Come on, you need to fight, general!" she left only Dawn in her right hand and turned the male around. His eyes were barely open, and what little sliver was visible in the grey-blue eyes was distorted by pain. The male was barely conscious.

"Torquil, fight! If not for anyone else, do it for Mairi. Come on!" Cassandrea pleaded and tried to hoist the general up.

But Torquil showed no sign of trying to help her with that. He averted his gaze, his body limp, and defeated.

"She's dead," he whispered, his voice weak and broken.

"No-"

A set of footsteps crept closer, and the siren swiftly turned around, flaring her wings over the general. Her blade concealed under the wing, she stared at the approaching male. The same blonde warrior who smiled at her in the city and eagerly brought his lips to her hand in his horse form. She thought they had been searching for treats, and now she realised he had been looking for her scent. Cassandrea snarled.

"I am not here to hurt you," the male looked at the general and tilted his head, "or him if he's so important to you. Although he would deserve it."

Cassandrea had a thousand things on her mind; she wanted to scream at the blond kelpie, but none of those words passed her lips. Her throat was too tight. Her lips too dry. She pulled Torquil closer to her body, not knowing what else to do. She would kill the male if he stepped any closer. But then what? There were hundreds like him in the marshes. And hundreds of things worse than him.

"I am Cale," the man continued, wisely staying where he was. "Kerr sent me to get you out of here."

"Liar!" she hissed immediately.

Cale raised his eyebrow.

"You are all liars!" the words suddenly sprung out of her mouth, hurtful and vile. "Your whole damn race are liars and murderers!"

Cale didn't show any reaction to that. But he did extend his hand towards her.

"Nevertheless, he's sent me to help you. Of course, you can always just fly away, right?"

He looked at the general in her arms, then back at her. Cassandrea followed his gaze. She knew that. All of that. But she couldn't leave Torquil to be captured. If only because he knew too much. She could kill him, but she wasn't sure she could handle that kind of pain on top of everything else. So she thought hard. The male in front of her didn't move. He stayed his hand earlier when he could have killed her. There was no reason why he should do that only to kill her later. And Kerr... As much as she hated him, as much as he betrayed her and the entire army, he also stopped the kappa from coming after her.

"How?" she asked.

"I'll carry you. Both. Though I still think you should leave him. He is a terribly grumpy old man, your general."

"I don't care what you think," Cassandrea snapped.

"Alright," Cale held his arms up, "both it is."

And in a flash of blue light, he shifted into a gorgeous palomino stallion with a shining creamy mane.

Cassandrea hesitated. However, one look around her was all she needed to confirm that this was her only choice to get Torquil out. The fighting was still heavy. There were shrieks of pain coming from the thick fog surrounding her, clashes of blades, and faint green flashes of light. Fae magic. Some of them must have been alive after all. Still fighting. Maybe if she got to them... The horse snorted as if he could tell where her thoughts were going. He scratched his hoof against the ground and shook his mane. Cassandrea hissed at him, but she got up and dragged Torquil's immense weight towards the beast. Only with the aid of her wings was she able to hurl the general over Cale's back, and while she would have preferred flying, she had to sit behind the male to hold him in place.

"Try anything and you are dead," she warned the kelpie.

The horse gave her a look, but he made no gesture to indicate he understood. So Cassandrea wrapped her injured arm around Torquil's body and held Dawn in the other, her head constantly turning left and right and scanning the battlefield for any incoming danger. Her arm was still bleeding, torn, and painful, but she didn't dare to take her attention away from her surroundings for long enough to bandage it.

There were too many enemies around her. The banshees. The blue and yellow lights she now recognised to be will-o'-the-wisps. The kelpies and kappas and some small crouched figures popping out of the heather and disappearing again. Yet it was as if none of them could see her. As if she were invisible. And that made the journey all the more eerie. She felt like some sort of a wraith. Death itself riding through the battlefield. Cursed to see her soldiers dying all around her but unable to help them. And each step and each sight and each scream was clawing at her soul, eating more of it and leaving nothing but void behind. Kerr did this to her. He and his false king. She hated him. Hated that she had to accept his help. Cale's help. Hated that she had to look and do nothing in order to save Torquil. Hated that she knew she wouldn't be able to do anything, even if she wouldn't have to save Toquil. Hated how useless she felt. How tiny in the grand scale of things. Maybe, she thought, maybe she should get off the horse and fight. Fight until some of these beasts killed her. Then, at least, her heart would stop hurting.

And as if the gods obliged her plea, the horse below her

suddenly jerked and lunged off the path and into the murky waters of a peatbog. Cassandrea yelped, her mouth instantly filling with ice-cold water, the bog closing over her head. She was wrong. Cale didn't want to help them after all. He was drowning them. And she doomed them both.

Not thinking about it, she angled her sword and plunged it into the kelpie's body. She tried to pull it out again, but it got stuck, so she let go and grabbed the general instead. She had to get up. Up. She kicked against Cale's hairy body to propel herself towards the surface, but something big bumped into her side and steered her off the course. The water was dark and full of blood, and the bump pushed all air out of her lungs. She tried not to lose her grip on Torquil and extended her wings to use them as fins, but a sharp pain pierced through her ankle, and she could feel claws wrapping around it and pulling her down. Down. Away from the light. Away from everything. She let go of Torquil and pushed him up. Maybe at last he could make it if she couldn't. She could see his body moving up. For a moment. Before his armour started pulling him down again. Cassandrea would cry out her desperation if she could. It was hopeless. Everything was hopeless. She tried to kick the arm holding her, but she knew that even if she freed herself, she wouldn't have enough strength to get to the surface. The claws moved up her body, grabbed her waist and pushed her below, and then they wrapped around her neck. And that was it. Cassandrea froze completely, and her mind went dark. She couldn't move. Couldn't breathe. Couldn't think. She would have loved to fight or at least feel sorry for herself, but the truth was, all she could feel was... nothing. There was an absolute empty void in both her heart and the swamp surrounding her. She couldn't even tell if her eyes were opened or closed. Couldn't move her arms to fight. So she just stared into the darkness, motionless, her body sinking deeper and deeper, a satisfied voice hissing into her ear. Cassandrea opened her mouth to take the last breath of water she knew would end it all, but she never got to do so. Something light flashed in front of her eyes and tore into the kappa. The water around her moved, and it swirled and grabbed her paralysed body and pushed her up with such strength it forced her to close her mouth again. Suddenly she could feel and command her limbs once more. She could think. And then her head popped out of the water next to Torquil's, and she took a breath. The deepest breath she had ever taken. It tasted of iron.

At first she thought it was the general and his magic that pulled them out, but Torquil was unconscious, held on the surface by the currents alone. Then she thought it was Kerr, but the banks of the bog were empty. Then it must have been Cale. But there was no horse and no blond mane to be found. The water around her was dark with blood. His blood, she realised. From how she stabbed him.

"Cale?" she called, but nobody replied.

It didn't matter, she told herself. She had to get out of the bog. Get Torquil out. And stop her arm from bleeding. Her ankle. Her waist. She hadn't even realised in how much pain she was until she collapsed into the heather next to Torquil, sobbing at every move she had to make to drag him that far. Weak. She felt so weak. And she hated it. She hated everything. For a few long breaths, she just laid there, weeping. She gave up. She had given up in the waters. And still the gods wanted to punish her further and spat her out. For what? Just to spite her? Her eyes moved to Torquil, who was still unconscious. And suddenly the fear for his life became stronger than her need for self-pity. She crawled next to the man and heaved the warrior on his side. She grabbed him by his stomach and threw her fingers in his throat while her wings strained to lift her up enough to make her arm squeeze his stomach. It probably looked ridiculous, as she flapped like a trapped pigeon trying to fly, but it worked. Torquil coughed. And sputtered. Then vomited out what looked like at least half of the swamp.

Her muscles burning from the strain and the exhaustion, Cassandrea helped the male heave the remaining water from his stomach and lungs before she dared to let go of him. Her wounds needed some care, too. So she took off her jacket and shirt and tore the shirt into long linen strips. She didn't care that Torquil was watching her. That he could see her body. If he had anything to say about it, he could go to hell. But he remained quiet, even as she wrapped the strips first around her arm, then the male's chest, then her own waist, and finally her ankle. The wounds were bad, but their magic would take care of them. Eventually. Unless they bled out first. She put her jacket back on and looked at Torquil.

The general could barely stay awake, let alone move on his

own, so she took a hold of his wrists and turned him on his back. Then she started walking. Carefully. She forced her feet to take one step at a time, and each step that faltered, she corrected with her wings. It was slow. Too slow. But she was moving. Staggering on the soaked ground, she cursed everything and everybody that got her into this situation. She cursed the swamp, cursed Kerr and his entire kelpie kind, cursed Terren and his cursed beasts, and most of them all she cursed herself. For falling for Kerr. For suggesting the cut through the marshes. For believing, even for one moment, that there was light and colour in this world. Pure fury and disgust filled her heart as she was dragging the fallen general on. But it was that darkness and fury that kept her going and gave her the strength to push on. For as long as her body would last.

Chapter 15

Her body, as it turned out, lasted exactly eight hours. Eight hours of dragging, half-flying, and hiding from the beasts prowling the marshes. She felt like a bird caught in a snare. With Torquil being the snare. Her wings were working relentlessly on easing his weight for her, but she was exhausted and hungry, and her whole body was hurting like it had never been before. She knew all too well that she was leaving a blood trail behind the size of a dragon, and she dreaded the moment something would decide to follow it. So she didn't dare to stop and rest. She knew that the southeast end of the marshes was only a few hours away, with Achaross being in that direction. However, she couldn't go that way. That was where General T'aar was expecting them.

Cassandrea had no doubt about that. Not anymore, knowing the kappas were on the other king's side. Her best chance was to sneak through the enemy lines on the south-southeast side of the marshes. Between Achaross and Finpool. Too close to Terren for her own liking, but she was a tiny speck on the land and his focus was on the sea, so she was willing to risk it. Anything that would get her out of the swamp.

The fog was still covering most of the land, and only thanks to the warm south breeze whispering into her ear, she knew the way to go. The marshland didn't lose any of its danger. The kappas may not have been hunting her at that moment, but she was sure that was only because of the abundance of other prey. Sometimes she felt she was being watched by the tiny creatures in the heather, and several times she had to avert her gaze from a stray will-o'-the-wisp not to be swayed off the right direction. Once she met a fae-seeker, but the beast just sniffed her and moved on. She wondered if any more of them survived. If they didn't, it was a significant loss on their side. Next to the three thousand soldiers and gods knew how many ships. Cassandrea gritted her teeth.

A few times she thought she saw figures in the fog. Dark and tall ones. Some were surrounded with a faint green glow akin to a magical shield. They could have been their fae, but Cassandrea wasn't willing to risk approaching them. They could have been enemies just as easily. So she kept trudging forth hour by hour until her legs simply gave up and she fell into the heather next to Torquil.

"You lasted longer than I thought you would," the general said.

Cassandrea jerked her head in his direction and noticed his eyes were open for once. She snarled at him out of habit, but she didn't really feel it this time. It didn't mean anything. Nothing did.

"I am tired," she whispered and curled into a tiny ball among the swamp flora. "You are welcome to use your own legs."

"How many?" he asked.

That question made her heart ache with an unbearable loss and desperation. She did not want to be the one to tell him and make him feel the same. So she didn't say anything.

"How many?" he repeated.

Cassandrea didn't answer. What point would it have to do so? It wouldn't change anything. But the general understood the meaning of her silence anyway.

"All of them then," he said unusually quietly.

She didn't deny it, and he didn't say anything after that. They were both just lying on the ground and staring into nothingness.

*

The sun was high in the sky, its yellow ring barely visible through the fog and retaining an eerie aura, by the time Cassandrea's body healed enough to allow her to move again. Torquil was sleeping or unconscious, which one, she didn't know. Either way, his eyes were closed when she leaned over him and grabbed his arms to continue their graceless track. He was alive, and that was good enough.

The swamps seemed endless. Several times she wondered whether she hadn't lost her way and gone in the wrong direction altogether. But the southern wind always came back to reassure her. She was just damn slow with the general dragging her down, and being stuck with her own thoughts in the eerie silence wasn't helping one bit. She wanted to tell Torquil she was sorry. To let him see the guilt and regret in her. But he was unconscious and the more she thought about it, the more her throat clenched and her breathing caught. So she didn't. Not that it would have changed anything, anyway.

She also didn't dare to cry her pain out, but when the pressure in her chest became unbearable, she opened her mouth and screamed without a sound, tears running down her cheeks and freezing into a chilling crust on her skin. There was nothing left in her but a gaping void. She was thirsty. And hungry. And weak. But she no longer felt it. Sometimes she checked the general only to see pain carved in his expression as his body was slowly stitching the mangled flesh together. She didn't envy him. At least she had the physical labour to focus on while he had nothing but his thoughts.

By the end of the second day, she had finally reached the edge of the marsh. She expected tears of relief when her boots met rocky ground and she felt the slight rise of the foothills, but they didn't come. As if the void snuffed them out as well. So she just kept going until she found a sheltered spot between the rocks, and there she dropped the general and curled into a ball again, desperately needing some rest.

When she woke up, the fog was gone and the sky was full of stars. Beautiful shining stars. She had never been happier to see them.

"You should have let me die there," Torquil finally decided to speak up, his eyes blankly staring into the same night sky.

Cassandrea didn't feel like amusing him with nonsense like that. She felt bad enough for her own situation to bother with understanding.

"Look who decided to grace me with his presence," she snorted.

"I mean it," the general said.

"So do I," Cassandrea shrugged, "you are a good commander. We need you alive."

"I doubt the king will feel that way."

Cassandrea's hands closed into fists. She knew that was true. And she was just as guilty of this failure as he was. Was she going through all of this just to be killed by her king? No, he wouldn't do that to her. He wouldn't-

The stars suddenly flickered, and some big shadow passed over a bunch of them. At first she thought it was a cloud, but it was too fast for one. And too suspiciously shaped. She gasped for air and tried to melt into the stones.

Torquil must have seen it as well, because he said, "I trained him, you know?"

She needed to tell him to shut up, but she couldn't get a sound out of her throat. It was one thing to face a friendly dragon and an entirely different one to face a hostile one. But the general continued, whether she wanted him to or not.

"Two hundred years ago. He was so young back then. And so sad. He was always... so sad."

The shadow disappeared, and the stars smiled down at Cassandrea, bright as ever. She thanked them for their warning, took a deep breath, and turned her head to look at Torquil.

"Why him?" she asked. "Why did Valderan pick *him?*"

But the general didn't reply; his mind lost to oblivion once more.

*

On the dawn of the third day, Torquil finally woke up properly. To Cassandrea's biggest relief, he stopped talking about death and decided to walk with just a minor support. It was such a big change that the siren felt her feet were already a thousand pounds lighter. And she wasn't even using her wings. The landscape was constantly rising and then dropping beneath their feet, leading them through the low hills between Achaross and Finpool. The last obstacle before crossing what Cassandrea expected to be the current frontlines. Hopefully uncontested as of yet.

The siren swept back a few strands from her face as she paused next to a small evergreen tree that jutted at the side of a few boulders. Her hair felt thick and greasy and damp from the accumulated sweat. All kinds of small things got stuck between the strands: foliage, dirt, dead bugs and gods knew what else, making the silken smooth strands feel like gritted parchment and gravel.

"We are about a day's march away from Thandor's crossing," Torquil said, looking down the hill. "With a boat, we can make our way down the river at night and make it to Ithyren without having to cross either of the lost territories."

The general's words were firm, assertive. Cassandrea was relieved about that; hearing his will to live returning was as much of a good sign as it was a reminder for her to keep on going. Even if the male's heart was filled with similar grief as hers. Guilt. For surviving where most had not. But there was a new fire in him now, a fire that burnt more vibrantly than she had ever seen in anyone. The beautiful iron eyes were keen. Sharp. Attentive. And they were filled with purpose. He hadn't thanked her for saving him. He didn't need to. And she didn't want him to, either.

"Can we assume the town is still ours?" she found herself asking.

The general looked down the hillside that rolled into the vast, green valley beneath. The snow had melted almost entirely and first daffodils and pansies were reaching for the sunlight that was caressing the landscape. Spring had brought death upon them. Death and destruction. And betrayal. Cassandrea closed her eyes and felt the soft southern wind kiss her cheeks and wipe away the tears that had tried to come.

"No. We can't assume anything," the general said quietly, "but we have to try."

She knew that. She knew why, too. There was still a chance Mairi had made it to Ithyren. They had to try.

They didn't speak much for the rest of the day. The only stops they made were to rest and eat whatever meagre meals they could muster. They didn't dare to set up a fire, in the fear of patrols or wandering warbands. As the evening fell upon them, Cassandrea and Torquil found their way to the bank of a river that would eventually lead them to Thandor's Crossing, a large town that overlooked the three rivers that crossed and mixed together to lead towards Ithyren, and ultimately, to the sea. Following the river from a short distance away, the general and the siren quietly approached a small cottage near the rapids, right on the town's outskirts. There was a candle lit in the window, and melancholic songs accompanied its lonesome flame. The siren halted. The general gave her a look of worry, but Cassandrea looked at the candle and pressed her hand to her heart when she caught the words and the melody of the song.

"They're singing for the lost battalions."

"Then the town has not fallen," the general said. His voice was hollow, but relief was visible in his eyes.

They made their way to the front door, and the laments of the fallen soldiers were brought to an abrupt halt as the general's fist banged on the door two times. A short, complete silence followed. Then a series of footsteps thundered on the floor and the tall door was flung open. The man who opened it was as wide as a barn's wall, portly, and tall enough that he would need to crouch to walk under a shop sign. Dark, weather-beaten skin and greying hair covered both his head and his jaw. The man wore heavy-duty linen clothes that had weathered many storms, and the ferryman's sleeves were rolled up to his elbows, revealing his muscled forearms. The man's eyes were suspicious and seeing he held his hand behind his back, Cassandrea assumed there was a weapon in it, ready to be plunged at whoever was coming. But the weapon fell as the man took one look at the warrior that had banged their door.

"General Torquil," the man said, almost reverently. He stepped aside, allowing the old fae warrior and the siren to enter, and everyone inside gasped at the sight of them.

Cassandrea looked around. It was a small, humble home. One room for sleeping, one room for bathing, and one room for everything else. In that common room, two fae soldiers sat around a small, thick wooden table, their eyes glazed and distant from the horrors they had seen. A woman, presumably the ferryman's wife, was sobbing at a small stove while she was heating what smelled like mulled wine. Another woman, much younger, was sitting on a bench near the window, staring at a candle, also with tears in her eyes.

The soldiers twitched and struggled to get up as soon as Torquil's form filled the door frame, but the general shook his head and stopped them with a commanding gesture.

"At ease, boys," he managed. His voice was thin. So, so incredibly thin. Defeated.

Cassandrea couldn't bear it. So she looked at the ferryman, who in the meantime put away the weapon he had held behind him—a gigantic fishing hook that would have been big enough for grounding a drake.

"We need a passage to Ithyren if you can spare a boat that far."

The ferryman turned to the siren. Without a hesitation, he nodded, swiftly glancing at the two soldiers, then his wife.

"Absolutely, my lady," he said quickly, his deep voice filling the house. "I will take you to Ithyren. That's not a problem. At all."

"Thank you," Torquil replied instead of Cassandrea, his eyes staying on the soldiers, "are you two coming with us?"

"Of course, general," the younger one said, "but don't you want to eat first?"

"No," Torquil's gaze drifted away at those words and the male turned, "I will wait outside for you. Take your time."

And he was gone.

Cassandrea briefly considered going after him, but then she decided to be the more practical one.

"We will need some supplies. Food. Blankets. Water. Can you spare anything?"

The ferryman's wife squirmed at that, but her husband nodded.

"I will find something."

"Thank you."

She looked at the wife and pulled out the pouch Kerr gave her what seemed like aeons ago. She opened it and squinted when the emerald necklace blinked into her face. With an aching heart, she reached inside, pulled out two golden coins, and laid them on the table.

"For your trouble," she said, and hid the rest of her treasure inside her pocket.

This was not how she had envisioned spending it.

Chapter 16

Dawn was still an hour away when Kerr left Achaross and headed towards the old-growth Saemach forest south of the city walls. It was a beautiful place full of painfully fresh air, moss, old fallen trunks overgrown with lichen, and tall windthrows looking like wraiths with their roots up in the air. There wasn't much light under the foliage, and the little sunshine the leaves let through had a strange grey and green hue to it. The forest was extraordinarily quiet, with high humidity and moss silencing even the bugs and birds living there. Kerr was walking slowly, taking his time climbing over the fallen trees and avoiding the crooked forms of their still-growing brethren. He avoided touching any, not wishing to upset some dryad or a forest fae, yet he couldn't help but marvel at the beauty of this place. In many ways, it was similar to his marshlands. Wild. Primeval. Lonely. Attracting those who didn't feel at home in the overorganised world of humans. Kerr knew all too well why the person he was meeting had picked this spot to do so. He felt it in the roots, in the lichen caressing his shoulders, and in the water dripping from leaves and needles and squelching in the moss beneath his feet—the ancient magic protecting Saemach.

Kerr bent down and slipped under a fallen tree that was blocking his way to a natural opening. Well, natural. There was a small swamp there, preventing the growth of any taller trees. In the centre of the wetland rose a low hill, and three standing stones towered proudly on top of it, reaching towards the skies.

Crossing the swamp was no feat for the kelpie, but he still took his time and did it deliberately to provide enough warning for the person waiting amidst the standing stones. Male. Dressed in green and black, clothes sewn out of a simple fabric and decorated only with a silver thread. He was young, or he seemed to be. Younger than most of them. In reality, Kerr knew he was over two hundred years old. Not that anybody could tell until he opened his eyes. Eyes that were closed now while the thin male was sitting in the grass on top of the hill, his back leaned against the central standing stone, a crown of soft blond hair shining in the rising sun.

Terren.

Kerr's king.

The fourth most powerful being in the world.

"Lord Terren."

The dragon king didn't open his eyes when Kerr climbed the hill and stopped next to him. He didn't have to.

"You are concerned," he said as a way of greeting, his voice gentle and soft like a gurgling stream. "Didn't you win?"

"I did," Kerr looked down at his hands. "We did."

"And did you let them go?" Terren asked.

"I did."

"Good," the dragon weighed every word. "Is that what you are upset about?"

Kerr hesitated. He didn't want to start an argument he knew he couldn't win. However, the battle and the aftermath were eating at his heart, not allowing him to rest.

"Why?" he asked finally.

But Terren didn't reply to that. He had never replied to anything significant.

"Wasn't it your plan?" he inquired instead.

"Yes," Kerr nodded, "mine and T'aar's."

"And it worked," the dragon mused.

"In a way," Kerr sighed and leaned against the closest menhir, "but we could have taken the general and the siren with us. They would have been better off here."

The dragon finally opened his eyes and looked at Kerr with a gaze that was much, much older than the male's real age.

"Would they agree?"

Kerr stared into those emerald eyes with narrow pupils like he had so many times before and tried to find anything to object to. A reason to disagree. Because he did disagree. But it was so hard...

"No," he said finally and hated himself for it.

"You cannot help people who do not wish to be helped, Kerr," the dragon said gently, his gaze understanding and soothing and his voice sad in a way that made Kerr's heart ache. "Not yet."

"So you've said."

"And you agreed."

"I did," the kelpie lord nodded, "but I may have been wrong to do so."

"Give it time."

Kerr thrust his hands into his pockets and closed his eyes.

"My people are ready to join Rheon's forces and march east," he said to change the topic.

This time it was Terren who hesitated, and that sadness laid even heavier in his voice when he replied.

"I am afraid it will be just you and T'aar for now."

"Why?" Kerr asked, and for some unknown reason, his chest tightened while he was waiting for the reply.

"Rheon has been captured at Boulderhelm."

Kerr's heart stopped.

"No," he breathed out and ran his fingers through his hair, suddenly unsure what to do with himself. "How sure are you?"

"It is a certainty; I am afraid," the king said, his emerald eyes studying Kerr.

"Alright," the kelpie male nodded, "then we have to get him out. I'll talk to T'aar. We can-"

"Kerr," the dragon stopped him with the same peaceful and sad voice as before, "I do not want you to extract him."

"What?" Kerr stared hard at his king, stupefied. "You cannot possibly... You... You are not serious."

"I am," the dragon said with that deadly calm Kerr simply couldn't share.

"They are going to kill him!"

"That is a possibility. Although I find it highly unlikely."

"You cannot know that."

Terren didn't say anything to that.

"You cannot know that," Kerr repeated and took a step closer, "and even if they don't kill him, they will hurt him. Hell, he knows things they can't learn."

"Kerr," Terren remained unfazed by anything the kelpie Lord threw at him, "I do not wish for you to extract him. Is that clear?"

"Why?!" Kerr huffed, utterly infuriated.

"Because you will only endanger yourself. And others. Rheon is out of our reach at the moment. And we better..."

"He is like your son! Are you just going to let them execute him? Torture him? Use him against you?"

That finally seemed to have some effect on the young king as he turned away from Kerr and stared into the deep green of the forest. Yet his mind seemed set.

"Will you respect my wish, Kerr?" he asked.

The kelpie lord gritted his teeth and nodded.

"Of course, My Lord."

"Good. That is all. Meet T'aar and send me a plan for our

advance south."

"I will, My Lord."

Kerr bowed and turned around to walk back into the city. He felt the dragon's eyes on him as he trudged through the swamps and even long after that when there were trees and branches between them. Terren requested that he did nothing. Nothing about his friend who got captured by the evil lurking south. And he promised to respect that wish. Because it was a wise wish, and Terren was right. Trying to break out Valderan's prisoner was a fool's errand. A suicide. So it was wise to agree not to do that.

However, Kerr had lied, promising that.

And he hated how good at it he was.

Chapter 17

Two days after leaving Thandor's crossing, Cassandrea and Torquil arrived in Ithyren. They spent a day looking for Mairi, but instead of getting word of her, they discovered that King Valderan had relocated to the city of Dranast. Given both Mairi and Ronan were sent to meet the king, following in their footsteps was the best chance they had to find her. And the place they had to go to anyway. So Dranast it was—the City of Enlightenment.

With its academies, institutes, schools, and libraries, Dranast was a sought-after location for knowledge and learning, tucked away on the far side of the Western Weald where it bordered the Midlands. The city was carved into a mountain range that made it easy to defend and difficult to siege, and much to Cassandrea's dismay, there was no large river connecting to it, meaning their somewhat comfortable, albeit cold, method of transportation by boat was no longer viable. General Torquil had suggested that Cassandrea rode a horse, but she wasn't willing to entertain the idea. The sole thought made her shudder so violently she was certain she would be sick if she had to sit on top of one of those beasts. So she opted to fly. No matter how exhausted she was and how much Daelith and Thasarius, the two fae soldiers, tried to coax her to ride with them or at least use their steeds, she wouldn't go near the creatures. She couldn't. She couldn't even try.

However, the journey took three weeks on horseback. It was a long time for the siren to keep flying above them. She could have made the trek faster and cut over the forests, but she refused to leave Torquil's side. Even when the general told her to go and stop stalling, she told him no. She had sworn to herself they would arrive at Valderan's court together. Face the king together. So she tried flying even if it drew every ounce of her energy.

Then finally, on the thirteenth day, exhausted and on the brink of a collapse, she attempted to overcome the fear and fed a beautiful palomino mare an apple. Yet as soon as the horse turned its golden head towards her, she felt a cold grip of icy waters closing around her and a familiar tang of blood in her mouth. Her breath laboured and thin, she stood there, frozen like a salt statue, her mind swirling in the deep abyss of the bog.

She had no idea for how long she had been petrified, silent

tears rolling down her cheeks, stuck in that perpetual torment inside her head. Trembling, gasping for air, for nothing. The next time she registered her surroundings, she was sitting at the campfire, the general speaking to her calmly. After that, nobody offered her a ride again. And she was grateful for it.

She spent her nights drifting further and further away from the males, preferring solitude and silence. Safety. She trusted the general and the two warriors enough, but she couldn't find peace around the campfire, no matter how hard she had tried. As a result, she frequently wandered off to a location beneath a tree or up on a branch to which she had tied herself, spending hours watching the moon and stars flicker between the leaves before falling asleep. It wasn't a good sleep and she hated every second of it. More often than not, it offered her only pain and terrifying memories.

During those nights when she couldn't fall asleep, she spent her time honing, sharpening and polishing her one remaining blade, Dusk. Its twin sister Dawn had been lost, drowned in that cursed bog. Or perhaps that worthless kelpie had taken it with him, hopefully to his own watery grave. That suited Cassandrea just fine. For her, there was no dawn. Not anymore. And it was in nights like those when Kerr's words came back haunting her. Tormenting her.

"Promise me, Cass," he had said, *"that you will always find something to laugh about."*

Cassandrea snarled as the whetstone sang against the steel. She made a new promise to Kerr. She promised that the next time she would see him, she would plunge Dusk into his rotten, lying heart.

*

At last, the mountain road gave way to the pale stone bridges leading to the city itself. Their arches reached across the deep ravines between the mountain pass and the city itself, stretching for several miles, high above the deadly drops into the rocky bedrock. Cassandrea landed nearby, hiding her wings, and walked at a respectable distance from the horses, but close enough to be recognised as one of the party. Before reaching the bridges, they were halted and approached by six guards, all clad in silver armour with white bone-inlaid ornaments that curved around their breastplates and pauldrons in cloud-like curls, led by a young fae captain. Their helmets were tall and slim, pointed, and had long tufts of platinum hair that were whipping in the winds like delicate quicksilver flags.

"State your business," the captain said, only to stop dead in his tracks as he recognised the general. The hand he had lifted in order to halt the incoming party dropped down.

"General Torquil," the male addressed the warrior, his head suddenly bowing down in respect. "We've heard the news-"

"Everyone's heard the bloody news. I'm here to see the king," the general snarled and Cassandrea gasped in shock.

Torquil had never addressed any men in arms like that. Not his own, not even the auxiliary forces. Luckily the captain took no offence. He inclined his head and gestured towards the city.

"Of course," was all he offered as he stepped aside.

The five guardsmen all took a curious look at the last remnants of the mighty army that had sailed north as their captain addressed the general one last time.

"May the pyres light your path," he said quietly.

But none of the travellers bothered to reply. The general just nodded and ushered his horse to move and the rest followed.

The city of Dranast was breathtaking. It was a marvel built of white stone. The same white stone forming the mountain range behind it, the two wonders blending perfectly from afar. And as the party crossed the last long stone bridge to the city and stepped inside its walls, the full beauty and magnificence of the City of Enlightenment unfurled before them. Its bleached stone walls were decorated with blue and silver paints, making them delicate and airy. Tall towers and spires pierced the sky, reaching for the clouds with their pointed pinnacles and sharp pointed banners flying in the winds. High, elegant archways welcomed the travellers passing through the city gates and led them towards palaces and buildings with stained glass panes that let light in and painted the floors with beautiful pictures of the rainbow mosaics.

As they continued through the city, Cassandrea noticed some beautiful pillars carved with ornate motifs and themes of clouds and stars that would have drawn her closer had it been on any other day. All around them, the sound of rushing water could be heard. There were no rivers leading to Dranast, but several waterfalls coming from the nearby mountains roared down around the city to a deep mountain lake beneath.

Cassandrea would have shed a tear in awe had she not been so exhausted. However, in her current mood, she just gave them a disinterested glance and kept walking.

Soon they got closer to the city market and the scents of the city started wrapping themselves around the group, tempting them again, this time with fresh bread, baked with herbs and spices Cassandrea had never smelled before. Something prickly and acidic wafted from a teahouse nearby and the siren's mouth watered just from the smell of it. But she didn't want to stop. Not yet. She was afraid that if she halted, she wouldn't be able to get up ever again. But the general had different plans for them.

"We will rest here. I will send word of our arrival, and we'll wait for the king's summons." Torquil's tone left little room for a debate. Not that Cassandrea wanted to argue with him, anyway. She simply nodded, as did Daelith and Thasarius.

The siren found a nearby tavern, booked a room, prepared a hot bath, and soaked in it for hours. Only once her body had been soaked so thoroughly she could feel her skin shrivelling up and the water grew cold and unpleasant did she finally get out and collapse into a bed. She did not remember much after that.

*

A few hours later, her door practically broke inward with a deafening crash, and Cassandrea was brutally thrown out of her sleep. Immediately, she drew a dagger from under her pillow and raised it, only to see a young male in the doorway, utter pain and relief in his expression. He was panting, like he had been running for miles, and his face was slightly red from the exercise. The male was handsome, in a sweet, charming way, with a boyish gleam to his eyes, one iris emerald green, one royal blue. His olive skin was flawless, and his scruffy hair was a mix of auburn and chestnut, resembling the coat of a fox. But the male wasn't a shapeshifter or fae. He was a teg. A creature that was more human-looking than its fae cousins but equally beautiful. Curious and cunning in nature, tegs were often mischievous and playful and delighted in a mix of teasing and trickery. But there were none of those qualities visible on this male's face now. Only worry. And relief when he finally beheld the siren.

"Ash…" Cassandrea croaked.

Her throat stung, and she dropped the dagger on her bed. The teg closed the door behind him and promptly rushed to her, enclosing her in a tight embrace.

"I've heard the news, I thought—" he couldn't finish his words.

Swallowing, Cassandrea shook her head.

"Don't," she pleaded, "don't say it."

Ashban was as close to a brother as Cassandrea could have wished for. He shared years with her in captivity and then he shared years with her in freedom. And these days he was sharing years of working for King Valderan alongside her. Her only friend. Only family she had.

The male fell silent as he took a deep breath and swallowed whatever he was planning to say. Cassandrea couldn't get any words out either. She felt like she was about to break. About to shatter into a million pieces. She knew that Ashban was the only person who would have known why. Would have understood how it felt. Not only the loss of an army, but the betrayal... Ashban would have understood.

But still, the words didn't come. Or any tears. Cassandrea leaned back from the embrace, and the male gave her a long look. His sad gaze turned even darker as he took in her injuries. The dishevelled look. The gaunt face and the hollow stare. He even seemed to notice that she had only one blade left. But he didn't mention it. Instead, he brought his tanned fingers to her unkempt hair, inspecting it carefully.

"You look like shit," he stated.

Cassandrea snorted, yet there was a listless smile tugging at the corner of her mouth. She could give him that much. Give him something. He deserved it.

"I wish I could tell you that I'm here to catch up and have you tell me all about what happened," the teg started, and his expression made Cassandrea frown with suspicion, "but word's on the street that Ronan had caught general Nightshade, and he brought him here for interrogation."

Hatred engulfed her heart at that. She glanced at Ashban, who was staring at his fingers, suddenly finding them very interesting.

"I figured you'd like to know. He's currently boasting all about it at the bazaar to anyone who cares to listen," he continued while Cassandrea threw her blanket off and started gathering her clothes.

"Wait," the teg said.

She halted.

"I got you some new clothes. You can't meet him... and the king, looking like that."

Cassandrea's heart stopped.

"He summoned me?"

Ashban nodded.

"When?"

The teg offered her a sealed note. It had the king's golden wax stamp, still intact, heavy and thick over the yellow parchment. Cassandrea broke it and read the note. It was short, brutal, and efficient.

"Halls of Reflection, sundown."

Cassandrea folded the note and looked out of the window. Midday. She would have a few hours to burn. Enough time to squeeze out what she could from Ronan.

Ashban gave her a new set of leathers, a brown vest and black trousers, a pair of boots and a thin, airy shirt she could only guess the material of, and a long dark grey cloak with a wide trimmed hood, which she immediately changed into. And she had to admit, it helped. She felt like a new person. Ready to face the city and the king. As if she had shed a part of her old shell alongside those crusted clothes.

"Well, are you coming?" she waved Ashban over and rushed

outside.

She knew her brother didn't need to hear anything more. Definitely not her thanks or reassurances. He knew her too well to expect either.

*

Ronan truly was not hiding his achievement. He was sitting outside a teahouse, his back propped against thick ultramarine and cerulean pillows, the silvery mouthpiece of a hookah in his fingers, and a wide, smug grin reaching from ear to ear. When he spotted Cassandrea and Ashban, the already half-closed eyes drooped, and his lips curled into a cruel smile.

"The prodigal daughter returns," he drawled, taking a long drag, then exhaling the smoke in a casual, nonchalant manner.

"I heard you pulled off a feat of strength, Ronan," Cassandrea said, dismissing the insult entirely.

Normally, it would have irritated Ronan, but the changeling was riding a good drift from his pipe, and his mood was as high as him. So he grinned, his sharp teeth flashing dangerously.

"That I did," he said sluggishly and he gestured at the pillows in front of him.

Cassandrea sat down, Ashban next to her.

"Tell me," she encouraged the older male.

Ronan grinned. There was nothing else he wanted to do more.

"Would you believe that Boulderhelm was a perfect hideout

for a monster like him?" he started, smiling to himself as he leaned his back into the plush pillows. He hooked his leg and rested his arm against the knee, letting the silvery mouthpiece dangle from his relaxed fingers.

"He was brutalising the slaves. Sure, he was 'freeing' them," Ronan accentuated his words with an elegant move of his fingers, "but only after he'd had his fun with them."

He made a show of shuddering at his own words.

"What?!" Cassandrea breathed out.

"That's sickening," Ashban snarled.

"Oh yes. But what do you expect from a mixed-breed mutt like him? He's hardly a human, hardly fae, either," Ronan chortled, "and he also razed the nearby village, torched it down completely. Flooded the mines, too, after the rest of the slaves hid from him. Then he left them to drown there. Just so we would lose the site."

Cassandrea's blood began to boil. Wasn't it enough to drown three thousand soldiers in the bog? Now this? Infuriated, her hands balled into fists as she stared at Ronan.

"You've brought him here?" she asked.

The changeling nodded slowly. Smugly.

"And I intend to have a jolly good time ripping all his secrets from his flesh."

Cassandrea couldn't help but feel a bitter flush of glee in her soul.

"Good," she said. Good that at least one monster was about to suffer. "I want in."

Ronan looked at her and chuckled, "You don't say."

"I want in," she insisted. "I have questions to ask. I need to-"

"How about no?" Ronan grinned, bathing in the power he had. "He is my prisoner."

"Ronan-"

Her words died out as General Torquil's shadow slid over her and the male's towering figure stopped by her side.

"Cassandrea," he said firmly, "we need to go."

The siren hadn't even realised how late it had become. It was almost sundown already. She quickly bid her goodbyes to both Ronan and Ashban, the first just chortling and waving her off, the second giving her a concerned look, and she followed Torquil towards the Halls of Reflection.

The temple they walked in had once been a sacred place for rites and rituals of ancient magic, and it certainly looked the part. Sky-high vaulted ceilings with elaborate, vibrant paintings of constellations and sacred animals were passing into towering windows painted with shades of blue and decorated with silver and white motifs of stars, moonlight, and exotic birds. The floor tiles formed a miniscule mosaic, each tile not larger than a fingernail, and the patterns whirled in shapes of clouds and waves pouring all over the floor. And what was more important—in the very centre of the biggest hall stood the most sacred creature of them all.

King Valderan in his human form.

*

The king's unusual eyes took them in; his pupils dilated in the shadows of the temple, filling almost the whole golden eyes with an unending void Cassandrea felt resonating in her soul. It was as if he knew. As if he knew everything. As if he had looked right into her soul and weighed it. And suddenly she wanted to fall to her knees and cry and beg him for forgiveness. Not to save her life, but to end it. To end it before she could make even worse mistakes than she had already made.

However, her king's gaze moved to Torquil, and the shimmer of kindness he had always had for Cassandrea vanished like a smoke in the wind. And the general kneeled down. Cassandrea followed suit and lowered her head. And in that moment she had no idea why she had made any future plans besides this meeting. She should have said goodbye to Ashban instead. For it was all ending right there and then. She closed her eyes and waited for it.

"General," the king said, and his voice could have been mistaken for kind if it didn't have that challenging tail only somebody with Cassandrea's ears could hear. "You have lost almost four thousand of my men."

Torquil neither tried to deny it nor justify it.

"I have."

The king stepped closer, and Cassandrea shivered. Power was radiating from the male even in his human form and right now that power was utterly terrifying.

"Explain it to me," the king said softly, standing now right above the general. A perfect position to strike, Cassandrea noted.

Yet she wouldn't even dream about trying to defy such a strike. They would have deserved it. Both of them.

"I didn't foresee his strategy, My Lord. He surrounded us and lured us into a trap. Through the spy we were told we could trust."

Now, Cassandrea thought. Now it would come. Torquil would tell her king all about her foolishness. All about Kerr and how she suggested going through the marshes. And then...

"I listened to his advice to take my men through the marshes to Achaross, and they were..." Torquil gulped before he could continue, "slaughtered. Almost all of them."

Cassandrea gave the general a side glance. He didn't say it. Why didn't he say it?

"My men butchered, my ships lost, my cities razed, and yet, here you are, Torquil, unscathed."

Cassandrea gulped. The king's voice was so silky and so quiet that she had to strain her ears to hear it.

"I wouldn't be, were it not for your spy," Torquil said firmly. "Cassandrea saved my life. At a great personal cost."

"Did she now?" Valderan turned to the siren, and her blood froze in her veins.

This was wrong. It was all wrong. He should be with her. She was the one who trusted Kerr. The one who caused the whole disaster. She opened her mouth to tell the king, but the king's hand landed on her shoulder and squeezed it. And with it, the words evaporated from her mind. He didn't hate her. He should hate her...

"She dragged me for days to get me out of the battlefield," Torquil confirmed.

"How impressive," Valderan said, and the hand slowly slid from Cassandrea's shoulder as he turned to the general. "No less than what I would have expected from you. Yet, unlike her, you've failed. The man who taught Terren all about strategy. How did you not see this coming?"

"It wasn't his strategy, My Lord," Torquil said unusually confidently, "it was too ruthless to be his plan. Terren wouldn't have sacrificed a whole city to trap us."

Cassandrea drew a sharp breath at that. Too ruthless for the dragon king? What nonsense was that? Terren had thrown the whole country into war to get the throne. She felt Valderan's gaze on her again and tried to silence her heart and her thoughts.

"You disagree."

"My king."

"Interesting," Valderan mused and took her in for the second time. "Observe, Torquil."

Cassandrea felt her king's fingers under her chin as he raised her head up and forced her to look straight into his black, endless eyes.

"The most beautiful creature," Valderan continued, holding Cassandrea's gaze with a kind smile addressed only to her, "is a loyal one. Her small heart is aching for the soldiers *you* have lost."

Torquil held his tongue.

"If you cannot deal with Terren's new strategist, find him and silence him," Valderan spoke up again, still looking at

Cassandrea, his fingers idly stroking her cheek, "and remember, I might need you, but I do not need your cousin. Or your daughter."

It was spoken so casually that Cassandrea didn't fully grasp what had been said until she heard Torquil's sharp inhale. Mairi was alive, she realised. She was alive and... threatened to. And the general... he had a daughter, too? But most of all, Valderan didn't seem to be in the mood to kill Torquil, and that filled her heart with careful optimism. Especially when he smiled at her again and asked, "Don't you have a prophecy for me, Cassandrea?"

"I do," she breathed out. Gods, she almost forgot about that amidst all the turmoil. "I asked the seer what would help you win the war, my king. The answer was something or somebody called Garoth. I believe it may be the name of a sword or a person owning it. A sword of fire."

"Garoth," Valderan repeated, still stroking her cheek, as if he wanted to express his gratitude. And he was so gentle and kind. He had forgiven them. Both of them. Cassandrea's heart skipped a beat and then started beating like she was in a frenzy. Yes, she could live for this. For her king. For his kindness.

"You two will find this Garoth for me," the king nodded, "and then we will end this war."

He let go of Cassandrea's face and took a step back. But as he did that, the siren felt a rush of courage and purpose surging through her veins.

"I would like to start by interrogating your prisoner, my king," she dared to say.

The king halted and looked back at her.

"Which prisoner?"

"Your newest one. General Rheon Nightshade. I believe he may have a lot of information that could be useful to us."

Valderan pondered about it.

"Ronan is already interrogating him."

"I know," she nodded, a malicious, confident spirit taking hold of her heart, "but Ronan also sent us into a trap when he employed Terren's double spy. Did he not?"

A flash of amusement flickered through Valderan's eyes, and the dilated pupils constricted, leaving space for his royal gold.

"You are a dangerous foe to have, Cassandrea. I like that."

For a moment, he rubbed his fingers together in thought, but then he nodded.

"You may have the general. Make him suffer in ways Terren can't even imagine. For all of us."

Cassandrea swiftly nodded, bowing her head so low she nearly touched the ground.

"For all of us, my king."

And just like that, the darkest day of Cassandrea's life turned a lot brighter.

ChapteR 18

"You what?!"

Ronan was fuming as Cassandrea slipped the sealed note over to his hands. Stacks of paper unfurled and scattered around as the changeling banged both his fists against the wooden top of his desk. An inkwell tilted and toppled, spilling the midnight blue liquid all over the parchments. Ronan stood up, his fingers reaching for her neck.

"Wrangle your emotions, changeling," she snarled back at him, "for it is by the king's decree."

Ronan seethed as he broke the king's golden seal and opened the letter. His ever-shifting eyes darted from one line to another. Then he returned to the beginning and started reading it all over again. And again, as if not understanding. Confusion flickered in his eyes.

Cassandrea extended her palm over the desk.

"The key, Ronan," she crooned.

If Ronan had possessed an inch of magic in his cursed blood, the king's letter would have combusted. But he didn't. He crumpled it up in his fist, clenched so tight his knuckles turned white. Then, without saying another word, he pulled a drawer open and dug out a small iron key that he threw on the table.

"Get out," he spat the words out like they were on fire.

Cassandrea picked up the key and obliged.

Spending time with Ronan was not among her favourite past times, although now she was feeling a warm wave of satisfaction washing over her at the sight of his anger.

She had made barely ten full steps outside the office when a shadow loomed over her. Torquil. He had been waiting for her. Cassandrea was startled and came to a halt, bracing herself for whatever harsh words he was about to deliver. Craning her head up to meet the warrior's gaze, what she saw made her blink in surprise. The cold grey-blue eyes didn't seem angry with her. No. The general did look angry and sad, but it wasn't aimed at her. Cassandrea felt her heart withering and mouth drying up as she tried to muster something to say to him. A way to thank him for taking the fall for her. But before she had the chance to do so or to ask his reasons for it, the old warrior spoke.

"You're nothing to him, Cassandrea," Torquil said, his voice low and quiet, as he offered his warning. "Remember that."

Feeling the confusion and a sudden spike of anger roiling in her gut, Cassandrea opened her mouth to protest. To remind him that he had no idea just how close she was to the king, but the male spoke up again, his eyes briefly flitting to Ronan's office door.

"Whatever it is you do to the prisoner," he demanded, "make sure it will get us the information we need. For with every action you take there, you will be drawing the ire of people who will kill you for it if they win this war."

Cassandrea frowned, tilting her head. Her eyes narrowed.

"Why did you take the fall?" she asked quietly, her eyes looking for some answer in the general's eyes. An answer, a scheme, malice... something. But there was nothing. Just silver lining his grey irises.

"I was hoping he'd kill me."

Cassandrea's chest tightened. She wanted to tell him she knew. That she knew how that felt. But the words wouldn't pass her lips.

"But I wasn't lucky," Torquil finished and shrugged while a hateful smirk twisted his lips.

Then he hesitated. As if he was waiting for her to say something. And she wanted to. She wanted to, so, so much. But she didn't. Couldn't. So Torquil eventually turned and took a step away from her.

"We need to find that... Garoth," she finally blurted up. It wasn't what she should have said, but it was something. A new purpose. For both of them.

Torquil nodded, but he didn't react to it as enthusiastically as she had hoped.

"I'll contact you about it," he said only. And kept walking.

*

Dranast was a city of knowledge and as such, it didn't have a proper prison. However, even the priests and magicians sometimes needed things to be contained. Usually something magical and dangerous. So Dranast had a very specific place of confinement. Designed to keep in the strongest of creatures and the oddest of nightmares.

Cassandrea had never seen the dungeons before, but she had heard rumours about their mirror walls, enchanted to reflect any spell on those who cast it, voidleaf gardens for magical nullifying tattoos and special poisons that would make even the dragon kings sick.

Rumours that were true, she realised, as she caught her own reflection in a line of mirrors decorating not just the walls of the dungeon but the floor and ceiling as well. The guards assured her that they could move the prisoner into a cell without these preventive measures should she want to use her magic on him, but for now, she just wanted to get acquainted with what she was dealing with.

Her steps were light and she couldn't help the feeling of excitement settling in her chest. A loyal creature, Valderan had called her. A beautiful, loyal creature. And he was right. She would prove it to him. She would show him that not everybody was a traitor. That she wouldn't hurt him like Terren. And she would prove it to him by getting this Garoth. And by making their enemies suffer and regret the day they turned against them. For she felt her king's pain more than he knew. Ryker. Kerr. Her own kind. She knew betrayal maybe better than the king himself.

The corridor ended with a huge iron door and Cassandrea stopped in front of it. There were two torches on each side, prepared for whoever was going in. The siren grabbed one, pushed the key inside the keyhole and turned it. The door opened and the cell greeted her with a gust of icy cold wind. There was no light inside. No fire. It reeked of blood, both fresh and old, that had long since become a part of the room. The light of the torch flickered in a dozen mirrors and sent shadows and glints dancing across the cell so fast it took Cassandrea a good minute to adjust her sight and understand what she was looking at.

There was a column in the centre of the room and at its base, there was a male kneeling on the ground, his hands tied around the column and a dried puddle of blood beneath him. No, not so dried; some of it was fresh. And it smelled of... autumn?

The male's head was hanging low, making it impossible to see his features, but there was something oddly familiar about him. About the towering build, broad shoulders, and a tuft of short black hair, uneven and tousled and matted with blood clots. Cassandrea raised her torch at the same time as the prisoner raised his head and a dozen pairs of shining white eyes flashed at her from all directions. She took an instinctive step back and drew a sharp breath.

It was him.

The monster from the cliffs.

General Rheon Nightshade.

EVELYN A. BERNARD

Evelyn A. Bernard
Oaths of Land and Sea
Cover illustration: Ondřej Mašek

www.ingramcontent.com/pod-product-compliance
Ingram Content Group UK Ltd.
Pitfield, Milton Keynes, MK11 3LW, UK
UKHW040814240425
5607UKWH00028B/386

9 798230 474661